Greatest Short Stories

VOLUME VI

—

FOREIGN

P. F. COLLIER & SON CORPORATION
PUBLISHERS   **NEW YORK**

CONTENTS

1

CONTENTS

THE ACCURSED HOUSE

BY ÉMILE GABORIAU

THE ACCURSED HOUSE

BY ÉMILE GABORIAU

THE Vicomte de B——, an amiable and charming young man, was peacefully enjoying an income of 30,000 livres yearly, when, unfortunately for him, his uncle, a miser of the worst species, died, leaving him all his wealth, amounting to nearly two millions.

In running through the documents of succession, the Vicomte de B—— learned that he was the proprietor of a house in the Rue de la Victoire. He learned, also, that the unfurnished building, bought in 1849 for 300,000 francs, now brought in, clear of taxes, rentals amounting to 82,000 francs a year.

"Too much, too much, entirely," thought the generous vicomte, "my uncle was too hard; to rent at this price is usury, one can not deny it. When one bears a great name like mine, one should not lend himself to such plundering. I will begin to-morrow to lower my rents, and my tenants will bless me."

With this excellent purpose in view, the Vicomte de B—— sent immediately for the

Translated by E. C. Waggener. Copyright, 1891, by The Current Literature Publishing Company.

concièrge of the building, who presented himself as promptly, with back bent like a bow.

"Bernard, my friend," said the vicomte, "go at once from me and notify all your tenants that I lower their rents by one-third."

That unheard-of word "lower" fell like a brick on Bernard's head. But he quickly recovered himself; he had heard badly; he had not understood.

"Low—er the rents!" stammered he. "Monsieur le Vicomte deigns to jest. Lower! Monsieur, of course means to raise the rents."

"I was never more serious in my life, my friend," the vicomte returned; "I said, and I repeat it, lower the rents."

This time the *concièrge* was surprised to the point of bewilderment—so thrown off his balance that he forgot himself and lost all restraint.

"Monsieur has not reflected," persisted he. "Monsieur will regret this evening. Lower the tenants' rents! Never was such a thing known, monsieur! If the lodgers should learn of it, what would they think of monsieur? What would people say in the neighborhood? Truly—"

"Monsieur Bernard, my friend," dryly interrupted the vicomte, "I prefer, when I give an order, to be obeyed without reply. You hear me —go!"

Staggering like a drunken man, Monsieur Bernard went out from the house of his proprietor.

All his ideas were upset, overthrown, confounded. Was he, or was he not, the plaything of a dream, a ridiculous nightmare? Was he himself Pierre Bernard, or Bernard somebody else?

"Lower his rents! lower his rents!" repeated he. "It is not to be believed! If indeed the lodgers had complained! But they have not complained; on the contrary, all are good payers. Ah, if his uncle could only know this, he would rise from the tomb! His nephew has gone mad, 'tis certain! Lower the rents! They should have this young man up before a family council; he will finish badly! Who knows—after this—what he will do next? He lunched too well, perhaps, this morning."

And the worthy Bernard was so pale with emotion when he reentered his lodge, so pale and spent, that on seeing him enter, his wife and daughter Amanda exclaimed as with one voice:

"Goodness! what is it? What has happened to you now?"

"Nothing," responded he, with altered voice, "absolutely nothing."

"You are deceiving me," insisted Madame Bernard, "you are concealing something from me; do not spare me; speak, I am strong—what did the new proprietor tell you? Does he think of turning us off?"

"If it were only that! But just think, he told me with his own lips, he told me to—ah! you will never believe me—"

7

"Oh, yes; only do go on."

"You will have it, then!— Well, then, he told me, he ordered me to notify all the tenants that ·—*he lowered their rents one-third!* Did you hear what I said?—*lowered* the rents of the tenants—"

But neither Madame nor Mademoiselle Bernard heard him out—they were twisting and doubling with convulsive laughter.

"Lower!" repeated they; "ah! what a good joke, what a droll man! Lower the tenants' rents."

But Bernard, losing his temper and insisting that he must be taken seriously in his own lodge, his wife lost her temper too, and a quarrel followed! Madame Bernard declaring that Monsieur Bernard had, beyond a doubt, taken his fantastic order from the bottom of a litre of wine in the restaurant at the corner.

But for Mademoiselle Amanda the couple would undoubtedly have come to blows, and finally Madame Bernard, who did not wish to be thought demented, threw a shawl over her head and ran to the proprietor's house. Bernard had spoken truly; with her own two ears, ornamented with big, gilded hoops, she heard the incredible word. Only, as she was a wise and prudent woman, she demanded "a bit of writing" to put, as she said, "her responsibility under cover."

She, too, returned thunderstruck, and all the evening in the lodge, father, mother, and daughter deliberated.

Should they obey? or should they warn some relative of this mad young man, whose common sense would oppose itself to such insanity?

They decided to obey.

Next morning, Bernard, buttoning himself into his best frock coat, made the rounds of the three-and-twenty lodges to announce his great news.

Ten minutes afterward the house in the Rue de la Victoire was in a state of commotion impossible to describe. People who, for forty years had lived on the same floor, and never honored each other with so much as a tip of the hat, now clustered together and chatted eagerly.

"Do you know, monsieur?"

"It is very extraordinary."

"Simply unheard of!"

"The proprietor's lowered my rent!"

"One-third, is it not? Mine also."

"Astounding! It *must* be a mistake!"

And despite the affirmations of the Bernard family, despite even the "bit of writing" "under cover," there were found among the tenants doubting Thomases, who doubted still in the face of everything.

Three of them actually wrote to the proprietor to tell him what had passed, and to charitably warn him that his *concièrge* had wholly lost his mind. The proprietor responded to these skeptics, confirming what Bernard had said. Doubt, therefore, was out of the question.

Then began reflections and commentaries.

"*Why* had the proprietor lowered his rents?"

"Yes, *why?*"

"What motives," said they all, "actuate this strange man? For certainly he must have grave reasons for a step like this! An intelligent man, a man of good sense, would never deprive himself of good fat revenues, well secured, for the simple pleasure of depriving himself. One would not conduct himself thus without being forced, constrained by powerful or terrible circumstances."

And each said to himself:

"*There is something under all this!*"

"But what?"

And from the first floor to the sixth they sought and conjectured and delved in their brains. Every lodger had the preoccupied air of a man that strives with all his wits to solve an impossible cipher, and everywhere there began to be a vague disquiet, as it happens when one finds himself in the presence of a sinister mystery.

Some one went so far as to hazard:

"This man must have committed a great and still hidden crime; remorse pushes him to philanthropy."

"It was not a pleasant idea, either, the thought of living thus side by side with a rascal; no, by no means; he might be repentant, and all that, but suppose he yielded to temptation once more!"

10

"The house, perhaps, was badly built?" questioned another, anxiously.

"Hum-m, so-so! no one could tell; but all knew one thing—it was very, very old!"

"True! and it had been necessary to prop it when they dug the drain last year in the month of March."

"Maybe it was the roof, then, and the house is top-heavy?" suggested a tenant on the fifth floor.

"Or perhaps," said a lodger in the garret "there is a press for coining counterfeit money in the cellar; I have often heard at night a sound like the dull, muffled thud of a coin-stamper."

The opinion of another was that Russian, maybe Prussian, spies had gained a lodgment in the house, while the gentleman of the first story was inclined to believe that the proprietor purposed to set fire to his house and furniture with the sole object of drawing great sums from the insurance companies.

Then began to happen, as they all declared, extraordinary and even frightful things. On the sixth and mansard floors it appeared that strange and absolutely inexplicable noises were heard. Then the nurse of the old lady on the fourth story, going one night to steal wine from the cellar, encountered the ghost of the defunct proprietor—he even held in his hand a receipt for rent—by which she knew him!

And the refrain from aloft to cellar was:

"There *is* something under all this!"

11

From disquietude it had come to fright; from fright it quickly passed to terror. So that the gentleman of the first floor, who had valuables in his rooms, made up his mind to go, and sent in notice by his clerk.

Bernard went to inform the proprietor, who responded:

"All right, let the fool go!"

But next day the chiropodist of the second floor, though he had naught to fear for his valuables, imitated the gentleman beneath him. Then the bachelors and the little households of the fifth story quickly followed his example.

From that moment it was a general rout. By the end of the week, everybody had given notice. Every one awaited some frightful catastrophe. They slept no more. They organized patrols. The terrified domestics swore that they too would quit the accursed house and remained temporarily only on tripled wages.

Bernard was no more than the ghost of himself; the fever of fear had worn him to a shadow.

"No," repeated his wife mournfully at each fresh notification, "no, it is *not* natural."

Meanwhile three-and-twenty "For Rent" placards swung against the facade of the house, drawing an occasional applicant for lodgings.

Bernard—never grumbling now—climbed the staircase and ushered the visitor from apartment to apartment.

"You can have your choice," said he to the people that presented themselves, "the house is entirely vacant; all the tenants have given notice as one man. They do not know why, exactly, but things have happened, oh! yes, *things!* a mystery such as was never before known—*the proprietor has lowered his rents!"*

And the would-be lodgers fled away affrighted.

The term ended, three-and-twenty vans carried away the furniture of the three-and-twenty tenants. Everybody left. From top to bottom, from foundations to garret, the house lay empty of lodgers.

The rats themselves, finding nothing to live on, abandoned it also.

Only the *concièrge* remained, gray green with fear in his lodge. Frightful visions haunted his sleep. He seemed to hear lugubrious howlings and sinister murmurs at night that made his teeth chatter with terror and his hair erect itself under his cotton nightcap. Madame Bernard no more closed an eye than he. And Amanda in her frenzy renounced all thought of the operatic stage and married—for nothing in the world but to quit the paternal lodge—a young barber and hair-dresser whom she had never before been able to abide.

At last, one morning, after a more frightful nightmare than usual, Bernard, too, took a great resolution. He went to the proprietor, gave up his keys, and scampered away.

．　．　．　．　．　．　．　．　．

And now on the Rue de la Victoire stands the abandoned house, "The Accursed House," whose history I have told you. Dust thickens upon the closed slats, grass grows in the court. No tenant ever presents himself now; and in the quarter, where stands this Accursed House, so funereal is its reputation that even the neighboring houses on either side of it have also depreciated in value.

Lower one's rents!! Who would think of such a thing!!!

THE CLOAK

BY NIKOLAI VASILIEVITCH GOGOL

THE CLOAK

BY NIKOLAI VASILIEVITCH GOGOL

IN the department of—but it is better not to mention the department. There is nothing more irritable than departments, regiments, courts of justice, and, in a word, every branch of public service. Each individual attached to them nowadays thinks all society insulted in his person. Quite recently a complaint was received from a justice of the peace, in which he plainly demonstrated that all the imperial institutions were going to the dogs, and that the Czar's sacred name was being taken in vain; and in proof he appended to the complaint a romance, in which the justice of the peace is made to appear about once in every ten lines, and sometimes in a drunken condition. Therefore, in order to avoid all unpleasantness, it will be better to designate the department in question as a certain department.

So, in a certain department there was a certain official—not a very high one, it must be allowed —short of stature, somewhat pock-marked, red-haired, and short-sighted, with a bald forehead, wrinkled cheeks, and a complexion of the kind known as sanguine. The St. Petersburg climate was responsible for this. As for his official status,

17

he was what is called a perpetual titular councilor, over which some writers make merry and crack their jokes, obeying the praiseworthy custom of attacking those who can not bite back.

His family name was Bashmatchkin. This name is evidently derived from *bashmak* (shoe); but when, at what time, and in what manner, is not known. His father and grandfather, and all the Bashmatchkins, always wore boots, which only had new heels two or three times a year. His name was Akakiy Akakievitch. It may strike the reader as rather singular and far-fetched; but he may rest assured that it was by no means far-fetched, and that the circumstances were such that it would have been impossible to give him any other.

This was how it came about.

Akakiy Akakievitch was born, if my memory fails me not, in the evening on the 23d of March. His mother, the wife of a Government official, and a very fine woman, made all due arrangements for having the child baptized. She was lying on the bed opposite the door; on her right stood the godfather, Ivan Ivanovitch Eroshkin, a most estimable man, who served as presiding officer of the senate; and the godmother, Anna Semenovna Byelobrushkova, the wife of an officer of the quarter, and a woman of rare virtues. They offered the mother her choice of three names, Mokiya, Sossiya, or that the child should be called after the martyr Khozdazat. "No,"

said the good woman, "all those names are poor."
In order to please her, they opened the calendar
at another place; three more names appeared,
Triphiliy, Dula, and Varakhasiy. "This is a
judgment," said the old woman. "What names!
I truly never heard the like. Varadat or Varukh
might have been borne, but not Triphiliy and
Varakhasiy!" They turned to another page and
found Pavsikakhiy and Vakhtisiy. "Now I see,"
said the old woman, "that it is plainly fate. And
since such is the case, it will be better to name
him after his father. His father's name was
Akakiy, so let his son's be Akakiy too." In this
manner he became Akakiy Akakievitch. They
christened the child, whereat he wept, and made
a grimace, as though he foresaw that he was to
be a titular councilor.

In this manner did it all come about. We have
mentioned it in order that the reader might see
for himself that it was a case of necessity, and
that it was utterly impossible to give him any
other name. When and how he entered the department, and who appointed him, no one could
remember. However much the directors and
chiefs of all kinds were changed, he was always
to be seen in the same place, the same attitude,
the same occupation; so that it was afterward
affirmed that he had been born in undress uniform with a bald head.

No respect was shown him in the department.
The porter not only did not rise from his seat

when he passed, but never even glanced at him, any more than if a fly had flown through the reception-room. His superiors treated him in coolly despotic fashion. Some subchief would thrust a paper under his nose without so much as saying "Copy," or "Here's a nice, interesting affair," or anything else agreeable, as is customary among well-bred officials. And he took it, looking only at the paper, and not observing who handed it to him, or whether he had the right to do so; simply took it, and set about copying it.

The young officials laughed at and made fun of him, so far as their official wit permitted; told in his presence various stories concocted about him, and about his landlady, an old woman of seventy; declared that she beat him; asked when the wedding was to be; and strewed bits of paper over his head, calling them snow. But Akakiy Akakievitch answered not a word, any more than if there had been no one there besides himself. It even had no effect upon his work: amid all these annoyances he never made a single mistake in a letter. But if the joking became wholly unbearable, as when they jogged his hand, and prevented his attending to his work, he would exclaim, "Leave me alone! Why do you insult me?" And there was something strange in the words and the voice in which they were uttered. There was in it something which moved to pity; so much that one young man, a newcomer, who, taking pattern by the others, had permitted him-

self to make sport of Akakiy, suddenly stopped
short, as though all about him had undergone a
transformation and presented itself in a different
aspect. Some unseen force repelled him from
the comrades whose acquaintance he had made,
on the supposition that they were well-bred and
polite men. Long afterward, in his gayest moments, there recurred to his mind the little official
with the bald forehead, with his heart-rending
words, "Leave me alone! Why do you insult
me?" In these moving words, other words re-
sounded—"I am thy brother." And the young
man covered his face with his hand; and many a
time afterward, in the course of his life, shud-
dered at seeing how much inhumanity there is in
man, how much savage coarseness is concealed
beneath delicate, refined worldliness, and even, O
God! in that man whom the world acknowledges
as honorable and noble.

It would be difficult to find another man who
lived so entirely for his duties. It is not enough
to say that Akakiy labored with zeal: no, he
labored with love. In his copying he found a
varied and agreeable employment. Enjoyment
was written on his face: some letters were even
favorites with him, and when he encountered
these he smiled, winked, and worked with his lips,
till it seemed as though each letter might be read
in his face, as his pen traced it. If his pay had
been in proportion to his zeal, he would, perhaps,
to his great surprise, have been made even a

councilor of state. But he worked, as his companions, the wits, put it, like a horse in a mill.

Moreover, it is impossible to say that no attention was paid to him. One director, being a kindly man, and desirous of rewarding him for his long service, ordered him to be given something more important than mere copying. So he was ordered to make a report of an already concluded affair to another department; the duty consisting simply in changing the heading and altering a few words from the first to the third person. This caused him so much toil that he broke into a perspiration, rubbed his forehead, and finally said: "No, give me rather something to copy." After that they let him copy on forever.

Outside this copying, it appeared that nothing existed for him. He gave no thought to his clothes; his undress uniform was not green, but a sort of rusty-meal color. The collar was low, so that his neck, in spite of the fact that it was not long, seemed inordinately so as it emerged from it, like the necks of those plaster cats which wag their heads and are carried about upon the heads of scores of image sellers. And something was always sticking to his uniform, either a bit of hay or some trifle. Moreover, he had a peculiar knack, as he walked along the street, of arriving beneath a window just as all sorts of rubbish was being flung out of it; hence he always bore about on his hat scraps of melon rinds and other such

articles. Never once in his life did he give heed
to what was going on every day in the street;
while it is well known that his young brother
officials train the range of their glances till they
can see when any one's trouser-straps come un-
done upon the opposite sidewalk, which always
brings a malicious smile to their faces. But
Akakiy Akakievitch saw in all things the clean,
even strokes of his written lines; and only when
a horse thrust his nose, from some unknown quarter, over his shoulder, and sent a whole gust of
wind down his neck from his nostrils, did he observe that he was not in the middle of a page, but
in the middle of the street.

On reaching home he sat down at once at the
table, supped his cabbage-soup up quickly, and,
swallowed a bit of beef with onions, never notic-
ing their taste, and gulping down everything with
flies and anything else which the Lord happened
to send at the moment. His stomach filled, he
rose from the table and copied papers which he
had brought home. If there happened to be none,
he took copies for himself, for his own gratifica-
tion, especially if the document was noteworthy,
not on account of its style, but of its being addressed to some distinguished person.

Even at the hour when the gray St. Petersburg sky had quite disappeared, and all the
official world had eaten or dined, each as he
could, in accordance with the salary he received
and his own fancy; when all were resting from

the departmental jar of pens, running to and fro
from their own and other people's indispensable
occupations, and from all the work that an uneasy
man makes willingly for himself, rather than
what is necessary; when officials hasten to dedi-
cate to pleasure the time which is left to them,
one bolder than the rest going to the theatre;
another into the street, looking under all the bon-
nets; another wasting his evening in compliments
to some pretty girl, the star of a small official
circle; another—and this is the common case of
all—visiting his comrades on the fourth or third
floor, in two small rooms with an anteroom or
kitchen, and some pretensions to fashion, such as
a lamp or some other trifle, which has cost many
a sacrifice of dinner or pleasure trip; in a word,
at the hour when all officials disperse among the
contracted quarters of their friends, to play whist
as they sip their tea from glasses with a kopek's
worth of sugar, smoke long pipes, relate at times
some bits of gossip which a Russian man can
never, under any circumstances, refrain from,
and, when there is nothing else to talk of, repeat
eternal anecdotes about the commandant to whom
they had sent word that the tails of the horses on
the Falconet Monument had been cut off, when
all strive to divert themselves, Akakiy Akakievitch indulged in no kind of diversion. No one
could ever say that he had seen him at any kind
of evening party. Having written to his heart's
content, he lay down to sleep, smiling at the

thought of the coming day—of what God might send him to copy on the morrow.

Thus flowed on the peaceful life of the man, who, with a salary of four hundred rubles, understood how to be content with his lot; and thus it would have continued to flow on, perhaps, to extreme old age were it not that there are various ills strewn along the path of life for titular councilors as well as for private, actual, court, and every other species of councilor, even for those who never give any advice or take any themselves.

There exists in St. Petersburg a powerful foe of all who receive a salary of four hundred rubles a year, or thereabouts. This foe is no other than the northern cold, although it is said to be very healthy. At nine o'clock in the morning, at the very hour when the streets are filled with men bound for the various official departments, it begins to bestow such powerful and piercing nips on all noses impartially that the poor officials really do not know what to do with them. At an hour when the foreheads of even those who occupy exalted positions ache with the cold, and tears start to their eyes, the poor titular councilors are sometimes quite unprotected. Their only salvation lies in traversing as quickly as possible, in their thin little cloaks, five or six streets, and then warming their feet in the porter's room, and so thawing all their talents and qualifications for official service which had become frozen on the way.

Akakiy Akakievitch had felt for some time
that his back and shoulders suffered with peculiar poignancy in spite of the fact that he tried
to traverse the distance with all possible speed.
He began finally to wonder whether the fault
did not lie in his cloak. He examined it thoroughly at home, and discovered that in two places,
namely, on the back and shoulders, it had become
thin as gauze; the cloth was worn to such a degree
that he could see through it, and the lining had
fallen into pieces. You must know that Akakiy
Akakievitch's cloak served as an object of ridi-
cule to the officials; they even refused it the noble
name of cloak, and called it a cape. In fact, it
was of singular make; its collar diminishing year
by year, but serving to patch its other parts. The
patching did not exhibit great skill on the part
of the tailor, and was, in fact, baggy and ugly.
Seeing how the matter stood, Akakiy Akakievitch decided that it would be necessary to take
the cloak to Petrovitch, the tailor, who lived somewhere on the fourth floor, up a dark staircase,
and who, in spite of his having but one eye, and
pock-marks all over his face, busied himself in re-
pairing the trousers and coats of officials and
others; that is to say, when he was sober, and not
nursing some other scheme in his head.

It is not necessary to say much about this
tailor; but, as it is the custom to have the character of each personage in a novel clearly defined,
there is no help for it, so here is Petrovitch the

tailor. At first he was called only Grigoriy, and was some gentleman's serf; he commenced calling himself Petrovitch from the time when he received his free papers, and further began to drink heavily on all holidays, at first on the great ones, and then on all church festivals without discrimination, wherever a cross stood in the calendar. On this point he was faithful to ancestral custom; and when quarreling with his wife he called her a low female and a German. As we have mentioned his wife, it will be necessary to say a word or two about her. Unfortunately, little is known of her beyond the fact that Petrovitch has a wife, who wears a cap and a dress, but can not lay claim to beauty; at least, no one but the soldiers of the guard even looked under her cap when they met her.

Ascending the staircase which led to Petrovitch's room—which staircase was all soaked with dish-water and reeked with the smell of spirits which affects the eyes, and is an inevitable adjunct to all dark stairways in St. Petersburg houses—ascending the stairs, Akakiy Akakievitch pondered how much Petrovitch would ask, and mentally resolved not to give more than two rubles. The door was open; for the mistress, in cooking some fish, had raised such a smoke in the kitchen that not even the beetles were visible. Akakiy Akakievitch passed through the kitchen unperceived, even by the housewife, and at length reached a room where he beheld Petrovitch seated on a large unpainted table, with his legs tucked under him like a Turkish pasha. His feet were bare, after the fashion of tailors as they sit at work; and the first thing which caught the eye 'was his thumb, with a deformed nail thick and strong as a turtle's shell. About Petrovitch's neck hung a skein of silk and thread, and upon his knees lay some old garment. He had been trying unsuccessfully for three minutes to thread his needle, and was enraged at the darkness and even at the thread, growling in a low voice, "It won't go through, the barbarian! You pricked me, you rascal!"

Akakiy Akakievitch was vexed at arriving at the precise moment when Petrovitch was angry; he liked to order something of Petrovitch when the latter was a little downhearted, or, as his wife expressed it, "when he had settled himself with brandy, the one-eyed devil!" Under such circumstances, Petrovitch generally came down in his price very readily, and even bowed and returned thanks. Afterward, to be sure, his wife would come, complaining that her husband was drunk, and so had fixed the price too low; but if only a ten-kopek piece were added, then the matter was settled. But now it appeared that Petrovitch was in a sober condition, and therefore rough, taciturn, and inclined to demand, Satan only knows what price. Akakiy Akakievitch felt this, and would gladly have beat a retreat; but he was in for it. Petrovitch screwed up his one eye very intently at him; and Akakiy Akakievitch involuntarily said: "How do you do, Petrovitch?"

"I wish you a good-morning, sir," said Petrovitch, squinting at Akakiy Akakievitch's hands, to see what sort of booty he had brought.

"Ah! I—to you, Petrovitch, this—" It must be known that Akakiy Akakievitch expressed himself chiefly by prepositions, adverbs, and scraps of phrases which had no meaning whatever. If the matter was a very difficult one, he had a habit of never completing his sentences; so that frequently, having begun a phrase with the words, "This, in fact, is quite—" he forgot to go on, thinking that he had already finished it.

"What is it?" asked Petrovitch, and with his one eye scanned Akakievitch's whole uniform from the collar down to the cuffs, the back, the tails, and the button-holes, all of which were well known to him, since they were his own handiwork. Such is the habit of tailors; it is the first thing they do on meeting one.

"But I, here, this—Petrovitch—a cloak, cloth —here you see, everywhere, in different places, it is quite strong—it is a little dusty, and looks old, but it is new, only here in one place it is a little— on the back, and here on one of the shoulders, it is a little worn, yes, here on this shoulder it is a little—do you see? that is all. And a little work—"

Petrovitch took the cloak, spread it out, to

begin with, on the table, looked hard at it, shook his head, reached out his hand to the window-sill for his snuff-box, adorned with the portrait of some general, though what general is unknown, for the place where the face should have been had been rubbed through by the finger, and a square bit of paper had been pasted over it. Having taken a pinch of snuff, Petrovitch held up the cloak, and inspected it against the light, and again shook his head. Then he turned it, lining upward, and shook his head once more. After which he again lifted the general-adorned lid with its bit of pasted paper, and, having stuffed his nose with snuff, closed and put away the snuff-box, and said finally, "No, it is impossible to mend it; it's a wretched garment!"

Akakiy Akakievitch's heart sank at these words.

"Why is it impossible, Petrovitch?" he said, almost in the pleading voice of a child; "all that ails it is that it is worn at the shoulders. You must have some pieces——"

"Yes, patches could be found, patches are easily found," said Petrovitch, "but there's nothing to sew them to. The thing is completely rotten; if you put a needle to it—see, it will give way."

"Let it give way, and you can put on another patch at once."

"But there is nothing to put the patches on to; there's no use in strengthening it; it is too far gone. It's lucky that it's cloth; for, if the wind were to blow, it would fly away."

"Well, strengthen it again. How this, in fact."

"No," said Petrovitch decisively, "there is nothing to be done with it. It's a thoroughly bad job. You'd better, when the cold winter comes on, make yourself some gaiters out of it, because stockings are not warm. The Germans invented them in order to make more money." Petrovitch loved, on all occasions, to have a fling at the Germans. "But it is plain you must have a new cloak."

At the word "new," all grew dark before Akakiy Akakievitch's eyes and everything in the room began to whirl round. The only thing he saw clearly was the general with the paper face on the lid of Petrovitch's snuff-box. "A new one?" said he, as if still in a dream: "why, I have no money for that."

"Yes, a new one," said Petrovitch, with barbarous composure.

"Well, if came to a new one, how it?"

"You mean how much would it cost?"

"Yes."

"Well, you would have to lay out a hundred and fifty or more, said Petrovitch, and pursed up his lips significantly. He liked to produce powerful effects, liked to stun utterly and suddenly and then to glance sidewise to see what face the stunned person would put on the matter.

"A hundred and fifty rubles for a cloak!"

shrieked poor Akakiy Akakievitch, perhaps for
the first time in his life, for his voice had always
been distinguished for softness.

"Yes, sir," said Petrovitch, "for any kind of
cloak. If you have a marten fur on the collar, or
a silk-lined hood, it will mount up to two hundred."

"Petrovitch, please," said Akakiy Akakievitch
in a beseeching tone, not hearing, and not trying
to hear, Petrovitch's words, and disregarding all
his "effects," "some repairs, in order that it may
wear yet a little longer."

"No, it would only be a waste of time and
money," said Petrovitch; and Akakiy Akakievitch went away after these words, utterly dis-
couraged. But Petrovitch stood for some time
after his departure, with significantly compressed
lips, and without betaking himself to his work,
satisfied that he would not be dropped, and an
artistic tailor employed.

Akakiy Akakievitch went out into the street
as if in a dream. "Such an affair!" he said to himself: "I did not think it had come to—" and then
after a pause he added: "Well, so it is! see what
it has come to at last! and I never imagined that
it was so!" Then followed a long silence, after
which he exclaimed: "Well, so it is! see what already—nothing unexpected that it would be
nothing—what a strange circumstance!" So saying, instead of going home, he went in exactly
the opposite direction without himself suspecting

it. On the way a chimney-sweep bumped up against him and blackened his shoulder, and a whole hatful of rubbish landed on him from the top of a house which was building. He did not notice it; and only when he ran against a watchman, who, having planted his halberd beside him, was shaking some snuff from his box into his horny hand, did he recover himself a little, and that because the watchman said, "Why are you poking yourself into a man's very face? Haven't you the pavement?" This caused him to look about him, and turn toward home.

There only he finally began to collect his thoughts and to survey his position in its clear and actual light, and to argue with himself, sensibly and frankly, as with a reasonable friend, with whom one can discuss private and personal matters. "No," said Akakiy Akakievitch, "it is impossible to reason with Petrovitch now; he is that—evidently his wife has been beating him. I'd better go to him on Sunday morning; after Saturday night he will be a little cross-eyed and sleepy, for he will want to get drunk, and his wife won't give him any money; and at such a time a ten-kopek piece in his hand will—he will become more fit to reason with, and then the cloak, and that—" Thus argued Akakiy Akakievitch with himself, regained his courage, and waited until the first Sunday, when, seeing from afar that Petrovitch's wife had left the house, he went straight to him.

Petrovitch's eye was, indeed, very much askew after Saturday: his head drooped and he was very sleepy; but for all that, as soon as he knew what it was a question of, it seemed as though Satan jogged his memory. "Impossible," said he; "please to order a new one." Thereupon Akakiy Akakievitch handed over the ten-kopek piece. "Thank you, sir; I will drink your good health," said Petrovitch; "but as for the cloak, don't trouble yourself about it; it is good for nothing. I will make you a capital new one, so let us settle about it now."

Akakiy Akakievitch was still for mending it; but Petrovitch would not hear of it, and said: "I shall certainly have to make you a new one, and you may depend upon it that I shall do my best. It may even be, as the fashion goes, that the collar can be fastened by silver hooks under a flap."

Then Akakiy Akakievitch saw that it was impossible to get along without a new cloak, and his spirit sank utterly. How, in fact, was it to be done? Where was the money to come from? He might, to be sure, depend, in part, upon his present at Christmas; but that money had long been allotted beforehand. He must have some new trousers, and pay a debt of long standing to the shoemaker for putting new tops to his old boots, and he must order three shirts from the seamstress, and a couple of pieces of linen. In short, all his money must be spent; and even if

the director should be so kind as to order him to
receive forty-five rubles instead of forty, or even
fifty, it would be a mere nothing, a mere drop in
the ocean toward the funds necessary for a cloak;
although he knew that Petrovitch was often
wrong-headed enough to blurt out some out-
rageous price, so that even his own wife could
not refrain from exclaiming, "Have you lost your
senses, you fool?" At one time he would not
work at any price, and now it was quite likely
that he had named a higher sum than the cloak
would cost.

But although he knew that Petrovitch would
undertake to make a cloak for eighty rubles, still,
where was he to get the eighty rubles from? He
might possibly manage half; yes, half might be
procured, but where was the other half to come
from? But the reader must first be told where
the first half came from. Akakiy Akakievitch
had a habit of putting, for every ruble he spent,
a kopek into a small box, fastened with lock and
key, and with a slit in the top for the reception
of money. At the end of every half-year he
counted over the heap of coppers, and changed it
for silver. This he had done for a long time, and
in the course of years the sum had mounted up to
over forty rubles. Thus he had one-half on hand;
but where was he to find the other half? where
was he to get another forty rubles from? Akakiy
Akakievitch thought and thought, and decided
that it would be necessary to curtail his ordinary

expenses for the space of one year at least—to dispense with tea in the evening, to burn no candles, and, if there was anything which he must do, to go into his landlady's room and work by her light. When he went into the street he must walk as lightly as he could, and as cautiously, upon the stones, almost upon tiptoe, in order not to wear his heels down in too short a time; he must give the laundress as little to wash as possible; and, in order not to wear out his clothes, he must take them off as soon as he got home, and wear only his cotton dressing-gown, which had been long and carefully saved.

To tell the truth, it was a little hard for him at first to accustom himself to these deprivations; but he got used to them at length, after a fashion, and all went smoothly. He even got used to being hungry in the evening, but he made up for it by treating himself, so to say, in spirit, by bearing ever in mind the idea of his future cloak. From that time forth his existence seemed to become, in some way, fuller, as if he were married, or as if some other man lived in him, as if, in fact, he were not alone, and some pleasant friend had consented to travel along life's path with him, the friend being no other than the cloak, with thick wadding and a strong lining incapable of wearing out. He became more lively, and even his character grew firmer, like that of a man who has made up his mind and set himself a goal. From his face and gait, doubt and indecision, all hesitating and wavering traits, disappeared of themselves. Fire gleamed in his eyes, and occasionally the boldest and most daring ideas flitted through his mind; why not, for instance, have marten fur on the collar? The thought of this almost made him absent-minded. Once, in copying a letter, he nearly made a mistake, so that he exclaimed almost aloud, "Ugh!" and crossed himself. Once in the course of every month he had a conference with Petrovitch on the subject of the cloak, where it would be better to buy the cloth, and the color, and the price. He always returned home satisfied, though troubled, reflecting that the time would come at last when it could all be bought, and then the cloak made.

The affair progressed more briskly than he had expected. Far beyond all his hopes, the director awarded neither forty nor forty-five rubles for Akakiy Akakievitch's share, but sixty. Whether he suspected that Akakiy Akakievitch needed a cloak, or whether it was merely chance; at all events, twenty extra rubles were by this means provided. This circumstance hastened matters. Two or three months more of hunger and Akakiy Akakievitch had accumulated about eighty rubles. His heart, generally so quiet, began to throb. On the first possible day he went shopping in company with Petrovitch. They bought some very good cloth, and at a reasonable rate too, for they had been considering the matter for six months, and rarely let a month pass without

their visiting the shops to inquire prices. Petrovitch himself said that no better cloth could be
had. For lining, they selected a cotton stuff,
but so firm and thick that Petrovitch declared it
to be better than silk, and even prettier and more
glossy. They did not buy the marten fur because it was, in fact, dear, but in its stead they
picked out the very best of cat-skin which could
be found in the shop, and which might, indeed,
be taken for marten at a distance.

Petrovitch worked at the cloak two whole
weeks, for there was a great deal of quilting;
otherwise it would have been finished sooner. He
charged twelve rubles for the job; it could not
possibly have been done for less. It was all sewed
with silk, in small, double seams; and Petrovitch went over each seam afterward with his own
teeth.

It was—it is difficult to say precisely on what
day, but probably the most glorious one in
Akakiy Akakievitch's life, when Petrovitch at
length brought home the cloak. He brought it in
the morning, before the hour when it was necessary to start for the department. Never did a
cloak arrive so exactly in the nick of time, for the
severe cold had set in, and it seemed to threaten
to increase. Petrovitch brought the cloak himself as befits a good tailor. On his countenance
was a significant expression, such as Akakiy
Akakievitch had never beheld there. He seemed
fully sensible that he had done no small

deed, and crossed a gulf separating tailors who
only put in linings and execute repairs from
those who make new things. He took the cloak
out of the pocket-handkerchief in which he had
brought it. The handkerchief was fresh from
the laundress, and he put it in his pocket for use.
Taking out the cloak, he gazed proudly at it, held
it up with both hands, and flung it skilfully over
the shoulders of Akakiy Akakievitch. Then he
pulled it and fitted it down behind with his hand,
and he draped it around Akakiy Akakievitch
without buttoning it. Akakiy Akakievitch, like
an experienced man, wished to try the sleeves.
Petrovitch helped him on with them, and it turned
out that the sleeves were satisfactory also. In
short, the cloak appeared to be perfect and most
seasonable. Petrovitch did not neglect to observe that it was only because he lived in a narrow street, and had no signboard, and had known
Akakiy Akakievitch so long, that he had made it
so cheaply; but that if he had been in business on
the Nevsky Prospect he would have charged
seventy-five rubles for the making alone. Akakiy
Akakievitch did not care to argue this point with
Petrovitch. He paid him, thanked him, and set
out at once in his new cloak for the department.
Petrovitch followed him, and, pausing in the
street, gazed long at the cloak in the distance,
after which he went to one side expressly to run
through a crooked alley and emerge again into
the street beyond to gaze once more upon the

cloak from another point, namely, directly in front.

Meantime Akakiy Akakievitch went on in holiday mood. He was conscious, every second of the time, that he had a new cloak on his shoulders; and several times he laughed with internal satisfaction. In fact, there were two advantages, one was its warmth, the other its beauty. He saw nothing of the road, but suddenly found himself at the department. He took off his cloak in the anteroom, looked it over carefully, and confided it to the especial care of the attendant. It is impossible to say precisely how it was that every one in the department knew at once that Akakiy Akakievitch had a new cloak, and that the "cape" no longer existed. All rushed at the same moment into the anteroom, to inspect it. They congratulated him and said pleasant things to him, so that he began at first to smile and then to grow ashamed. When all surrounded him and said that the new cloak must be "christened," and that he must give a whole evening at least to this, Akakiy Akakievitch lost his head completely, and did not know where he stood, what to answer, or how to get out of it. He stood blushing all over for several minutes, and was on the point of assuring them with great simplicity that it was not a new cloak, that it was so and so, that it was in fact the old "cape."

At length one of the officials, a subchief probably, in order to show that he was not at all proud, and on good terms with his inferiors, said: "So be it, only I will give the party instead of Akakiy Akakievitch; I invite you all to tea with me to-night; it happens quite *à propos,* as it is my name-day." The officials naturally at once offered the subchief their congratulations, and accepted the invitation with pleasure. Akakiy Akakievitch would have declined, but all declared that it was discourteous, that it was simply a sin and a shame, and that he could not possibly refuse. Besides, the notion became pleasant to him when he recollected that he should thereby have a chance of wearing his new cloak in the evening also.

That whole day was truly a most triumphant festival day for Akakiy Akakievitch. He returned home in the most happy frame of mind, took off his cloak, and hung it carefully on the wall, admiring afresh the cloth and the lining. Then he brought out his old, worn-out cloak for comparison. He looked at it and laughed, so vast was the difference. And long after dinner he laughed again when the condition of the "cape" recurred to his mind. He dined cheerfully, and after dinner wrote nothing, but took his ease for a while on the bed, until it got dark. Then he dressed himself leisurely, put on his cloak, and stepped out into the street. Where the host lived, unfortunately, we can not say; our memory begins to fail us badly; and the houses and

41

streets in St. Petersburg have become so mixed up in our head that it is very difficult to get anything out of it again in proper form. This much is certain, that the official lived in the best part of the city; and, therefore, it must have been anything but near to Akakiy Akakievitch's residence. Akakiy Akakievitch was first obliged to traverse a kind of wilderness of deserted, dimly lighted streets; but in proportion as he approached the official's quarter of the city the streets became more lively, more populous, and more brilliantly illuminated. Pedestrians began to appear; handsomely dressed ladies were more frequently encountered; the men had otter-skin collars to their coats; peasant wagoners, with their gratelike sledges stuck over with brass-headed nails, became rarer; while, on the other hand, more and more drivers in red velvet caps, lacquered sledges, and bear-skin coats began to appear, and carriages with rich hammer-cloths flew swiftly through the streets, their wheels crunching the snow. Akakiy Akakievitch gazed upon all this as upon a novel sight. He had not been in the streets during the evening for years. He halted out of curiosity before a shop-window, to look at a picture representing a handsome woman, who had thrown off her shoe, thereby baring her whole foot in a very pretty way; while behind her the head of a man with whiskers and a handsome mustache peeped through the doorway of another room. Akakiy Akakievitch shook his head

and laughed, and then went on his way. Why
did he laugh? Either because he had met with a
thing utterly unknown, but for which every one
cherishes, nevertheless, some sort of feeling; or
else he thought, like many officials, as follows:
"Well, those French! What is to be said? If
they do go in anything of that sort, why—" But
possibly he did not think at all.

Akakiy Akakievitch at length reached the
house in which the subchief lodged. The subchief lived in fine style; the staircase was lit by a
lamp, his apartment being on the second floor.
On entering the vestibule, Akakiy Akakievitch
beheld a whole row of goloshes on the floor.
Among them, in the centre of the room, stood a
samovar, or tea-urn, humming and emitting
clouds of steam. On the walls hung all sorts of
coats and cloaks, among which there were even
some with beaver collars or velvet facings. Beyond, the buzz of conversation was audible, and
became clear and loud when the servant came out
with a trayful of empty glasses, cream-jugs, and
sugar-bowls. It was evident that the officials had
arrived long before, and had already finished their
first glass of tea.

Akakiy Akakievitch, having hung up his own
cloak, entered the inner room. Before him all at
once appeared lights, officials, pipes, and card-
tables; and he was bewildered by a sound of rapid
conversation rising from all the tables, and the
noise of moving chairs. He halted very awk-

wardly in the middle of the room, wondering what he ought to do. But they had seen him. They received him with a shout, and all thronged at once into the anteroom, and there took another look at his cloak. Akakiy Akakievitch, although somewhat confused, was frank-hearted, and could not refrain from rejoicing when he saw how they praised his cloak. Then, of course, they all dropped him and his cloak, and returned, as was proper, to the tables set out for whist.

All this, the noise, the talk, and the throng of people was rather overwhelming to Akakiy Akakievitch. He simply did not know where he stood, or where to put his hands, his feet, and his whole body. Finally he sat down by the players, looked at the cards, gazed at the face of one and another, and after a while began to gape, and to feel that it was wearisome, the more so as the hour was already long past when he usually went to bed. He wanted to take leave of the host; but they would not let him go, saying that he must not fail to drink a glass of champagne, in honor of his new garment. In the course of an hour, supper, consisting of vegetables, salad, cold veal, pastry, confectioner's pies, and champagne, was served. They made Akakiy Akakievitch drink two glasses of champagne, after which he felt things grow livelier.

Still, he could not forget that it was twelve o'clock, and that he should have been at home

long ago. In order that the host might not think
of some excuse for detaining him, he stole out of
the room quickly, sought out, in the anteroom, his
cloak, which, to his sorrow, he found lying on the
floor, brushed it, picked off every speck upon it,
put it on his shoulders, and descended the stairs
to the street.

In the street all was still bright. Some petty
shops, those permanent clubs of servants and all
sorts of folks, were open. Others were shut, but,
nevertheless, showed a streak of light the whole
length of the door-crack, indicating that they
were not yet free of company, and that probably
some domestics, male and female, were finishing
their stories and conversations, while leaving
their masters in complete ignorance as to their
whereabouts. Akakiy Akakievitch went on in a
happy frame of mind: he even started to run,
without knowing why, after some lady, who flew
past like a flash of lightning. But he stopped
short, and went on very quietly as before, wondering why he had quickened his pace. Soon
there spread before him those deserted street,
which are not cheerful in the daytime, to say nothing of the evening. Now they were even more
dim and lonely: the lanterns began to grow rarer,
oil, evidently, had been less liberally supplied.
Then came wooden houses and fences: not a soul
anywhere; only the snow sparkled in the streets
and mournfully veiled the low-roofed cabins with
their closed shutters. He approached the spot

where the street crossed a vast square with houses barely visible on its farther side, a square which seemed a fearful desert.

Afar, a tiny spark glimmered from some watchman's box, which seemed to stand on the edge of the world. Akakiy Akakievitch's cheerfulness diminished at this point in a marked degree. He entered the square, not without an involuntary sensation of fear, as though his heart warned him of some evil. He glanced back and on both sides, it was like a sea about him. "No, it is better not to look," he thought, and went on, closing his eyes. When he opened them, to see whether he was near the end of the square, he suddenly beheld, standing just before his very nose, some bearded individuals of precisely what sort he could not make out. All grew dark before his eyes, and his heart throbbed.

"But, of course, the cloak is mine!" said one of them in a loud voice, seizing hold of his collar. Akakiy Akakievitch was about to shout "watch" when the second man thrust a fist about the size of a man's head into his mouth, muttering, "Now scream!"

Akakiy Akakievitch felt them strip off his cloak and give him a push with a knee; he fell headlong upon the snow, and felt no more. In a few minutes he recovered consciousness, and rose to his feet; but no one was there. He felt that it was cold in the square and that his cloak was gone; he began to shout, but his voice did not appear to reach to the outskirts of the square. In despair, but without ceasing to shout, he started at a run across the square, straight toward the watch-box, beside which stood the watchman, leaning on his halberd, and apparently curious to know what kind of a customer was running toward him and shouting. Akakiy Akakievitch ran up to him, and began in a sobbing voice to shout that he was asleep and attended to nothing, and did not see when a man was robbed. The watchman replied that he had seen two men stop him in the middle of the square, but supposed that they were friends of his; and that, instead of scolding vainly, he had better go to the police on the morrow, so that they might make a search for whoever had stolen the cloak.

Akakiy Akakievitch ran home in complete disorder; his hair, which grew very thinly upon his temples and the back of his head, wholly disordered; his body, arms, and legs covered with snow. The old woman, who was mistress of his lodgings, on hearing a terrible knocking, sprang hastily from her bed, and, with only one shoe on, ran to open the door, pressing the sleeve of her chemise to her bosom out of modesty; but when she had opened it she fell back on beholding Akakiy Akakievitch in such a state. When he told her about the affair she clasped her hands, and said that he must go straight to the district chief of police, for his subordinate would turn up his nose, promise well, and drop the matter there. The very best thing to do, therefore, would be to go to the district chief, whom she knew, because Finnish Anna, her former cook, was now nurse at his house. She often saw him passing the house; and he was at church every Sunday, praying, but at the same time gazing cheerfully at everybody; so that he must be a good man, judging from all appearances. Having listened to this opinion, Akakiy Akakievitch betook himself sadly to his room; and how he spent the night there any one who can put himself in another's place may readily imagine.

Early in the morning he presented himself at the district chief's; but was told that this official was asleep. He went again at ten and was again informed that he was asleep; at eleven, and they said, "The superintendent is not at home;" at dinner time, and the clerks in the anteroom would not admit him on any terms, and insisted upon knowing his business. So that at last, for once in his life, Akakiy Akakievitch felt an inclination to show some spirit, and said curtly that he must see the chief in person; that they ought not to presume to refuse him entrance; that he came from the department of justice, and that when he complained of them, they would see.

The clerks dared make no reply to this, and one of them went to call the chief, who listened to the strange story of the theft of the coat. Instead of directing his attention to the principal points of the matter, he began to question Akakiy

Akakievitch: Why was he going home so late?
Was he in the habit of doing so, or had he been to
some disorderly house? So that Akakiy Akakievitch got thoroughly confused, and left him
without knowing whether the affair of his cloak
was in proper train or not.

All that day, for the first time in his life, he
never went near the department. The next day
he made his appearance, very pale, and in his old
cape, which had become even more shabby. The
news of the robbery of the cloak touched many;
although there were some officials present who
never lost an opportunity, even such a one as the
present, of ridiculing Akakiy Akakievitch. They
decided to make a collection for him on the spot,
but the officials had already spent a great deal in
subscribing for the director's portrait, and for
some book, at the suggestion of the head of that
division, who was a friend of the author; and so
the sum was trifling.

One of them, moved by pity, resolved to help
Akakiy Akakievitch with some good advice at
least, and told him that he ought not to go to the
police, for although it might happen that a police
officer, wishing to win the approval of his superiors, might hunt up the cloak by some means,
still his cloak would remain in the possession of
the police if he did not offer legal proof that it
belonged to him. The best thing for him, therefore, would be to apply to a certain prominent
personage; since this prominent personage, by

entering into relations with the proper persons, could greatly expedite the matter.

As there was nothing else to be done, Akakiy Akakievitch decided to go to the prominent personage. What was the exact official position of the prominent personage remains unknown to this day. The reader must know that the prominent personage had but recently become a prominent personage, having up to that time been only an insignificant person. Moreover, his present position was not considered prominent in comparison with others still more so. But there is always a circle of people to whom what is insignificant in the eyes of others is important enough. Moreover, he strove to increase his importance by sundry devices; for instance, he managed to have the inferior officials meet him on the staircase when he entered upon his service; no one was to presume to come directly to him, but the strictest etiquette must be observed; the collegiate recorder must make a report to the government secretary, the government secretary to the titular councilor, or whatever other man was proper, and all business must come before him in this manner. In Holy Russia all is thus contaminated with the love of imitation; every man imitates and copies his superior. They even say that a certain titular councilor, when promoted to the head of some small separate room, immediately partitioned off a private room for himself, called it the audience chamber, and posted at the door a lackey with red collar and braid, who grasped the handle of the door and opened to all comers; though the audience chamber would hardly hold an ordinary writing table.

The manners and customs of the prominent personage were grand and imposing, but rather exaggerated. The main foundation of his system was strictness. "Strictness, strictness, and always strictness!" he generally said; and at the last word he looked significantly into the face of the person to whom he spoke. But there was no necessity for this, for the half-score of subordinates, who formed the entire force of the office, were properly afraid; on catching sight of him afar off, they left their work, and waited, drawn up in line, until he had passed through the room. His ordinary converse with his inferiors smacked of sternness, and consisted chiefly of three phrases: "How dare you?" "Do you know whom you are speaking to?" "Do you realize who stands before you?"

Otherwise he was a very kind-hearted man, good to his comrades, and ready to oblige; but the rank of general threw him completely off his balance. On receiving any one of that rank he became confused, lost his way, as it were, and never knew what to do. If he chanced to be among his equals, he was still a very nice kind of man, a very good fellow in many respects, and not stupid; but the very moment that he found himself in the society of people but one rank lower than himself, he became silent; and his situation aroused sympathy, the more so as he felt himself that he might have been making an incomparably better use of his time. In his eyes there was sometimes visible a desire to join some interesting conversation or group; but he was kept back by the thought, "Would it not be a very great condescension on his part? Would it not be familiar? and would he not thereby lose his importance?" And in consequence of such reflections he always remained in the same dumb state, uttering from time to time a few monosyllabic sounds, and thereby earning the name of the most wearisome of men.

To this prominent personage, Akakiy Akakievitch presented himself, and this at the most unfavorable time for himself, though opportune for the prominent personage. The prominent personage was in his cabinet, conversing very gaily with an old acquaintance and companion of his childhood, whom he had not seen for several years, and who had just arrived, when it was announced to him that a person named Bashmatchkin had come. He asked abruptly: "Who is he?" "Some official," he was informed. "Ah, he can wait! this is no time for him to call," said the important man.

It must be remarked here that the important man lied outrageously: he had said all he had to say to his friend long before; and the conversation had been interspersed for some time with very long pauses, during which they merely slapped each other on the leg, and said: "You think so, Ivan Abramovitch?" "Just so, Stephan Varlamovitch!" Nevertheless, he ordered that the official should be kept waiting, in order to show his friend, a man who had not been in the service for a long time, but had lived at home in the country, how long officials had to wait in his anteroom.

At length, having talked himself completely out, and more than that, having had his fill of pauses, and smoked a cigar in a very comfortable armchair with reclining back, he suddenly seemed to recollect, and said to the secretary, who stood by the door with papers of reports, "So it seems that there is a tchinovnik waiting to see me. Tell him that he may come in." On perceiving Akakiy Akakievitch's modest mien and his worn undress uniform, he turned abruptly to him and said: "What do you want?" in a curt, hard voice, which he had practised in his room in private, and before the looking-glass, for a whole week before being raised to his present rank.

Akakiy Akakievitch, who was already imbued with a due amount of fear, became somewhat confused; and, as well as his tongue would permit, explained, with a rather more frequent addition than usual of the word "that," that his cloak was quite new and had been stolen in the most inhuman manner; that he had applied to him in order that he might, in some way, by his inter-

mediation—that he might enter into correspondence with the chief of police, and find the cloak.

For some inexplicable reason this conduct
seemed familiar to the prominent personage.
"What, my dear sir!" he said abruptly, "are you
not acquainted with etiquette? Where have you
come from? Don't you know how such matters
are managed? You should first have entered a
complaint about this at the court below: it would
have gone to the head of the department, then to
the chief of the division, then it would have been
handed over to the secretary, and the secretary
would have given it to me."

"But, your excellency," said Akakiy Akakievitch, trying to collect his small handful of wits,
and conscious at the same time that he was per-
spiring terribly, "I, your excellency, presumed to
trouble you because secretaries—are an untrust-
worthy race."

"What, what, what!" said the important personage. "Where did you get such courage?
Where did you get such ideas? What impudence
toward their chiefs and superiors has spread
among the young generation!" The prominent
personage apparently had not observed that
Akakiy Akakievitch was already in the neighborhood of fifty. If he could be called a young man,
it must have been in comparison with some one
who was seventy. "Do you know to whom you
speak? Do you realize who stands before you?
Do you realize it? do you realize it? I ask you!"

Then he stamped his foot and raised his voice to such a pitch that it would have frightened even a different man from Akakiy Akakievitch.

Akakiy Akakievitch's senses failed him; he staggered, trembled in every limb, and, if the porters had not run in to support him, would have fallen to the floor. They carried him out insensible. But the prominent personage, gratified that the effect should have surpassed his expectations, and quite intoxicated with the thought that his word could even deprive a man of his senses, glanced sidewise at his friend in order to see how he looked upon this, and perceived, not without satisfaction, that his friend was in a most uneasy frame of mind, and even beginning, on his part, to feel a trifle frightened.

Akakiy Akakievitch could not remember how he descended the stairs, and got into the street. He felt neither his hands nor feet. Never in his life had he been so rated by any high official, let alone a strange one. He went staggering on through the snowstorm, which was blowing in the streets, with his mouth wide open, the wind, in St. Petersburg fashion, darted upon him from all quarters, and down every cross street. In a twinkling it had blown a quinsy into his throat, and he reached home unable to utter a word. His throat was swollen, and he lay down on his bed. So powerful is sometimes a good scolding!

The next day a violent fever showed itself. Thanks to the generous assistance of the St.

Petersburg climate, the malady progressed more rapidly than could have been expected; and when the doctor arrived, he found, on feeling the sick man's pulse, that there was nothing to be done, except to prescribe a fomentation, so that the patient might not be left entirely without the beneficent aid of medicine; but at the same time he predicted his end in thirty-six hours. After this he turned to the landlady, and said: "And as for you, don't waste your time on him: order his pine coffin now, for an oak one will be too expensive for him." Did Akakiy Akakievitch hear these fatal words? and if he heard them, did they produce any overwhelming effect upon him? Did he lament the bitterness of his life? We know not, for he continued in a delirious condition. Visions incessantly appeared to him each stranger than the other. Now he saw Petrovitch and ordered him to make a cloak with some traps for robbers who seemed to him to be always under the bed; and cried every moment to the landlady to pull one of them from under his coverlet. Then he inquired why his old mantle hung before him when he had a new cloak. Next he fancied that he was standing before the prominent person listening to a thorough setting-down and saying: "Forgive me, your excellency!" but at last he began to curse, uttering the most horrible words, so that his aged landlady crossed herself, never in her life having heard anything of the kind from him, the more so, as those words followed directly

after the words "your excellency." Later on he
talked utter nonsense, of which nothing could be
made: all that was evident being that his inco-
herent words and thoughts hovered ever about
one thing, his cloak.

At length poor Akakiy Akakievitch breathed
his last. They sealed up neither his room nor his
effects, because, in the first place, there were no
heirs, and, in the second, there was very little to
inherit beyond a bundle of goose-quills, a quire of
white official paper, three pairs of socks, two or
three buttons which had burst off his trousers,
and the mantle already known to the reader. To
whom all this fell, God knows. I confess that the
person who told me this tale took no interest in
the matter. They carried Akakiy Akakievitch
out, and buried him.

And St. Petersburg was left without Akakiy
Akakievitch, as though he had never lived there.
A being disappeared, who was protected by none,
dear to none, interesting to none, and who never
even attracted to himself the attention of those
students of human nature, who omit no opportunity of thrusting a pin through a common fly,
and examining it under the miscroscope. A being who bore meekly the jibes of the department,
and went to his grave without having done one
unusual deed, but to whom, nevertheless, at the
close of his life, appeared a bright visitant in the
form of a cloak, which momentarily cheered his
poor life, and upon whom, thereafter, an intoler-

able misfortune descended, just as it descends upon the heads of the mighty of this world!

Several days after his death, the porter was sent from the department to his lodgings with an order for him to present himself there immediately; the chief commanding it. But the porter had to return unsuccessful, with the answer that he could not come; and to the question, "Why?" replied, "Well, because he is dead! he was buried four days ago." In this manner did they hear of Akakiy Akakievitch's death at the department; and the next day a new official sat in his place, with a handwriting by no means so upright, but more inclined and slanting.

But who could have imagined that this was not really the end of Akakiy Akakievitch, that he was destined to raise a commotion after death, as if in compensation for his utterly insignificant life? But so it happened, and our poor story unexpectedly gains a fantastic ending.

A rumor suddenly spread through St. Petersburg that a dead man had taken to appearing on the Kalinkin Bridge and its vicinity, at night, in the form of a tchinovnik seeking a stolen cloak, and that, under the pretext of its being the stolen cloak, he dragged, without regard to rank or calling, every one's cloak from his shoulders, be it catskin, beaver, fox, bear, sable; in a word, every sort of fur and skin which men adopted for their covering. One of the department officials saw the dead man with his own eyes, and immediately recognized in him Akakiy Akakievitch. This, however, inspired him with such terror that he ran off with all his might, and therefore did not scan the dead man closely, but only saw how the latter threatened him from afar with his finger. Constant complaints poured in from all quarters, of those who were exposed to the danger of a cold, on account of the frequent dragging off of their cloaks.

Arrangements were made by the police to catch the corpse, alive or dead, at any cost, and punish him as an example to others, in the most severe manner. In this they nearly succeeded; for a watchman, on guard in Kirushkin Alley, caught the corpse by the collar on the very scene of his evil deeds, when attempting to pull off the frieze cloak of a retired musician. Having seized him by the collar, he summoned, with a shout, two of his comrades, whom he enjoined to hold him fast, while he himself felt for a moment in his boot, in order to draw out his snuff-box, and refresh his frozen nose. But the snuff was of a sort which even a corpse could not endure. The watchman, having closed his right nostril with his finger, had no sooner succeeded in holding half a handful up to the left than the corpse sneezed so violently that he completely filled the eyes of all three. While they raised their hands to wipe them, the dead man vanished completely, so that they positively did not know whether they had actually had him in their grip at all. Thereafter

the watchmen conceived such a terror of dead
men that they were afraid even to seize the living,
and only screamed from a distance: "Hey, there!
go your way!" So the dead tchinovnik began to
appear, even beyond the Kalinkin Bridge, causing no little terror to all timid people.

But we have totally neglected that certain
prominent personage, who may really be considered as the cause of the fantastic turn taken by
this true history. First of all, justice compels us
to say that after the departure of poor, annihil-
ated Akakiy Akakievitch, he felt something like
remorse. Suffering was unpleasant to him, for
his heart was accessible to many good impulses,
in spite of the fact that his rank often prevented
his showing his true self. As soon as his friend
had left his cabinet he began to think about poor
Akakiy Akakievitch. And from that day forth
poor Akakiy Akakievitch, who could not bear up
under an official reprimand, recurred to his mind
almost every day. The thought troubled him to
such an extent that a week later he even resolved
to send an official to him, to learn whether he
really could assist him; and when it was reported
to him that Akakiy Akakievitch had died suddenly of fever, he was startled, harkened to the
reproaches of his conscience, and was out of sorts
for the whole day.

Wishing to divert his mind in some way, and
drive away the disagreeable impression, he set
out that evening for one of his friends' houses,

where he found quite a large party assembled.
What was better, nearly every one was of the
same rank as himself, so that he need not feel in
the least constrained. This had a marvelous
effect upon his mental state. He grew expan-
sive, made himself agreeable in conversation, in
short, he passed a delightful evening. After supper he drank a couple of glases of champagne—
not a bad recipe for cheerfulness, as every one
knows. The champagne inclined him to various
adventures; and he determined not to return
home, but to go and see a certain well-known
lady, of German extraction, Karolina Ivanovna,
a lady, it appears, with whom he was on a very
friendly footing.

It must be mentioned that the prominent personage was no longer a young man, but a good
husband, and respected father of a family. Two
sons, one of whom was already in the service; and
a good-looking, sixteen-year-old daughter, with
a rather *retroussé* but pretty little nose, came
every morning to kiss his hand, and say: *"Bon
jour,* papa." His wife, a still fresh and good-
looking woman, first gave him her hand to kiss,
and then, reversing the procedure, kissed his. But
the prominent personage, though perfectly satisfied in his domestic relations, considered it
stylish to have a friend in another quarter of the
city. This friend was scarcely prettier or
younger than his wife; but there are such puzzles
in the world, and it is not our place to judge

them. So the important personage descended the
stairs, stepped into his sledge, said to the coachman, "To Karolina Ivanovna's," and, wrapping
himself luxuriously in his warm cloak, found himself in that delightful frame of mind than which a
Russian can conceive nothing better, namely,
when you think of nothing yourself, yet when the
thoughts creep into your mind of their own accord, each more agreeable than the other, giving
you no trouble either to drive them away or seek
them. Fully satisfied, he recalled all the gay
features of the evening just passed, and all the
mots which had made the little circle laugh.
Many of them he repeated in a low voice, and
found them quite as funny as before; so it is not
surprising that he should laugh heartily at them.
Occasionally, however, he was interrupted by
gusts of wind, which, coming suddenly, God
knows whence or why, cut his face, drove masses
of snow into it, filled out his cloak-collar like a
sail, or suddenly blew it over his head with supernatural force, and thus caused him constant
trouble to disentangle himself.

Suddenly the important personage felt some
one clutch him firmly by the collar. Turning
round, he perceived a man of short stature, in an
old, worn uniform, and recognized, not without
terror, Akakiy Akakievitch. The official's face
was white as snow, and looked just like a corpse's.
But the horror of the important personage trans-
cended all bounds when he saw the dead man's

mouth open, and, with a terrible odor of the grave, give vent to the following remarks: "Ah, here you are at last! I have you, that—by the collar! I need your cloak; you took no trouble about mine, but reprimanded me; so now give up your own."

The pallid prominent personage almost died of fright. Brave as he was in the office and in the presence of inferiors generally, and although, at the sight of his manly form and appearance, every one said, "Ugh! how much character he has!" at this crisis, he, like many possessed of a heroic exterior, experienced such terror that, not without cause, he began to fear an attack of illness. He flung his cloak hastily from his shoulders and shouted to his coachman in an unnatural voice: "Home at full speed." The coachman, hearing the tone which is generally employed at critical moments, and even accompanied by something much more tangible, drew his head down between his shoulders in case of an emergency, flourished his whip, and flew on like an arrow. In a little more than six minutes the prominent personage was at the entrance of his own house. Pale, thoroughly scared, and cloakless, he went home instead of to Karolina Ivanovna's, reached his room somehow or other, and passed the night in the direst distress; so that the next morning over their tea his daughter said: "You are very pale to-day, papa." But papa remained silent, and said not a word to any one of what had happened to him, where he had been, or where he had intended to go.

This occurrence made a deep impression upon him. He even began to say: "How dare you? do you realize who stands before you?" less frequently to the under-officials, and, if he did utter the words, it was only after first having learned the bearings of the matter. But the most noteworthy point was that from that day forward the apparition of the dead tchinovnik ceased to be seen. Evidently the prominent personage's cloak just fitted his shoulders; at all events, no more instances of his dragging cloaks from people's shoulders were heard of. But many active and apprehensive persons could by no means reassure themselves, and asserted that the dead tchinovnik still showed himself in distant parts of the city.

In fact, one watchman in Kolomna saw with his own eyes the apparition come from behind a house. But being rather weak of body, he dared not arrest him, but followed him in the dark, until, at length, the apparition looked round, paused, and inquired: "What do you want?" at the same time showing such a fist as is never seen on living men. The watchman said: "It's of no consequence," and turned back instantly. But the apparition was much too tall, wore huge mustaches, and, directing its steps apparently toward the Obukhoff Bridge, disappeared in the darkness of the night.

CAVALLERIA RUSTICANA

BY GIOVANNI VERGA

GREATEST SHORT STORIES

CAVALLERIA RUSTICANA

BY GIOVANNI VERGA

AFTER Turridu Macca, Mistress Nunzia's son, came home from soldiering, he used to strut every Sunday, peacock-like, in the public square, wearing his rifleman's uniform, and his red cap that looked just like that of the fortune-teller waiting for custom behind the stand with the cage of canaries. The girls all rivaled each other in making eyes at him as they went their way to mass, with their noses down in the folds of their shawls; and the young lads buzzed about him like so many flies. Besides, he had brought back a pipe, with the king on horseback on the bowl, as natural as life; and he struck his matches on the back of his trousers, raising up one leg as if he were going to give a kick. But for all that, Master Angelo's daughter Lola had not once shown herself, either at mass or on her balcony, since her betrothal to a man from Licodia, who was a carter by trade, and had four Sortino mules in his stable. No sooner had Turridu heard the news than, holy great devil! but he wanted to rip him inside out, that was what he wanted to do to him, that fellow from Licodia.

Translated by Frederic Taber Cooper. Copyright, 1907, by P. F. Collier & Son.

However, he did nothing to him at all, but contented himself with going and singing every scornful song he knew beneath the fair one's window.

"Has Mistress Nunzia's Turridu nothing at all to do," the neighbors asked, "but pass his nights in singing, like a lonely sparrow?"

At last he came face to face with Lola, on her way back from praying to Our Lady of Peril; and at sight of him she turned neither white nor red, as though he were no concern of hers.

"It is a blessing to have sight of you!" said he.

"Oh, friend Turridu, I was told that you came back around the first of the month."

"And I too was told many other things besides!" he answered. "So it is true that you are going to marry Alfio the carter?"

"If such is the will of God!" answered Lola, drawing together beneath her chin the two corners of her herchief.

"You do the will of God by taking or leaving as it pays you best! And it was the will of God that I should come home from so far away to hear such fine news, Mistress Lola!"

The poor fellow still tried to make a show of indifference, but his voice had grown husky; and he walked on ahead of the girl with a swagger that kept the tassel of his cap dancing back and forth upon his shoulders. It really hurt the girl to see him with such a long face, but she had not the heart to deceive him with fair words.

"Listen, friend Turridu," she said at length, "you must let me go on to join the other girls. What would folks be saying if we were seen together?"

"That is true," replied Turridu; "now that you are to marry Alfio, who has four mules in his stable, it won't do to set people talking. My mother, on the other hand, poor woman, had to sell our one bay mule, and that little bit of vineyard down yonder on the highroad, during the time that I was soldiering. The time is gone when the Lady Bertha span; and you no longer give a thought to the time when we used to talk together from window to courtyard, and when you gave me this handkerchief just before I went away, into which God knows how many tears I wept at going so far that the very name of our land seemed forgotten. But now good-by, Mistress Lola, let us square accounts and put an end to our friendship."

Mistress Lola and the carter were married; and on the following Sunday she showed herself on her balcony, with her hands spread out upon her waist, to show off the big rings of gold that her husband had given her.

Turridu kept passing and repassing through the narrow little street, with his pipe in his mouth and his hands in his pockets, pretending indifference and ogling the girls; but inwardly he was eating his heart out to think that Lola's husband had all that gold, and that she pretended not even to notice him as he passed by.

"I'd like to take her from under his very eyes, the dirty dog!" he muttered.

Across from Alfio's house lived Master Cola, the vine-grower, who was rich as a porker, so they said, and had an unmarried daughter. Turridu said so much, and did so much, that Master Cola took him into his employ; then he began to haunt the house and make pretty speeches to the girl.

"Why don't you go and say all these fine things to Mistress Lola?" Santa answered him.

"Mistress Lola is a big lady! Mistress Lola is wife of one of the crowned heads now!"

"I suppose I am not good enough for the crowned heads."

"You are worth a hundred such as Lola; and I know one fellow who would never so much as look at Mistress Lola or her patron saint when you are around. For she isn't fit even to carry your shoes for you, indeed she isn't!"

"When the fox found that he couldn't reach the grapes—"

"He said, 'how lovely you are, you sweet little grape!'"

"Oh! come, hands off, friend Turridu."

"Are you afraid I am going to eat you?"

"No, I am not afraid of you nor of him you serve."

"Ah! your mother was from Licodia, we all

know that. Your blood boils quickly! Oh! I could eat you up with my eyes!"

"Then eat me up with your eyes, and leave no crumbs; but meanwhile pick up that bundle of twigs for me."

"For your sake I would pick up the whole house, that I would!"

To hide her blushes, she threw at him the fagot she happened to have in her hands, but for a wonder missed him.

"Cut it short! Talking doesn't bind fagots."

"If I was rich, I should be looking for a wife just like you, Santa!"

"I shall not marry a crowned head, as Mistress Lola did; but I shall have my dower, as well as she, when the Lord sends me the right man."

"We know that you are rich, yes, we know that!"

"If you know so much, then stop talking, for my father will soon be here, and I don't care to have him catch me in the courtyard."

The father began to make a wry face, but the girl pretended not to notice, for the tassel of the rifleman's hat had set her heart-strings quivering and was forever dancing before her eyes. After the father had put Turridu out of the door, the daughter opened her window to him, and would stand chatting with him all the evening, until the whole neighborhood could talk of nothing else.

"I am crazy about you," Turridu would say; "I am losing my sleep and my appetite."

"I don't believe it!"

"I wish I was the son of Victor Emanuel, so that I could marry you!"

"I don't believe it!"

"By our Lady, I could eat you up, like a piece of cake!"

"I don't believe it!"

"On my honor!"

"Oh, mother mine!"

Lola, listening night after night, hidden behind a pot of sweet basil, turning first pale and then red, one day called down to Turridu: "How is it, friend Turridu, that old friends no longer greet each other?"

"Alas!" sighed Turridu, "blessed is he who may greet you!"

"If you care to give me greeting, you know where my home is," answered Lola.

Turridu came back to greet her so often that Santa took notice of it, and closed her window in his face. The neighbors pointed him out with a smile or a nod of the head when he passed by in his rifleman's uniform. Lola's husband was away, making a circuit of the village fairs with his mules.

"On Sunday I mean to go to confession, for last night I dreamt of black grapes," said Lola.

"Wait a while! wait a while!" begged Turridu.

"No, now that Easter is so near, my husband would want to know why I have not been to confession."

"Ahah!" murmured Master Cola's Santa, waiting for her turn on her knees before the confessional where Lola was washing herself clean of her sins. "On my soul, it is not to Rome I would send you to do penance!"

Friend Alfio came home with his mules and a pretty penny of profit, and brought his wife a present of a fine new dress for the holidays.

"You do well to bring her presents," his neighbor Santa said to him, "for while you are away your wife has been trimming up the honor of your house!"

Master Alfio was one of those carters who wear the cap well down over one ear, and to hear his wife talked of in this fashion made him change color as though he had been stabbed. "Holy big devil!" he exclaimed, "if you have not seen aright, I won't leave you eyes to weep with, you and your whole family!"

"I have forgotten how to weep!" answered Santa; "I did not weep even when I saw with these very eyes Mistress Nunzia's son, Turridu, go in at night to your wife's house."

"Then it is well," replied Alfio; "many thanks to you."

Now that the husband was home again, Turridu no longer wasted his days in the little street, but drowned his sorrow at the tavern with his friends; and on Easter eve they had on the table a big dish of sausage. When Master Alfio came in, just from the way he fastened his eyes upon him, Turridu understood what business he had come on, and laid his fork down upon his plate.

"How can I serve you, friend Alfio?" he asked.

"Nothing important; friend Turridu, it is some time since I have seen you, and I wanted to talk with you of the matter that you know about."

Turridu had at once offered him a glass, but Alfio put it aside with his hand. Then Turridu arose and said to him: "Here I am, friend Alfio."

The carter threw an arm around his neck.

"If you will come to-morrow morning down among the prickly pears of Canziria, we can talk of this affair, friend Turridu."

"Wait for me on the highroad at sunrise, and we will go together."

With these words they exchanged the kiss of challenge. Turridu seized the carter's ear between his teeth, and thus solemnly bound himself not to fail him.

The friends had all silently withdrawn from the dish of sausage, and accompanied Turridu all the way to his home. Mistress Nunzia, poor woman, was accustomed to wait for him late every night.

"Mother," said Turridu, "do you remember when I went away to be a soldier, and you thought that I was never coming back! Give me a kiss, such as you gave me then, for to-morrow I am going on a long journey!"

Before daybreak he took his clasp-knife, which he had hidden under the straw at the time he went away as a conscript, and started with it for the prickly pears of Canziria.

"Holy Mother, where are you going in such a rage?" sobbed Lola in terror as her husband started to leave the house.

"I am not going far," answered Alfio, "but it will be far better for you if I never come back."

Lola, in her night-gown, prayed at the foot of her bed, and pressed to her lips the rosary which Fra Bernadino had brought her from the Holy Land, and recited all the Ave Marias that there were beads for.

"Friend Alfio," began Turridu after he had walked quite a bit of the way beside his companion, who remained silent, with his cap drawn over his eyes, "as true as God himself, I know that I am in the wrong, and I ought to let you kill me. But before I came here, I saw my old mother, who rose early to see me start, on the pretext that she had to tend the chickens; but her heart must have told her the truth. And as true as God himself, I am going to kill you like a dog, sooner than have the poor old woman weeping for me."

"So much the better," replied Master Alfio, stripping off his jacket, "strike your hardest, and so will I."

They were both worthy foes. Turridu received the first thrust, and was quick enough to catch it on his arm. When he paid it back, he gave good measure, and aimed for the groin.

"Ah, friend Turridu, you have really made up your mind to kill me?"

"Yes, I told you so; ever since I saw my old mother going out to feed the chickens, her face floats all the time before my eyes."

"Then open your eyes wide," Alfio called to him, "for I am going to square accounts with you."

And as he stood on guard, crouching over, so as to hold his left hand upon his wound which was aching, and with his elbow almost touching the ground, he suddenly caught up a handful of dust and threw it into his opponent's eyes.

"Oh!" howled Turridu, "I am done for!"

He sought to save himself by making desperate leaps backward; but Alfio overtook him with another blow in the stomach and a third in the throat.

"And the third is for the honor of my house, that you made free with. Now, perhaps, your mother will forget to feed her chickens."

Turridu stumbled about for a moment, here and there among the prickly pears, and then fell like a log. The blood gurgled in a crimson foam out of his throat, and he had no chance even to gasp out, "Oh, mother mine!"

RAILROAD AND CHURCH-YARD

BY BJÖRNSTJERNE BJÖRNSON

RAILROAD AND CHURCH-YARD

BY BJÖRNSTJERNE BJÖRNSON

I

KNUD AAKRE belonged to an old family in the parish, where it had always been renowned for its intelligence and its devotion to the public welfare. His father had worked his way up to the priesthood, but had died early, and as the widow came from a peasant stock the children were brought up as peasants. Knud had, therefore, received only the education afforded by the public schools of his day; but his father's library had early inspired him with a love of knowledge. This was further stimulated by his friend Henrik Wergeland, who frequently visited him, sent him books, seeds, and much valuable counsel. Following some of the latter, Knud early founded a club, which in the beginning had a very miscellaneous object, for instance: "to give the members practise in debating and to study the constitution," but which later was turned into a practical agricultural society for the entire bailiwick. According to Wergeland's advice, he also founded a parish library, giving his father's

Translated by Rasmus B. Anderson. Copyright, 1882, by Houghton, Mifflin & Co. All rights reserved.

books as its first endowment. A suggestion from the same quarter led him to start a Sunday-school on his gard, for those who might wish to learn writing, arithmetic, and history. All this drew attention to him, so that he was elected member of the parish board of supervisors, of which he soon became chairman. In this capacity he took a deep interest in the schools, which he brought into a remarkably good condition.

Knud Aakre was a short man, brisk in his movements, with small, restless eyes and very disorderly hair. He had large lips, which were in constant motion, and a row of splendid teeth which always seemed to be working with them, for they glistened while his words were snapped out, crisp and clear, crackling like sparks from a great fire.

Foremost among the many he had helped to gain an education was his neighbor Lars Högstad. Lars was not much younger than Knud, but he had developed more slowly. Knud liked to talk about what he read and thought, and he found in Lars, whose manner was quiet and grave, a good listener, who by degrees grew to be a man of excellent judgment. The relations between them soon became such that Knud was never willing to take any important step without first consulting Lars Högstad, and the matter on hand was thus likely to gain some practical amendment. So Knud drew his neighbor into the board of supervisors, and gradually into everything in which he himself took part. They always drove together to the meetings of the board, where Lars never spoke; but on the way back and forth Knud learned his opinions. The two were looked upon as inseparable.

.   .   .   .

One fine autumn day the board of supervisors convened to consider, among other things, a proposal from the bailiff to sell the parish grain magazine and with the proceeds establish a small savings-bank. Knud Aakre, the chairman, would undoubtedly have approved this measure had he relied on his unbiased judgment. But he was prejudiced, partly because the proposal came from the bailiff, whom Wergeland did not like, and who was consequently no favorite of Knud's either, and partly because the grain magazine had been built by his influential paternal grandfather and by him presented to the parish. Indeed, Knud was rather inclined to view the proposition as a personal insult, therefore he had not spoken of it to any one, not even to Lars, and the latter never entered on a topic that had not first been set afloat by some one else.

As chairman, Knud Aakre read the proposal without adding any comments; but, as was his wont, his eyes sought Lars, who usually sat or stood a little aside, holding a straw between his teeth—he always had one when he took part in a conversation; he either used it as a toothpick or he let it hang loosely in one corner of his mouth, turning it more rapidly or more slowly, according to the mood he was in. To his surprise Knud saw that the straw was moving very fast.

"Do you think we should agree to this?" he asked.

Lars answered dryly:

"Yes, I do."

The whole board, feeling that Knud held quite a different opinion, looked in astonishment at Lars, but the latter said no more, nor was he further questioned. Knud turned to another matter, as though nothing had transpired. Not until the close of the meeting did he resume the subject, and then asked, with apparent indifference, if it would not be well to send the proposal back to the bailiff for further consideration, as it certainly did not meet the views of the people, for the parish valued the grain magazine. No one replied. Knud asked whether he should enter the resolution in the register, the measure did not seem to be a wise one.

"Against one vote," added Lars. "Against two," cried another, promptly. "Against three," came from a third; and before the chairman could realize what was taking place, a majority had voted in favor of the proposal.

Knud was so surprised that he forgot to offer any opposition. He recorded the proceedings, and read, in a low voice: "The measure is recommended—adjourned."

His face was fiery red as he rose and put up the

minute-book; but he determined to bring forward
the question once more at the meeting of the representatives. Out in the yard, he put his horse
to the wagon, and Lars came and took his seat
at his side. They discussed various topics on
their way home, but not the one they had nearest
at heart.

The next day Knud's wife sought Lars's wife
to inquire if there was anything wrong between
the two men, for Knud had acted so strangely
when he came home. A short distance above the
gard buildings she met Lars's wife, who was on
her way to ask the same question, for her husband, too, had been out of sorts the day before.
Lars's wife was a quiet, bashful person, somewhat cowed, not by harsh words, but by silence,
for Lars never spoke to her unless she had done
something amiss, or he feared that she might do
wrong. Knud Aakre's wife, on the other hand,
talked more with her husband, and particularly
about the board, for lately it had taken his
thoughts, work, and affection away from her and
the children. She was as jealous of it as of a
woman; she wept at night over the board and
quarreled with her husband about it during the
day. But for that very reason she could say nothing about it now when for once he had returned
home unhappy; for she immediately became more
wretched than he, and for her life she could not
rest until she had discovered what was the matter.
Consequently, when Lars's wife could not give

her the desired information, she had to go out in the parish to seek it. Here she obtained it, and of course was at once of her husband's opinion; she found Lars incomprehensible, not to say wicked. When, however, she let her husband perceive this, she felt that as yet there was no breach between Lars and him; and, that, on the contrary, he clung warmly to him.

The representatives met. Lars Högstad drove over to Aakre in the morning; Knud came out of the house and took his seat beside him. They exchanged the usual greetings, spoke perhaps rather less than was their wont on the way, and not of the proposal. All the members of the board were present; some, too, had found their way in as spectators, which Knud did not like, for it showed that there was a stir in town about the matter. Lars was armed with his straw, and he stood by the stove warming himself, for the autumn was beginning to be cold. The chairman read the proposal, in a subdued, cautious manner, remarking when he was through that it must be remembered this came from the bailiff, who was not apt to be very felicitous in his proposals. The building, it was well known, was a gift, and it was not usual to part with gifts, especially when there was no need of doing so.

Lars, who never before had spoken at the meetings, now took the floor, to the astonishment of all. His voice trembled, but whether it did so out of regard for Knud, or from anxiety lest his own cause should be lost, shall remain unsaid. But his arguments were good and clear, and full of a logic and confidence which had scarcely been heard at these meetings before. And when he had gone over all the ground, he added, in conclusion:

"What does it matter if the proposal does come from the bailiff? This affects the question as little as who erected the building, or in what way it came into the public possession."

Knud Aakre had grown very red in the face (he blushed easily), and he shifted uneasily from side to side, as was his wont when he was impatient, but none the less did he exert himself to be circumspect and to speak in a low voice. There were savings-banks enough in the country, he thought, and quite near at hand, he might almost say *too* near. But if, after all, it was deemed expedient to have one, there were surely other ways of reaching it than those leading over the gifts of the dead and the love of the living. His voice was a little unsteady when he said this, but quickly recovered as he proceeded to speak of the grain magazine in itself, and to show what its advantages were.

Lars answered him thoroughly on the last point, and then added:

"However, one thing and another lead me to doubt whether this parish is managed for the sake of the living or the dead; furthermore, whether it is the love and hatred of a single family which

controls matters here, or the good of the whole."
Knud answered quickly: "I do not know
whether he who has just spoken has been least
benefited by his family—both by the dead and
by him who now lives."

The first shot was aimed at the fact that Knud's
powerful grandfather had saved the gard for
Lar's paternal grandfather, when the latter, on
his part, was absent on a little excursion to the
penitentiary.

The straw which long had been in brisk motion
suddenly became still.

"It is not my way to keep talking everywhere
about myself and my family," said Lars, then
turned again with calm superiority to the subject
under discussion, briefly reviewing all the points
with one definite object. Knud had to admit to
himself that he had never viewed the matter from
such a broad standpoint; involuntarily he raised
his eyes and looked at Lars, who stood before
him, tall, heavily built, with clearness on the vig-
orous brow and in the deep eyes. The lips were
tightly compressed, the straw still played in the
corner of his mouth; all the surrounding lines in-
dicated vigor. He kept his hands behind him,
and stood rigidly erect, while his voice was as
deep and as hollow as if it proceeded from the
depths of the earth. For the first time in his life
Knud saw him as he was, and in his inmost soul
he was afraid of him; for this man must always
have been his superior. He had taken all Knud

himself knew and could impart; he had rejected the tares and kept what produced this strong, hidden growth.

He had been fostered and loved by Knud, but had now become a giant who hated Knud deeply, terribly. Knud could not explain to himself why, but as he looked at Lars he instinctively felt this to be so, and all else becoming swallowed up in this thought he started up, exclaiming:

"But Lars! Lars! what in Heaven's name is the matter with you?" His agitation overcame him—"you, whom I have—you who have—"

Powerless to utter another word, he sat down; but in his effort to gain the mastery over the emotion he deemed Lars unworthy of seeing, he brought his fist down with violence on the table, while his eyes flashed beneath his stiff, disorderly hair, which always hung over them. Lars acted as if he had not been interrupted, and turning toward the others he asked if this was to be the decisive blow; for if such were the case there was no need for further remarks.

This calmness was more than Knud could endure.

"What is it that has come among us?" cried he. "We who have, until to-day, been actuated by love and zeal alone, are now stirred up against each other, as though goaded on by some evil spirit," and he cast a fiery glance at Lars, who replied:

"It must be you yourself who bring in this

spirit, Knud; for I have kept strictly to the matter before us. But you never can see the advantage of anything you do not want yourself; now we shall learn what becomes of the love and the zeal when once this matter is decided as we wish."

"Have I then illy served the interests of the parish?"

There was no reply. This grieved Knud, and he continued: "I really did persuade myself that I had acomplished various things—various things which have been of advantage to the parish; but perhaps I have deceived myself."

He was again overcome by his feelings; for his was a fiery nature, ever variable in its moods, and the breach with Lars pained him so deeply that he could scarcely control himself. Lars answered:

"Yes, I know you appropriate the credit for all that is done here, and if one should judge by the amount of speaking at these meetings, you certainly have accomplished the most."

"Is that the way of it?" shouted Knud, looking sharply at Lars. "Is it you who deserve the entire honor?"

"Since we must finally talk about ourselves," said Lars, "I am free to admit that every question has been carefully considered by both of us before it was introduced here."

Here little Knud Aakre regained his ready speech:

"Take the honor, in God's name; I am able to

live without it; there are other things harder to lose!"

Involuntarily Lars evaded his gaze, but said, as he set the straw in very rapid motion:

"If I were to express *my* opinion, I should say that there is not very much to take credit for. No doubt the priest and the schoolmasters are content with what has been done; but certainly the common people say that up to the present time the taxes of this parish have grown heavier and heavier."

Here arose a murmur in the crowd, and the people grew very restless. Lars continued:

"Finally, to-day we have a matter brought before us that might make the parish some little amends for all it has paid out; this is perhaps the reason why it encounters such opposition. This is a question which concerns the parish; it's for the good of all; it is our duty to guard it from becoming a mere family matter."

People exchanged glances, and spoke in half-audible tones; one of them remarked, as he rose to go for his dinner-pail, that these were the truest words he had heard in these meetings for many years. Now all rose from their seats, the conversation became general, and Knud Aakre, who alone remained sitting, felt that all was lost, fearfully lost, and made no further effort to save it. The truth was, he possessed something of the temperament attributed to Frenchmen: he was very good at a first, second, or even third attack, but poor at self-defense, for his sensibilities overwhelmed his thoughts. He was unable to comprehend this, nor could he sit still any longer, and so resigning his place to the vice-chairman, he left. The others could not refrain from a smile.

He had come to the meeting in company with Lars, but went home alone, although the way was long. It was a cold autumn day, the forest was jagged and bare, the meadow gray-yellow, frost was beginning here and there to remain on the roadside. Disappointment is a terrible companion. Knud felt so small, so desolate, as he walked along; but Lars appeared everywhere before him, towering up to the sky, in the dusk of the evening, like a giant. It vexed him to think it was his own fault that this had been the decisive battle; he had staked too much on one single little issue. But surprise, pain, anger, had mastered him; they still burned, tingled, moaned, and stormed within him. He heard the rumbling of cart-wheels behind him; it was Lars driving his superb horse past him, in a brisk trot, making the hard road resound like distant thunder. Knud watched the broad-shouldered form that sat erect in the cart, while the horse, eager for home, sped onward, without any effort on the part of Lars, who merely gave him a loose rein. It was but a picture of this man's power: he was driving onward to the goal! Knud felt himself cast out of his cart, to stagger on alone in the chill autumn air.

RAILROAD AND CHURCHYARD

In his home at Aakre, Knud's wife was waiting for him. She knew that a battle was inevitable; she had never in her life trusted Lars, and now she was positively afraid of him. It had been no comfort to her that he and her husband had driven away together; it would not have consoled her had they returned in the same way. But darkness had fallen and they had not come. She stood in the doorway, gazing out on the road in front of the house; she walked down the hill and back again, but no cart appeared.

Finally she hears a rattling on the hard road, her heart throbs as the wheels go round, she clings to the casement, peering out into the night; the cart draws near; only one is in it; she recognizes Lars, who sees and recognizes her, but drives past without stopping. Now she became thoroughly alarmed. Her limbs gave way under her, she tottered in and sank down on the bench by the window. The children gathered anxiously about her, the youngest one asked for papa; she never spoke with them except of him. He had such a noble disposition, and this was what made her love him; but now his heart was not with his family, it was engrossed in all sorts of business which brought him only unhappiness, and so they were all unhappy.

If only no misfortune had befallen him! Knud was so hot-tempered. Why had Lars come home alone? Why did he not stop? Should she run after him, or down the road after her husband?

She was in an agony of distress, and the children pressed around her, asking what was the matter. But this she would not tell them, so rising she said they must eat supper alone, then got everything ready and helped them. All the while she kept glancing out on the road. He did not come. She undressed the children and put them to bed, and the youngest repeated the evening prayer while she bowed over him. She herself prayed with such fervor in the words which the infant lips so soothingly uttered that she did not heed the steps outside.

Knud stood upon the threshold, gazing at his little company at prayer. The mother drew herself up; all the children shouted: "Papa!" but he seated himself at once, and said, softly: "Oh, let him say it once more!"

The mother turned again to the bedside, that he, meanwhile, should not see her face, for it would have seemed like intruding on his grief before he felt the need of revealing it. The little one folded its hands over its breast, all the rest did likewise, and it repeated:

" I, a little child, pray Heaven
That my sins may be forgiven;
With time, I'll larger, wiser grow,
And my father and mother joy shall know,
If only Thou, dearest, dearest Lord,
Will help me to keep Thy precious word!
And now to our Heavenly Father's merciful keeping
Our souls let us trust while we're sleeping."

What peace now fell upon the room! Not a minute had elapsed ere all the children were sleeping as in the arms of God; but the mother moved softly away and placed supper before the father, who was, however, unable to eat. But after he had gone to bed, he said:

"Henceforth I shall be at home."

And his wife lay at his side trembling with joy which she dared not betray; and she thanked God for all that had happened, for whatever it might be it had resulted in good!

II

In the course of a year Lars had become chairman of the parish board of supervisors, president of the savings-bank, and leading commissioner in the court of reconciliation; in short, he held every office to which his election had been possible. In the board of supervisors for the amt (county) he was silent during the first year, but the second year he created the same sensation when he spoke as in the parish board; for here, too, coming forward in opposition to him who had previously been the guiding power, he became victorious over the entire rank and file, and was from that time himself the leader. From this his path led him to the storthing (parliament), where his fame had preceded him, and where consequently there was no lack of challenges. But here, although steady and firm, he always remained retiring. He did not care for power, except where he was well known, nor would he

risk leadership at home by a possible defeat
abroad.

For he had a pleasant life at home. When he
stood by the church wall on Sundays, and the
congregation walked slowly past, saluting him
and stealing side glances at him, and one after
another paused in order to exchange a few words
with him—then truly it might be said that he
controlled the entire parish with a straw, for of
course this hung in the corner of his mouth.

He deserved his honors. The road leading to
the church, he had opened; the new church they
were standing beside, he had built; this and much
more was the fruit of the savings-bank which he
had founded and now managed himself. For its
resources were further made fruitful, and the
parish was constantly held up as an example to
all others of self-management and good order.

Knud Aakre had entirely withdrawn from the
field, although at first he attended a few of the
meetings of the board, because he had promised
himself that he would continue to offer his services, even if it were not altogether pleasing to
his pride. In the first proposal he had made he
became so greatly perplexed by Lars, who insisted upon having it represented in all its details,
that, somewhat hurt, he said: "When Columbus
discovered America he did not have it divided
into parishes and deaneries: this came gradually;" whereupon Lars, in his reply, compared
the discovery of America with Knud's proposal

—it so happened that this treated of stable improvements—and afterward Knud was known by no other name in the board than "Discovery of America." So Knud thought that as his usefulness had ceased, so too had his obligations to work, and he refused to accept further reelections.

But he continued to be industrious; and in order that he might still have a field for usefulness, he enlarged his Sunday-school, and placed it, by means of small contributions from the attendants, in communication with the mission cause, of which he soon became the centre and leader in his own and the surrounding counties. Thereupon Lars Högstad remarked, that if ever Knud undertook to collect money for any purpose, he must know beforehand that it was to do good thousands of miles from home.

There was, be it observed, no more strife between them. To be sure, they no longer associated with each other, but they bowed and spoke when they met. Knud always felt a little pain at the mere thought of Lars, but strove to suppress it, and persuade himself that matters could not have been otherwise. At a large wedding-party, many years afterward, where both were present and both were in good spirits, Knud mounted a chair and proposed a toast for the chairman of the parish board, and the first representative their amt had sent to the storthing! He spoke until he became deeply moved, and, as usual, expressed himself in an exceedingly handsome way. Every one thought it was honorably done, and Lars came up to him, and his gaze was unsteady as he said that, for much of what he knew and was, he was indebted to him.

At the next election of the board of supervisors Knud was again made chairman!

But had Lars Högstad foreseen what now followed, he would certainly not have used his influence for this. "Every event happens in its own time," says an old proverb, and just as Knud Aakre again entered the board, the best men of the parish were threatened with ruin, as the result of a speculation craze which had long been raging, but which now first began to demand its victims. It was said that Lars Högstad was the cause of this great disaster, for he had taught the parish to speculate. This penny fever had originated in the parish board of supervisors, for the board itself was the greatest speculator of all. Every one down to the laboring youth of twenty years desired in his transactions to make ten dollars out of one; a beginning of extreme avarice in the efforts to hoard, was followed by an excessive extravagance, and as all minds were bent only on money, there had at the same time developed a spirit of suspicion, of intolerance, of caviling, which resulted in lawsuits and hatred. This also was due to the example of the board, it was said, for among the first things Lars had done as chairman was to sue the venerable old priest for holding doubtful titles. The priest had lost, but had also immediately resigned. At that time some had praised, some censured this suit; but it had proved a bad example. Now came the consequences of Lars's management, in the form of loss to every single man of property in the parish, consequently public opinion underwent a sharp change! The opposing force, too, soon found a leader, for Knud Aakre had come into the board, introduced by Lars.

The struggle began forthwith. All those youths to whom Knud in his time had given instructions, were now grown up and were the most enlightened men in the parish, thoroughly at home in all its transactions and public affairs. It was against these men that Lars now had to contend, and they had borne him a grudge from their childhood up. When of an evening after one of these stormy proceedings he stood on the steps in front of his house, gazing over the parish, he could hear a sound as of distant rumbling thunder rising toward him from the large gards, now lying in the storm. He knew that the day they met their ruin, the savings-bank and himself would be overthrown, and all his long efforts would culminate in imprecations on his own head.

In these days of conflict and despair, a party of railroad commissioners, who were to survey the route for a new road, made their appearance one evening at Högstad, the first gard at the entrance to the parish. In the course of conversation during the evening, Lars learned that there was a question whether the road should run through this valley or another parallel to it.

Like a flash of lightning it darted through his mind that if he could succeed in having it laid here, all property would rise in value, and not only would he himself be saved but his fame would be transmitted to the latest posterity! He could not sleep that night, for his eyes were dazzled by a glowing light, and sometimes he could even hear the sound of the cars. The next day he went himself with the commissioners while they examined the locality; his horse took them, and to his gard they returned. The next day they drove through the other valley; he was still with them, and he drove them back again to his house. They found a brilliant illumination at Högstad; the first men of the parish had been invited to be present at a magnificent party given in honor of the commissioners; it lasted until morning. But to no avail, for the nearer they came to a final issue, the more plainly it appeared that the road could not pass through this locality without undue expense. The entrance to the valley lay through a narrow gorge, and just as it swung into the parish, the swollen river swung in also, so that the railroad would either have to take the same curve along the mountain that the highway now made, thus running at a needlessly high altitude and crossing the river twice, or it would have to run straight forward, and thus through

the old, now unused churchyard. Now the church
had but recently been removed, and it was not
long since the last burial had taken place there.

If it only depended on a bit of old churchyard,
thought Lars, whether or not this great blessing
came into the parish, then he must use his name
and his energy for the removal of this obstacle!
He at once set forth on a visit to the priest and
the dean, and furthermore to the diocese council;
he talked and he negotiated, for he was armed
with all possible facts concerning the immense
advantage of the railroad on one hand, and the
sentiments of the parish on the other, and actually succeeded in winning all parties. It was
promised him that by a removal of part of the
bodies to the new churchyard the objections
might be set aside, and the royal permission obtained for the churchyard to be taken for the line
of railroad. It was told him that nothing was
now needed but for him to set the question afloat
in the board of supervisors.

The parish had grown as excited as himself:
the spirit of speculation which for many years
had been the only one prevailing in the parish,
now became madly jubilant. There was nothing
spoken or thought of but Lars's journey and its
possible results. When he returned with the
most magnificent promises, they made much of
him; songs were sung in his praise; indeed, if at
that time the largest gards had gone to destruction, one after another, no one would have

paid any attention to it: the speculation craze had given way to the railroad craze.

The board of supervisors assembled: there was presented for approval a respectful petition, that the old churchyard might be appropriated as the route of the railroad. This was unanimously adopted; there was even mention of giving Lars a vote of thanks and a coffee-pot in the form of a locomotive. But it was finally thought best to wait until the whole plan was carried into execution. The petition came back from the diocese council, with a demand for a list of all bodies that would have to be removed. The priest made out such a list, but instead of sending it direct, he had his own reasons for sending it through the parish board. One of the members carried it to the next meeting. Here it fell to the lot of Lars, as chairman to open the envelope and read the list.

Now it chanced that the first body to be disinterred was that of Lars's own grandfather! A little shudder ran through the assembly! Lars himself was startled, but nevertheless continued to read. Then it furthermore chanced that the second body was that of Knud Aakre's grandfather, for these two men had died within a short time of each other. Knud Aakre sprang from his seat; Lars paused; everyone looked up in consternation, for old Knud Aakre had been the benefactor of the parish and its best beloved man, time out of mind. There was a dead silence, which lasted for some minutes. At last Lars cleared his throat and went on reading. But the further he proceeded the worse the matter grew; for the nearer they came to their own time, the dearer were the dead. When he had finished, Knud Aakre asked quietly whether the others did not agree with him in thinking that the air about them was filled with spirits. It was just beginning to grow dark in the room, and although they were mature men, sitting in numbers together, they could not refrain from feeling alarmed. Lars produced a bundle of matches from his pocket and struck a light, dryly remarking that this was no more than they knew before.

"Yes, it is," said Knud, pacing the floor, "it is more than I knew before. Now I begin to think that even railroads can be purchased too dearly."

These words sent a quiver through the audience, and, observing that they had better further consider the matter, Knud made a motion to that effect.

In the excitement which had prevailed, he said, the benefit likely to be derived from the road had been overestimated. Even if the railroad did not pass through this parish, there would have to be stations at both ends of the valley; true, it would always be a little more troublesome to drive to them than to a station right in our midst, yet the difficulty would not be so very great that it would be necessary because of it to violate the repose of the dead.

Knud was one of those who when his thoughts were once in rapid motion could present the most convincing arguments; a moment before what he now said had not occurred to his mind, nevertheless it struck home to all. Lars felt the danger of his position, and concluding that it was best to be cautious, apparently acquiesced in Knud's proposition to reconsider. Such emotions are always worse in the beginning, he thought; it is wisest to temporize with them.

But he had miscalculated. In ever-increasing waves the dread of touching the dead of their own families swept over the inhabitants of the parish; what none of them had thought of as long as the matter existed merely in the abstract, now became a serious question when it was brought home to themselves. The women especially were excited, and the road near the courthouse was black with people the day of the next meeting. It was a warm summer day, the windows were removed, and there were as many without the house as within. All felt that a battle was to be fought.

Lars came driving up with his handsome horse, and was greeted by all; he looked calmly and confidently around, not seeming to be surprised at anything. He took a seat near the window, found his straw, and a suspicion of a smile played over his keen face as he saw Knud Aakre rise to his feet to act as spokesman for all the dead in the old Högstad churchyard.

But Knud Aakre did not begin with the

churchyard. He began with an accurate exposition of how greatly the profits likely to accrue from having the railroad run through the parish had been overestimated in all this turmoil. He had positive proofs for every statement he made; he had calculated the distance of each gard from the nearest station. Finally he asked:

"Why has there been so much ado about this railroad, if not in behalf of the parish?"

This he could easily explain to them. There were those who had occasioned so great a disturbance that a still greater one was required to conceal it. Moreover, there were those who in the first outburst of excitement could sell their gards and belongings to strangers who were foolish enough to purchase. It was a shameful speculation which not only the living but the dead must serve to promote!

The effect of his address was very considerable. But Lars had once for all resolved to preserve his composure let come what would. He replied, therefore, with a smile, that he had been under the impression that Knud himself was eager for the railroad, and certainly no one would accuse him of having any knowledge of speculation. (Here followed a little laugh.) Knud had not evinced the slightest objection to the removal of the bodies of common people for the sake of the railroad; but when his own grandfather's body was in question then it suddenly affected the welfare of the whole community! He said no more, but looked with a faint smile at Knud, as did also several others. Meanwhile, Knud Aakre surprised both him and them by replying:

"I confess it; I did not comprehend the matter until it touched my own family feelings; it is possible that this may be a shame, but it would have been a far greater one not to have realized it at last—as is the case with Lars! Never," he concluded, "could this raillery have been more out of place; for to people with common decency the whole affair is revolting."

"This feeling is something that has come up quite recently," replied Lars; "we may, therefore, hope that it will soon pass over again. May it not perhaps help the matter a little to think what the priest, dean, diocese council, engineers, and government will all say if we first unanimously set the ball in motion, then come and beg to have it stopped? If we first are jubilant and sing songs, then weep and deliver funeral orations? If they do not say that we have gone mad in this parish, they must at all events say that we have acted rather strangely of late."

"Yes, God knows, they may well think so!" replied Knud. "We have, indeed, acted very strangely of late, and it is high time for us to mend our ways. Things have come to a serious pass when we can each disinter his own grandfather to make way for a railroad; when we can disturb the resting-place of the dead in order that our own burdens may the more easily be carried.

For is not this rooting in our churchyard in order
to make it yield us food the same thing? What
is buried there in the name of Jesus, we take up
in Moloch's name—this is but little better than
eating the bones of our ancestors."

'Such is the course of nature," said Lars,
dryly.

"Yes, of plants and of animals."

"And are not we animals?"

"We are, but also the children of the living
God, who have buried our dead in faith in Him:
it is He who shall rouse them and not we."

"Oh, you are talking idly! Are we not obliged
to have the graves dug up at any rate, when their
turn comes? What harm if it happen now?"

"I will tell you. What was born of them still
draws the breath of life; what they built up yet
remains; what they loved, taught, and suffered
for, lives about us and within us; and should we
not allow them to rest in peace?"

"Your warmth shows me that you are thinking of your own grandfather again," replied Lars,
"and I must say it seems to me high time the parish should be rid of *him*. He monopolized too
much space while he lived; and so it is scarcely
worth while to have him lie in the way now that
he is dead. Should his corpse prevent a blessing
to this parish that would extend through a hundred generations, we may truly say that of all
who have been born here, *he* has done us the
greatest harm."

Knud Aakre tossed back his disorderly hair, his eyes flashed, his whole person looked like a bent steel spring.

"How much of a blessing what you are speaking about may be, I have already shown. It has the same character as all the other blessings with which you have supplied the parish, namely, a doubtful one. It is true, you have provided us with a new church, but you have also filled it with a new spirit—and it is not that of love. True, you have furnished us with new roads, but also with new roads to destruction, as is now plainly manifest in the misfortunes of many. True, you have diminished our public taxes, but you have increased our private ones; lawsuits, promissory notes, and bankruptcies are no fruitful gifts to a community. And *you* dare to dishonor in his grave the man whom the whole parish blesses? You dare assert that he lies in our way; ay, no doubt he does lie in your way, this is plain enough now, for his grave will be the cause of your downfall! The spirit which has reigned over you, and until to-day over us all, was not born to rule but to enter into servitude. The churchyard will surely be allowed to remain in peace; but to-day it shall have one grave added to it, namely, that of your popularity, which is now to be buried there."

Lars Högstad rose, white as a sheet; his lips parted, but he was unable to utter a word, and the straw fell. After a few vain efforts to find and recover his powers of speech, he burst forth like a volcano with:

"And so these are the thanks I get for all my toil and drudgery! If such a woman-preacher is to be allowed to rule—why, then, may the devil be your chairman if ever I set my foot here again! I have kept things together until this day, and after me your trash will fall into a thousand pieces, but let it tumble down now—here is the register!" And he flung it on the table. "Shame on such an assembly of old women and brats!" Here he struck the table with great violence. "Shame on the whole parish that it can see a man rewarded as I am now."

He brought down his fist once more with such force that the great courthouse table shook, and the inkstand with its entire contents tumbled to the floor, marking for all future generations the spot where Lars Högstad fell in spite of all his prudence, his long rule, and his patience.

He rushed to the door and in a few moments had left the place. The entire assembly remained motionless; for the might of his voice and of his wrath had frightened them, until Knud Aakre, remembering the taunt he had received at the time of *his* fall, with beaming countenance and imitating Lars's voice, exclaimed:

"Is *this* to be the decisive blow in the matter?"

The whole assembly burst into peals of merriment at these words! The solemn meeting ended in laughter, talk, and high glee; only a few left the place, those remaining behind called for drink to add to their food, and a night of thunder succeeded a day of lightning. Every one felt as happy and independent as of yore, ere the commanding spirit of Lars had cowed their souls into dumb obedience. They drank toasts to their freedom; they sang, indeed, finally they danced, Knud Aakre and the vice-chairman taking the lead and all the rest following, while boys and girls joined in, and the young folks outside shouted "Hurrah!" for such a jollification they had never before seen!

III

Lars moved about in the large rooms at Högstad without speaking a word. His wife, who loved him, but always in fear and trembling, dared not come into his presence. The management of the gard and of the house might be carried on as best it could, while on the other hand there kept growing a multitude of letters, which passed back and forth between Högstad and the parish, and Högstad and the post-office; for Lars had claims against the parish board, and these not being satisfied he prosecuted; against the savings-bank, which were also unsatisfied, and so resulted in another suit. He took offense at expressions in the letters he received and went to law again, now against the chairman of the parish board, now against the president of the savings-bank. At the same time there were dreadful articles in the newspapers, which report attributed to him, and which were the cause of great dissension in the parish, inciting neighbor against neighbor. Sometimes he was absent whole weeks, no one knew where, and when he returned he lived as secluded as before. At church he had not been seen after the great scene at the representatives' meeting.

Then one Saturday evening the priest brought tidings that the railroad was to run through the parish after all, and across the old churchyard! It struck like lightning into every home. The unanimous opposition of the parish board had been in vain, Lars Högstad's influence had been stronger. This was the meaning of his journeys, this was his work! Involuntary admiration of the man and his stubborn persistence tended to suppress the dissatisfaction of the people at their own defeat, and the more they discussed the matter the more reconciled they became; for a fact accomplished always contains within itself reasons why it is so, which gradually force themselves upon us after there is no longer possibility of change. The people assembled about the church the next day, and they could not help laughing as they met one another. And just as the whole congregation, young and old, men and women, ay, even children, were all talking about Lars Högstad, his ability, his rigorous will, his immense influence, he himself with his whole household came driving up in four conveyances, one after the other. It was two years since his last visit there! He alighted and passed through the crowd, while all, as by one impulse, unhesitatingly greeted him, but he did not deign to bestow a glance on either side, nor to return a single salutation. His little wife, pale as death, followed him. Inside of the church the astonishment grew to such a pitch that as one after another caught sight of him they stopped singing and only stared at him. Knud Aakre, who sat in his pew in front of Lars, noticed that there was something the matter, and as he saw nothing remarkable in front of him, he turned round. He saw Lars bowed over his hymn-book, searching for the place.

He had not seen him since that evening at the meeting, and such a complete change he had not believed possible. For this was no victor! The thin, soft hair was thinner than ever, the face was haggard and emaciated, the eyes hollow and bloodshot, the giant neck had dwindled into wrinkles and cords. Knud comprehended at a glance what this man had gone through; he was seized with a feeling of strong sympathy, indeed, he felt something of the old love stirring within his breast. He prayed for Lars to his God, and made a resolute vow that he would seek him after service; but Lars had started on ahead. Knud resolved to call on him that evening. His wife, however, held him back.

"Lars is one of those," said she, "who can

scarcely bear a debt of gratitude: keep away from him until he has an opportunity to do you some favor, and then perhaps he will come to you!"

But he did not come. He appeared now and then at church, but nowhere else, and he associated with no one. On the other hand, he now devoted himself to his gard and other business with the passionate zeal of one who had determined to make amends in one year for the neglect of many; and, indeed, there were those who said that this was imperative.

Railroad operations in the valley began very soon. As the line was to go directly past Lars's gard, he tore down the portion of his house that faced the road, in order to build a large and handsome balcony, for he was determined that his gard should attract attention. This work was just being done when the temporary rails for the conveyance of gravel and timber to the road were laid and a small locomotive was sent to the spot. It was a beautiful autumn evening that the first gravel car was to pass over the road. Lars stood on his front steps, to hear the first signal and to see the first column of smoke; all the people of the gard were gathered about him. He gazed over the parish, illumined by the setting sun, and he felt that he would be remembered as long as a train should come roaring through this fertile valley. A sense of forgiveness glided into his soul. He looked toward the churchyard, a part of which still remained, with crosses bowed down to the ground, but a part of it was now the railroad. He was just endeavoring to define his own feeling when the first signal whistled, and presently the train came slowly working its way along, attended by a cloud of smoke, mingled with sparks, for the locomotive was fed with pine wood. The wind blew toward the house so that those standing without were soon enveloped in a dense smoke, but as this cleared away Lars saw the train working its way down through the valley like a strong will.

He was content, and entered his house like one who has come from a long day's work. The image of his grandfather stood before him at this moment. This grandfather had raised the family from poverty to prosperity; true, a portion of his honor as a citizen was consumed in the act, but he had advanced nevertheless! His faults were the prevailing ones of his time: they were based on the uncertain boundary lines of the moral conceptions of his day. Every age has its uncertain moral distinctions and its victims.

Honor be to him in his grave, for he had suffered and toiled! Peace be with him! It must be good to rest in the end. But he was not allowed to rest because of his grandson's vast ambition; his ashes were thrown up with the stones and the gravel. Nonsense! he would only smile at his grandson's work.

Amid thoughts like these Lars had undressed and gone to bed. Once more his grandfather's image glided before him. It was sterner now than the first time. Weariness enfeebles us, and Lars began to reproach himself. But he defended himself also. What did his grandfather want? Surely he ought to be satisfied now, for the family honor was proclaimed in loud tones above his grave. Who else had such a monument? And yet what is this? These two monstrous eyes of fire and this hissing, roaring sound belong no longer to the locomotive, for they turn away from the railroad track. And from the churchyard straight toward the house comes an immense procession. The eyes of fire are his grandfather's, and the long line of followers are all the dead. The train advances steadily toward the gard, roaring, crackling, flashing. The windows blaze in the reflection of the dead men's eyes. Lars made a mighty effort to control himself, for this was a dream, unquestionably.

There, now I am awake. Come on, poor ghosts!

And lo! they really did come from the churchyard, overthrowing road, rails, locomotive, and train, so that these fell with a mighty crash to the ground, and the green sod appeared in their stead, dotted with graves and crosses as before. Like mighty champions they advanced, and the hymn, "Let the dead repose in peace!" preceded them. Lars knew it; for through all these years it had been sighing within his soul, and now it had become his requiem; for this was death and death's visions. The cold sweat started out over his whole body, for nearer and nearer—and behold, on the window pane! there they are now, and he heard some one speak his name. Overpowered with dread he struggled to scream; for he was being strangled, a cold hand was clenching his throat, and he regained his voice in an agonized "Help me!" and awoke. The window had been broken in from the outside; the pieces flew all about his head. He sprang up. A man stood at the window, surrounded by smoke and flames.

"The gard is on fire, Lars! We will help you out!" It was Knud Aakre.

When Lars regained his consciousness, he was lying outside in a bleak wind, which chilled his limbs. There was not a soul with him; he saw the flaming gard to the left; around him his cattle were grazing and making their voices heard; the sheep were huddled together in a frightened flock; the household goods were scattered about, and when he looked again he saw some one sitting on a knoll close by, weeping. It was his wife. He called her by name. She started.

"The Lord Jesus be praised that you are alive!" cried she, coming forward and seating herself, or rather throwing herself down in front of him. "O God! O God! We surely have had enough of this railroad now!"

"The railroad?" asked he, but ere the words had escaped his lips a clear comprehension of the case passed like a shudder over him; for, of course, sparks from the locomotive that had fallen among the shavings of the new side wall had been the cause of the fire. Lars sat there brooding in silence; his wife, not daring to utter another word, began to search for his clothes. He accepted her attentions in silence, but as she knelt before him to cover his feet, he laid his hand on her head. Falling forward she buried her face in his lap and wept aloud. Many eyed her curiously. But Lars understood her and said: "You are the only friend I have."

Even though it had cost the gard to hear these words, it mattered not to her; she felt so happy that she gained courage, and rising up and looking humbly into her husband's face, she said:

"Because there is no one else who understands you."

Then a hard heart melted, and tears rolled down the man's cheeks as he clung to his wife's hand.

Now he talked to her as to his own soul. Now too she opened her mind to him. They also talked about how all this had happened, or rather he listened while she told about it. Knud Aakre had been the first to see the fire, had roused his people, sent the girls out over his parish, while he had hastened himself with men and horses to the scene of the conflagration, where all were sleeping. He had engineered the extinguishing of the flames and the rescuing of the household goods, and had himself dragged Lars from the burning room, and carried him to the left side of the house from whence the wind was blowing and had laid him out here in the churchyard.

And while they were talking of this, some one came driving rapidly up the road and turned into the churchyard, where he alighted. It was Knud, who had been home after his church-cart —the one in which they had so many times ridden together to and from the meetings of the parish board. Now he requested Lars to get in and ride home with him. They grasped each other by the hand, the one sitting, the other standing.

"Come with me now," said Knud.

Without a word of reply, Lars rose. Side by side they walked to the cart. Lars was helped in; Knud sat down beside him. What they talked about as they drove along, or afterward in the little chamber at Aakre, where they remained until late in the morning, has never been known. But from that day they were inseparable as before.

As soon as misfortune overtakes a man, every one learns what he is worth. And so the parish undertook to rebuild Lars Högstad's houses, and to make them larger and handsomer than any others in the valley. He was reelected chairman, but with Knud Aakre at his side; he never again failed to take counsel of Knud's intelligence and heart—and from that day forth nothing went to ruin.

THE VENDEAN MARRIAGE

BY JULES GABRIEL JANIN

THE VENDEAN MARRIAGE

BY JULES GABRIEL JANIN

SO YOU have never heard the circumstances of Monsieur Baudelot de Dairval's marriage, the man who died four years ago, and was so mourned by his wife that she died a week later herself, good lady? Yet it is a story worth telling.

It happened in the Vendée, and the hero, a Vendean, brave, young, daring, and of fine family, died tranquilly in his bed without ever suspecting that there would be a second Vendée.

Baudelot de Dairval was the grandson of that César Baudelot who is mentioned in the Memoirs of the Duchess of Orleans, own mother of the regent Louis Philippe. This woman, who has thrown such contempt on the greatest names of France, could not help praising César de Baudelot. Saint-Simon, skeptic and mocker, but good fellow withal, also spoke highly of him. So you'll understand that bearing such a name young Henri was not lost to report in the first Vendée, to protest arms in hand against the excesses of the Revolution. Baudelot was a Vendean simply because a man of his name and nature could be nothing else. He fought like his associates, neither more nor less. He was the friend of Cathelmeau and of all the others. He took part in those battles of giants; he took part fighting stoutly, and then laughing and singing as soon as he no longer heard the cries of the wounded. What wars, what livid tempests were ever like those? But it is not my business to tell again the story so often told.

But I want to tell you that one day, surprised at a farm by a detachment of Blues, Baudelot unexpectedly called together his troop. "My friends," said he, "this farm is surrounded. You must all escape! Take with you the women and children. Rejoin our chief, Cathelmeau. As for me, I'll stay and defend the gate. I certainly can hold it alone for ten minutes. Those three thousand out there would massacre us all. Good-by, good-by, my brave fellows! Don't forget me! It's my turn to-day. You'll get yourselves killed to-morrow!"

In those exceptional times and in that exceptional war, nothing seemed astonishing. Men did not even think of those rivalries in heroism so frequent in elegant warfare. In such a struggle of extermination there was no time to pose for sublimity of soul. Heroism was quite unaffected. So Baudelot's soldiers judged for themselves that their chief spoke sensibly, and obeyed as simply as he had commanded. They withdrew by the roof, taking away the women and children.

Baudelot remained at the door making noise enough for forty, haranguing, disputing and discharging his gun. One would have thought a whole regiment ready to fire was stationed there, and the Blues held themselves on the alert. Baudelot remained on the defensive as long as he had any voice. But when that failed and he thought his troop must have reached a place of safety, he tired of the warlike feint. He felt ill at ease at thus commanding the absent; and keeping quiet, he merely propped up the door as it was shaken from outside. This lasted several minutes, then the door cracked, and the Blues began to fire through the fissures. Baudelot was not wounded, and as his meal had been interrupted, he returned to the table and tranquilly ate some bread and cheese, and emptied a pitcher of country wine, thinking meanwhile that this was his last repast!

Finally the Blues forced the door and rushed in. It took them some minutes to clear away obstructions, and to recognize each other in the smoke of their guns. These soldiers of the Republic hunted eagerly with look and sword for the armed troop which had withstood them so long. Judge their surprise at seeing only a tall, very handsome young man, calmly eating black bread moistened with wine. Dumb with astonishment the conquerors stopped and leaned on their guns, and thus gave Henri Baudelot time to swallow his last mouthful.

"To your health, gentlemen!" he said, lifting his glass to his lips. "The garrison thanks you for the respite you have granted." At the same time he rose, and going straight to the Captain, said: "Monsieur, I am the only person in this house. I am quite ready for death."

Then he kept quiet, and waited. To his great surprise he was not shot at once. Perhaps he had fallen into the hands of recruits so little exercised as to delay twenty-four hours before killing a man. Perhaps his captors were moved by his coolness and fine bearing, and were ashamed at setting three hundred to kill one. We must remember that in that sad war there were French feelings on both sides.

So they contented themselves with tying his hands and leading him, closely watched, to a manor on the outskirts of Nantes, which, once an attractive country-seat, had now become a kind of fortress. Its master was no other than the chief of the Blues, who had captured Baudelot. This Breton, a gentleman although a Blue, had been one of the first to share revolutionary transports. He was one of those nobles so heroic to their own injury, who renounced in a day fortunes, coats of arms, and their own names, forgetting both what they had promised their fathers and what they owed to their sons, equally oblivious of past and future, and unfortunate victims of the present. But we will not reproach them, for either they died under the stroke of the Revolution, or lived long enough to see that all their sacrifices were vain.

Baudelot de Dairval was confined in the donjon, or, rather, in the pigeon-house of his conqueror. The doves had been expelled to give place to Chouan captives. Still covered with shining slates, still surmounted by its creaking weather-cock, this prison had retained a calm, gracious air, and it had not been thought necessary to bar the openings by which the pigeons came and went. Much as ever, a little straw had been added to the usual furniture.

At first the dovecote of a country manor struck him as a novel prison. He decided that as soon as his hands were free he would compose a romance upon it, with a guitar accompaniment. While thus thinking, he heard a violin and other instruments playing a joyful march. By piling up the straw against the wall and leaning on it with his elbow, Baudelot could look out of one of the openings. He saw a long procession of young men and pretty women in white gowns, preceded by village fiddlers, and all merry and joyous. As it passed at the foot of the dovecote, a pretty girl looked up attentively. She was fair, slender and dreamy-looking. Baudelot felt that she knew of the prisoner, and he began to whistle the air of Richard, "In an Obscure Tower," or something of the kind. For this young man was versed in all kinds of combats and romances, equally skilful with sword and guitar, an adept at horsemanship, a fine dancer, a true gentleman of wit and sword, such as are manufactured no more.

The wedding procession passed, or, at least, if not a wedding it was a betrothal, and Baudelot stopped singing. He heard a sound at his prison door; some one entered.

It was the master of the house himself. He had been a Marquis under Capet, now he called himself simply Hamelin. He was a Blue, but a good fellow enough. The Republic ruled him body and soul; he lent his sword and his castle. But he had not become cruel or wicked in its service. The morning of this very day, Captain Hamelin, for so he had been appointed by the Republic, learned that some Chouans were at his farm, had headed a detachment of Blues and postponed his betrothal. You know how he had seized Baudelot. As soon as the Chouan was in keeping the Captain had returned to his betrothal feast, and this is the reason why he did not shoot his prisoner at once or take him to Nantes.

Captain Hamelin was not thorough a Blue as to have quite forgotten the hospitable old customs of Bretagne soil. Therefore, while his friends were sitting down to table, he felt it incumbent to call upon his captive.

"Can I do anything for you, monsieur?" he asked.

"Monsieur," said Baudelot, bowing, "I should like the use of at least one of my hands."

"Your hands shall be unbound, monsieur," answered Hamelin; "if you will promise not to try to escape. But before you promise, remember that at six o'clock to-morrow morning you will surely be taken to Nantes."

"And shot at eight o'clock just as surely?" asked Baudelot.

Captain Hamelin was silent.

"Very well, monsieur," said Baudelot. "Unbind my hands and unless I'm delivered, I give my word as a gentleman and a Christian to stay here like a pigeon with clipped wings."

Captain Hamelin could not help smiling at his prisoner's allusion, and untied his hands.

"Now," said Baudelot, stretching his arms like a man stiff from sleep, "now, monsieur, I thank you, and am truly your servant until to-morrow. It will not be my fault if my gratitude does not last longer!"

Captain Hamelin said: "If you have any last arrangements—a will to make, for instance—I will send you writing materials." He was touched, for he was not a Breton for nothing.

"Seeing this, Baudelot took his hand. "Do you know," he said sadly, "that simple word 'will' wounds me more than the words 'death at Nantes!' It recalls that all my friends are dead. There is no one to whom I can bequeath my name, my sword, my love and my hate, and these are all I have left. Yet, it must be sweet to dispose of a fortune, to be generous even beyond the tomb; and while writing last benefits, to imagine the tears of joys and sorrow they will cause. That is sweet and honorable, isn't it, Captain? I must not think of it."

"I will send you some dinner," said Hamelin. "This is my day of betrothal, and my table is better provided than usual. My fiancée herself shall serve you, monsieur."

In one of the highest apertures of his cage, Baudelot saw a daisy which had been sown there by one of the first occupants of the dovecote. The pretty flower swayed joyously in the wind, and he gathered it and offered it to the Captain.

"It is our custom at home, Captain, to offer the bride a gift. Be so good as to give yours this little flower, which has blossomed in my domain. And now, good night. I have kept you from your loves long enough. May God remember your kindness toward me! Good-by. Best wishes! Send me some supper, for I'm hungry and need rest."

And they separated with friendly looks.

Dinner was brought the young Vendean by a pretty Breton girl with white teeth, rosy lips and the pensive air which befitted a shy country maiden, who had already seen so many proscripts. She served him zealously, and gave him no peace if he did not eat of this or that dish, drink this or that wine. It was a magnificent repast. The dovecote grew fragrant. It was almost like the time when the winged occupants of the tower gathered crumbs from the feast. As the girl was pouring champagne, Baudelot said to her:

"What is your name, my child?"

"My name is Marie," she answered.

"The same as my cousin's," went on the young man; "and how old are you, Marie?"

"Seventeen years," said Marie.

"The age of my cousin," said Baudelot, and as he thought of his pretty cousin butchered by the executioner, his heart almost failed him. But he blushed to weep before this child in whose eyes tears were gathering, and as he could not speak, he held out his glass. But the glass was full, and in the last rays of the sun the champagne sparkled joyously, for wine sparkled and spring bloomed even during the Terror. Seeing that his glass was full, Baudelot said:

"You have no glass, Marie?"

"I am not thirsty," said Marie.

"Oh!" said Baudelot, "this bright wine does not like to be drunk by a man alone. It is convivial by nature, and rejoices to be among boon companions. It is the great support of the Fraternity of which you have heard so much, my poor Marie, and which men really comprehend so little. Be friendly; dip your lips in my glass, my pretty Breton, if you would have me drink champagne once more before I die," and he lifted the glass to Marie's lips. She held them out, but at the words, "to die," her heart overflowed, and copious tears rolled into the joyous wine.

"To your health, Marie!" said Baudelot, and drank both wine and tears.

Just then they heard the horn, the hautboys, and the violins. "What's that?" said the young man setting down his glass. "God bless me, it's a ball!"

"Alas!" said Marie, "alas! yes, its a ball. My young mistress did not want dancing, but her lover and her father insisted. She is very unhappy this evening."

"Oh!" said the young Vendean, "my good Marie, if you are as kind as I think, you'll do something for me! Go, run, fly, tell your mistress that Count Baudelot de Dairval, Colonel of Light Horse, requests permission to pay her his respects. Or, no; find my host, not his bride, and tell him that his prisoner is very dull, that the noise of the ball will prevent his sleeping, that the night will be long and cold, that it's a charity to snatch an unhappy young man from the sad thoughts of his last night, that I beg him, in Heaven's name, to let me attend his ball. Tell him he has my word of honor not to try to escape. Tell him all that, Marie; and tell him whatever else comes into your heart and mind. Speak loud enough for your mistress to hear and be interested; and, thanks to you, Marie, I'm sure he will yield. Then, child, if I am invited, send your master's valet. Tell him to bring me clean linen and powder. There must be some powder still left in the castle. Tell him to bring me one of his

master's coats, and get them to lend me my
sword just for the evening. I will not unsheath
it. So, Marie, go, child!" And the prisoner
hurried her off and held her back in a way to
make one both laugh and cry.

A few minutes later Captain Hamelin's valet
appeared in the dovecote. He was a good old
fellow, faithful to powder and to all the old customs. Although a member of the municipal
council, he was an honest man, devoted to
Monsieur Robespierre only because he alone in
all republican France had dared to continue
powder, ruffles, and embroidered vest.

He brought a complete suit, which Captain
Hamelin had ordered when younger and a Marquis, to visit the court and see the King when
there was a court and a King. This suit was
very rich and handsome, the linen very white,
the shoes very fine. Baudelot's host had forgotten nothing, not even the perfumes and cos-
metics of an old-time Marquis. Baudelot confided his head to the valet, who adorned it com-
plaisantly, not without profound sighs of regret.
Baudelot was young and handsome, but had not
been groomed for some time. Therefore when
he saw himself dressed, curled and fresh shaven,
his eyes animated by a good meal and by the
music in the distance, he could not help smiling
with self-content and recalling his beautiful
nights at the "bal masqué" and at the opera with
the Count de Mirabeau.

He lacked only his sword, which was given him at the door with a reminder of his promise. It was night when he crossed the garden to the ballroom.

All the most beautiful republican ladies of the province were there. But you know women are not so revolutionary that they do not feel aristocratic sympathy for a young and handsome gentleman who is to be shot on the morrow.

To return to our story. The betrothal ball had begun. The financée was Mademoiselle de Mailly, grandniece of the beautiful De Mailly so beloved of Madame de Maintenon. She was a sad young blonde, evidently unhappy at dancing and marrying in that period of proscription. She was one of those strong spirits which seem weak until a certain fatal hour has sounded, when apparent weakness becomes invincible energy. The heroine replaces the little girl, and the ruins of a whole world could not intimidate her, who, until then, trembled at the least sign of displeasure.

Eleanor de Mailly was then very dejected. The friends of her childhood imitated her silence and despondency. Never before was Bretagne feast so gloomy. Nothing went as it should, neither dance nor dancers, and there was general lack of ease. The young men did not even try to please the pretty girls, and when the ball had scarcely begun every one wished it would end.

Suddenly the door into the great hall opened, and every one looked that way. There entered a pretty court gentleman, a lost type, a handsome officer, smiling and well dressed. He had the dress and elegant bearing of court. This apparition was in charming contrast with the dulness of the gathering. The men and women who were bluest at heart were delighted to find with them this remnant of the old French society so suddenly blotted out, alas! And, indeed, it was charming to see this young proscript, whom death on the morrow awaited, entering into this republican company, recalling its gaiety, and thinking of nothing but to be agreeable and please the ladies, faithful to the end of his calling of French gentleman!

His entrance took only a minute. Once in the room, he gave himself up to the ball and went to invite the first woman he saw. It was the blond girl whom he had noticed in the garden. She accepted without hesitation, remembering that republican death, the most unpleasant of all deaths, was offering her partner a bloody hand. When the men saw Baudelot dancing, doomed as he was, they blushed at their own lack of ardor. All the women were invited to dance at once, and accepted in order to see Baudelot nearer. So, thanks to the victim, the ball grew really gay.

Baudelot heartily shared this convulsive pleasure. His smile was not forced; his dance was light and graceful. He alone was genuinely entertained. The others amused themselves in very terror, and became almost delirious at sight of

this beautiful youth, who was king of the fête far
more than the bridegroom. Animated by such
passion, terror, and bloody interest, the ball took
possession of all. Baudelot was everywhere,
saluting old ladies like the King of France, and
young ones with joy and admiration, talking to
men in the mad language of youth and of nature
mixed with wit.

The more he yielded to this frank and natural
gaiety, the more he forgot that the night was advancing with frightful rapidity. And the later it
grew the more the women trembled in their hearts
at the thought that he must really die, for they
were near the epoch of old French honor, which
made Baudelot's presence at the ball the sign
that there was no hope for him. They knew his
word bound him faster than iron chains could
have done. They knew that both Baudelot and
Hamelin were doing right. Baudelot's pleasure
did no wrong to the committee of public safety.
As you may imagine, then, looks and smiles were
very tender, and more than one sigh escaped at
sight of the handsome proscript. As for him,
drunk with success, he had never been so full of
love and passion. So when he went to dance for
the third time with the queen of the ball, the
blond fiancée, he felt her little hand trembling
and trembled in his turn.

For when he glanced at her she was pale and
exhausted.

"What is the matter, Eleanor?" he asked.

"What is the matter, madame? Out of pity for your partner, do not tremble and grow so pale!"

Then turning toward the window curtains, which were moving to the dance music, she pointed out the dawning light.

"It is morning," she said.

"Ah, well!" said Baudelot, "what does it matter? It is morning. I have passed the most beautiful night of my life. I have seen you and loved you and been able to tell you I love you, for you know the dying don't lie. And now, good-by, Eleanor, good-by! Be happy and accept the blessing of the Chouan!"

It was the custom in Brittany at the end of the last square dance to kiss the lady on the forehead. The dance finished, Baudelot pressed his lips to Eleanor's brow. She grew faint and stood motionless, her brow supported by his lips. Then she recovered herself and Baudelot led her to a seat. She made him sit down beside her and said:

"Listen, you must go. Listen, they are harnessing the horses to take you to Nantes. Listen, in two hours you will be dead. Fly, then! If you wish, I will go with you. Then they will say you fled out of love, not from fear. Listen, if you will not escape alone, or with me, I will throw myself under the wheels of the carriage, and you will pass over my broken body!"

She said this in a low tone, without looking at him, and almost smiling, as though speaking of another ball.

Baudelot did not listen, but he looked at her with a joy in his heart such as he never before felt.

"How I love her!" he said to himself. He answered: "You know very well that is impossible, Eleanor. Oh, yes; if I were free, you should have no husband but me, but I do not belong either to myself or to you. So good-by, beautiful angel, and if you love me give me back the wild flower I sent you from my prison. Give it back, Eleanor. The little flower has been on your breast, it will help me to die."

At that moment Eleanor looked like death. There was a solemn silence. The music had stopped, and daylight was filling the room.

Suddenly there was a great noise of horses and riders.. It seemed to come from Nantes, and all the women moved spontaneously to protect Baudelot with their bodies, but his own soldiers appeared to deliver him. They were in the garden; they forced their way into the house, crying:

"Baudelot! Baudelot!"

They were astonished enough to find their young leader, not loaded with irons, but surrounded by handsomely dressed ladies and himself adorned as they had never beheld him.

Baudelot's first question was:

"Gentlemen, did you enter the pigeon-house?"

"Yes," was the answer. "That's where we began, Captain. Neither you nor the pigeons will find it again. The pigeon-house is torn down."

"Then," said Baudelot, drawing his sword, "I am released from my word. Thanks, my brave fellows!"

Then he took off his hat.

"Madame," he said very gently, "receive the humble gratitude of the captive."

He asked for a carriage.

"One is already harnessed, Captain," said one of his soldiers. "The owner of the house tells us it was to take you to Nantes."

Just then Baudelot noticed Hamelin bound with the fetters he himself had worn.

"Service for service, Captain," he said; "only, instead of untying your cords, allow me to cut them. No one shall wear them again."

Then, as he saw Eleanor recovering herself, he continued:

"Captain Hamelin, this period of civil war and spilled blood is too sad for betrothals. One can't tell whether there will be prisoners to watch in the morning or enemies to receive in the evening. Postpone your marriage, I beg of you. See, your fiancée herself wishes you to do so. My noble young lady, allow the poor Chouan to escort you back to your home at Mailly, will you not?"

And soon all the young Chouans galloped away, rejoicing to have delivered their Captain, and glorious in the rising sun. Poor fellows, they had so little time left, most of them, for the sunshine!

There are men who seem immortal whatever

they do. Baudelot de Dairval was not killed although he did not leave Vendée for an hour. When his country was less inundated with blood he married Eleanor de Mailly, and Captain Hamelin witnessed the wedding contract.

THE YOUNG GIRL OF TREPPI

BY PAUL JOHANN LUDWIG HEYSE

THE YOUNG GIRL OF TREPPI

BY PAUL JOHANN LUDWIG HEYSE

ON a height of the Apennines where the mountains rise between Tuscany and the northern part of the Papal States stands a lonely village of herdsmen called Treppi. The paths that lead up to it are none of them accessible by wagon. The road for post and vetturino, away toward the south, many an hour's travel, goes winding in and out over the mountains in a wide, roundabout course. By way of Treppi pass only the peasants who have business with the herdsmen, and occasionally a painter or pedestrian who wishes to avoid the highways, and during the night-time the contrabbandieri, or smugglers, with their pack-horses that know better than any of them the way over the rocky passes leading to the desolate village.

It was about the middle of October, a time when the evenings on these heights usually grow clearer. But now, after the heat of the day, a fine mist had rolled up out of the ravines and was spreading itself slowly over the bare, rocky outlines of the majestic highlands. It was perhaps nine o'clock at night. In the lowly, scattered huts of stone, which by day were guarded only by the very old women and the very young children, still feebly glimmered the lights of their hearth-fires. Around the hearths, over which the big kettle swung, the herdsmen and their families lay sleeping; the dogs stretched themselves beside the ashes; on a heap of hides some sleepless old grandmother was still sitting up, perhaps mechanically plying her spindle back and forth while she mumbled prayers or rocked a child that slept restlessly in its cradle. Through holes in the walls, as big as your hand, the night air oozed damp and earthy, and from the hearth-fire that was quickly burning out, smothered by the fog, the smoke choked thickly back and rolled along the ceiling of the huts without seeming to trouble the old woman in the least. After a while she, too, slept as well as she could, with her eyes wide open.

In one home alone was there sign of life. Like the others, this hut was but one story high; but the stones were better laid, the door was wider and higher, and against the broad, square building that formed the dwelling proper were supported various sheds, lean-to stalls, and a well-bricked oven. Before the door of the house stood a group of packed horses, from whose noses a young lad was tugging away at the empty meal-bags, while from the house came six or seven armed men out into the mist and hastily got their horses ready. As they started, a very old dog that was lying near the door waved his tail in a leisurely fashion;

then he lifted himself wearily from the ground and swung slowly into the hut, where the fire was still burning brightly. By the hearth stood his mistress, facing the fire, her straight figure motionless, her arms hanging down by her hips. As the dog touched her hand with his soft nose, she turned, startled out of a reverie. "Fuoco," she said, "poor dog, you are sick!"

The dog whined and moved his tail gratefully. Then he crept near to the hearth onto an old hide and stretched himself there, coughing and moaning.

In the mean time some of the servants had come in and seated themselves around the great table before the empty platters which the departing contrabbandieri had just left. An old maidservant now filled them again with polenta from the great kettle, and taking her own platter sat down with the others. As they ate, not a word was spoken; the fire crackled, the dog moaned hoarsely in his sleep, the grave young girl sat down on the stone slab of the hearth, leaving untouched the small plate of polenta which the maid had placed before her, and gazed about the hall, lost in self-forgetfulness. The mist was now standing before the door like a white wall. But behind the edge of the crags the half-moon rose clear into the heavens.

Up the street came a sound like the beating of hoofs and footsteps. "Pietro!" called the young mistress of the house in a quiet, reminding tone.

A tall fellow rose quickly from the table and disappeared into the fog.

The footsteps and voices were now heard coming nearer; at length the horse stopped before the hut. Still a little while and three men appeared under the doorway and entered with a curt "good evening." Pietro approached the young woman who was gazing without interest into the fire. "They are two men from Porretta," he said to her, "without any merchandise; they are guiding a signor over the mountains, whose passport is not in order."

"Nina!" called the young woman. The old serving-maid got up and came toward the hearth.

"It isn't that they only want to eat, padrona," continued the fellow. "Maybe the signor can have a night's lodging, too. He wishes to go no farther before daybreak."

"Make up a straw bed for him in the lean-to." Pietro nodded and went back to the table.

The three had taken their places without the servants deigning to give them any particular attention. Two of them were contrabbandieri, well armed, their cloaks thrown lightly about them, their hats drawn well down over their foreheads. They nodded a friendly greeting to the others, as to old acquaintances, and after they had given place to their companion, they made the sign of the cross, and began to eat.

The gentleman who had come with them ate nothing. He removed the hat from his high

brow, passed his hand through his hair, and let
his eyes wander over the place and the company.
On the walls he read the sacred texts drawn in
charcoal, saw in the corner the picture of the
Madonna with the little lamp burning before it,
and close by the fowls asleep on their perches;
then the ears of corn, strung in rows, hanging
from the ceiling; a board with jugs and wicker
bottles on it, hides and baskets arranged in rows
one upon the other. At last his eyes were arrested by the young woman at the hearth. Her
dark profile showed severe and beautiful against
the flickering glow of the fire, a great mass of
black braids coiled low on her neck, her hands
were lying locked together over one knee, while
her other foot rested on the stone floor of the hall.
What her age was he could not guess. But by
her bearing he knew that she was mistress of the
house.

"Have you any wine in the house, padrona?"
he then asked. Scarcely had he spoken these
words when the young girl sprang up as if struck
by lightning, and stood rigidly by the hearth with
both arms supporting her against the ledge. At
the same instant the dog, too, started out of his
sleep. A savage growl broke from his coughing
breast. The stranger saw all at once four kin-
dling eyes fastened upon him.

"May I not ask if you have wine in the house,
padrona?" he now repeated. Before the last
word was finished, the dog, howling loudly,

sprang upon him with unaccountable fury and with his teeth tore the cloak from the man's shoulders, and would have broken loose upon him again and again had not a sharp command from his mistress restrained him.

"Back, Fuoco, back! Peace, be quiet!" The dog stood in the middle of the room, beating heavily with his tail, his eyes fixed on the stranger. "Shut him up in the stall, Pietro!" said the young woman, half-aloud. She stood at the hearth, rigid as always, and, as Pietro hesitated, repeated the order. For the nightly place of the old dog had been for years by the hearth. The servants whispered one to the other, the dog followed reluctantly, and from without the howling and whining penetrated unpleasantly into the room until it seemed to cease from sheer exhaustion. In the mean time the maid-servant, at a sign from her mistress, had brought wine. The stranger drank, handed the beaker to his companion, and fell into silent reflection over the surprising disturbance he had so unwittingly caused. One after the other the servants put down their spoons and passed out with a "good night, padrona!" At last the three were alone with their hostess and the old serving-maid.

"The sun rises at four o'clock," said one of the contrabbandieri to the stranger. "Excellency, it is not necessary to start much earlier to be at Pistoja in good time. It's on account of the horse, that must have his six hours' rest."

"Very good, my friend. Go and sleep!"

"We will awaken you, Excellency."

"By all means," replied the stranger. "Though Madonna knows, I do not often sleep six hours at a stretch. Good night, Carlone; good night, Master Giuseppe!"

The men removed their hats respectfully and stood up. One went to the hearth and said: "Padrona, I have a message from Costanzo from Bologna, who wants to know if it was at your house he left his knife lying last Saturday."

"No," she said sharply and impatiently.

"I told him you would have sent it back to him long ago if it had been there. And then—"

"Nina," she broke in, "show them the way to the lean-to if they have forgotten it."

The maid-servant rose. "I was only going to say, Padrona," continued the man calmly, with a quiet twinkle in his eyes, "that this gentleman here would not look twice at his money if you gave him a softer bed than ours. That is what I wanted to tell you, Padrona, and now may the Blessed Virgin send you a good night, Signora Fenice!"

With that he turned to his companion, and, like him, bowed low before the picture in the corner, crossed himself, and with the serving-maid both left the room. "Good night, Nina!" called the young girl. The old woman turned at the threshold, made a sign of inquiry, then closed the door behind her quickly and obediently. Scarcely were they alone, when Fenice took up the brass lamp that stood at the side of the hearth and quickly lighted it. The fire was gradually dying out in the hearth; the three tiny, red flames of the lamp lighted only one small corner of the room. The darkness seemed to have made the stranger drowsy, for he was sitting at the table, his head lying on his arms, his cloak wrapped close about him as if he intended to pass the night that way. Then he heard his name called; he looked up. The lamp was burning on the table before him; opposite stood the young padrona who had called him. With irresistible power her look drew his toward her. "Filippo," said she, "don't you know me any more?" For a long time he looked searchingly into the beautiful face which was all aglow in the light of the lamp, and still more so from anxiety. The long, yielding eyelashes, as they slowly lifted and fell, softened the severity of the forehead and of the slenderly formed nose. Her mouth was a bloom of the rosiest youth; only, when it was silent it had a touch of resignation, sorrow, and wildness, which the dark eyes did not contradict.

And now, as she stood at the table, the stern beauty of her figure showed itself, especially the superb lines of her neck and throat. Nevertheless, after a minute's thought, Filippo said:

"Truly, I do not know you, Padrona."

"It is not possible," she said, in a strange, deep tone of assurance. "You have had seven years to be thinking about me. It is a long time—surely long enough for the picture to have made an impression."

This unlooked-for reply seemed all at once to break the spell of his preoccupation. "Of course, my girl," said he, "who thinks for seven years of nothing else save the beautiful head of a young woman must come at last to know it by heart."

"Yes," said she with meaning, "it is quite true, you said so then, that you would think of nothing else."

"Seven years ago? Seven years ago I was a light-hearted, joking fellow. And you believed that in good faith?"

She nodded three times, earnestly. "Why should I not believe it? Indeed, I have even learnt it through my own experience that you said right."

"Child," said he with a relenting look that well became his determined features, "I am sorry. Seven years ago, very likely, I still thought all women knew that the tender words of men were worth little more than the counters which we occasionally exchange for ringing gold, a matter of course that has been expressly agreed upon beforehand. What did I not think of you women seven years ago! Now, truly, I seldom think of you at all. Dear child, there are things so much more important to think about."

She was silent, as if she understood nothing of

147

all this and was willing to wait quietly until he said something that really concerned her.

"It is surely beginning to dawn upon me," he said after a moment's thought, "that I have traveled over this part of the mountain before. Perhaps I should have recognized this village and this house if it had not been for the mist. Yes, yes, it is the place in the mountains, of course, where the doctor sent me seven years ago, and where I stormed up and down the most inaccessible places, like a fool."

"I was sure of it," she said, and a little ray of joy lighted on her lips. "I was sure you could not have forgotten. The dog, Fuoco, certainly did not forget it, neither his old hate of you— nor I—my old love." She said this so cheerfully and with such assurance that he looked at her with increasing surprise.

"I do seem to remember now a young girl," said he, "whom I met once on a height of the Apennines, and who guided me to the home of her parents. I should otherwise have been obliged to pass the night on the cliffs. I even remember that I was pleased—"

"Yes," she broke in, "very much!"

"But I didn't please the maiden. I had a long conversation with her, to which she contributed not above ten words. When I thought at last to awaken the sleeping, sullen, sad little mouth with a kiss—I see her now as she sprang away from me to one side and picked up a stone in each hand, so that I hardly came off without being well stoned. If *you* are the maiden, how is it that you now talk to me about your old love?"

"I was fifteen years of age, Filippo, and very shy. I was always defiant and solitary, and did not know how to express myself. And then, too, I was afraid of my parents, who were still living at that time, as you afterward came to know. My father controlled many herds and herdsmen, and this inn here. There has been little change since then. Only he orders and scolds here no more—may his soul rest in Paradise! And before my mother I was shyest of all. Do you not know, you were sitting then at this very spot and praised the wine we had brought from Pistoja? I heard no more than this. My mother was looking sharply at me, so I went out and placed myself behind the window so that I could still look at you. You were younger, of course, but not better looking. You have to-day the same eyes with which you used to conquer when you wished, and the same mysterious voice which so aroused the jealousy of the dog, poor beast! Till then I had loved no one but him! He knew it, that I loved you more, he knew it better than you did."

"He was like a mad dog that night, and justly," said Filippo. "A wonderful night! But you had seriously bewitched me, Fenice. I know that I had no rest when you were unwilling to return to the house again, that I started up and went out to look for you. I caught one glimpse

149

of the little white kerchief you wore on your head, and then no more of you, for you sprang into the room next to the stable."

"That was my bedroom, Filippo. You did not dare to go in there."

"But I was going to. I still remember how long I stood and knocked and begged, bad fellow that I was, and thought that I should lose my head if I could not see you once more."

"Your head? No, your heart, you said. I remember all the circumstances, the words, everything!"

"Yet you wished to know nothing of them then."

"I was in a mood to die. I stood in the farthest corner and thought that if only I could still the beating of my heart, creep to the door, put my mouth to the crack through which you were speaking, I could feel your breath."

"Foolish, doting time of youth! If your mother had not come I might have been standing there still; for in the mean time you might have opened the door. I am almost ashamed, even now, to think how I went away in vexation and fury, and had a long dream about you all that night."

"I sat up in the dark and watched," said she. "Toward morning I fell asleep, and when I awoke and saw the sun—where were you? No one spoke of it to me, and I dared not ask. To see a human face was hateful to me, just as if they had killed you so that I should not see you any more. Out I rushed, running and then stopping still, up and down the mountain, all the time calling for you, cursing you, for because of you I could now love no more. At last I came down into the valley; then I got frightened and turned back again. I had been away two days when I got home. My father beat me and my mother would not speak to me. They knew very well why I had run away. And the dog went with me, good Fuoco; but when I shouted your name out into the stillness, he growled."

There followed a pause, while the eyes of the two rested on each other. Then Filippo spoke: "How long have your parents been dead?"

"Three years. They died that same week— may their souls rest in Paradise! Then I went to Florence."

"To Florence?"

"Yes, you said you were going to Florence. The wife of the café-keeper outside the walls over there by the side of San Miniato, to her some of the smugglers directed me. For one month I lived there, and every day they sent into the city to make inquiries about you. In the evenings I went down there myself and looked for you. At last we heard that you had gone long since—no one quite knew whither."

Filippo stood up and restlessly paced the room. Fenice turned toward him, her eyes followed him, yet she showed no sign of agitation, such as now moved him. Finally he came up to her, looked at her a moment, and then said:

"And to what purpose do you confess all this to me, poveretta?"

"I have been seven years getting my courage together. Oh! if I had only confessed to you then, it would not have caused me so much sorrow, this cowardly heart. But I knew that you must come back, Filippo; only that it would last for such a long time, that I did not know—that made me sad. I am a child to speak so. Why trouble myself about what is past? Filippo, you are there, and I am here and yours always, always!"

"Dear child," he began softly, and then silenced what was on the tip of his tongue. But she did not perceive how quietly and thoughtfully he was standing before her, staring vacantly beyond her toward the wall. She continued speaking calmly; it was as if the words had long become familiar to her, as if she had imagined them a thousand times in her loneliness: He will come and thus and so will you speak to him.

"I had many an opportunity to marry up here, and while I was at Florence. I wanted you only. When they implored me and spoke honeyed words to me, your voice sounded out of that faraway night, your speeches that were sweeter than all other words in the world. For several years now they have been leaving me in peace, although I am not old yet, and am still as—fair as

ever I was. It was as if they all knew you were
coming back soon." Then again: "Where are
you going to take me now? Will you remain up
here? No, for you, that will never do. Since I
was in Florence I have learned that life in the
mountains is dreary. We will sell the house and
the herds, then I shall be rich. I am tired of the
wild life of these people up here. In Florence
they had to teach me all a young city woman
should know, and they were astonished how
quickly I learned everything. Truly I had little
time to spare, and all my dreams kept telling me
that it would be up here where you would seek me
again. I inquired, too, of a fortune-teller, and it
has all turned out just as she said."

"And if I already have a wife?"

She looked straight at him from her full height.
"You are only wishing to prove me, Filippo!
You have no wife. That, too, the fortune-teller
told me. But where you lived, that she did not
know."

"You are right, Fenice, I have no wife. But
whence does she know, or you, that I shall ever
be willing to take one?"

"How could you *not* wish for me?" said she
with unshaken confidence.

"Sit down here by me, Fenice! I have much
to tell you. Give me your hand; promise that
you will hear me patiently to the end, my poor
little friend!" As she did none of all these things,
he continued with a quickening pulse, standing

in front of her, his eyes resting sadly upon her, while her own, as if foreboding something that would threaten her very life, now closed and now strayed to the ground.

"For years I have been compelled to keep away from Florence," he began. "As you know, there were at that time those political uprisings, that kept wavering so long, this way and that. I am a lawyer, and so know hosts of people, and write and receive a great number of letters throughout the year. Added to this, I was an independent, spoke my mind when it was necessary and was heartily hated, although I never wished to thrust any hand of mine into their secret game. Finally it became necessary for me to fly if I wished to escape an endless trial and imprisonment that would be neither for profit nor purpose. I went to Bologna, practised law for a living, and saw few people, women least of all; for of the gay young fellow for whom you have been wearing your heart out for seven years, there is nothing left, except that my head, or my heart, if you will, is still ready to burst if I can not be conquering something—in these days to be sure something other than the bolt of a pretty girl's bedroom door. You have heard, perhaps, how at the last there was also a disturbance at Bologna. They had arrested certain highly respected men, among them one whose way of living I had known for a long time, and knew, too, that his spirit was far from these matters. After that a miserable government undertook to reform matters, much as if a sickness had broken out among your sheep and you sent a wolf into the fold. But that is neither here nor there. Enough that my friend begged me to plead his cause for him, and that I helped him to gain his freedom. No sooner had this become known, when one day a wretched fellow came running up to me on the street and covered me with insults. I could not get rid of him except by thrusting him aside with my arm against his chest, for he was intoxicated. Scarcely had I found myself out of the crowd and had stepped into a café, when there came toward me a relative of this man, also intoxicated, not with wine but with venom and anger, and upbraided me as if I had been guilty of answering words with blows, instead of doing what every man of honor would have done. I answered as calmly as I could, for I now perceived that the whole affair was a preconcerted plan of the government to force me shamelessly into a duel. So one word led to another until my enemy at last won his game. He pretended that he was obliged to go into Tuscany, and insisted that the affair should be settled over there. I agreed, for it was time that one of us calm members should prove to the hot-heads that the cause of our restraint was not lack of spirit, but simply the hopelessness of all private intrigue when opposed to such superior power. But when, the day before yesterday, I applied for a passport, it was refused me—unless I were willing to give my reason; these were the orders of the supreme authority, so they said. It was now clear to me that they wanted either to draw me into disgrace by causing me to miss the duel, or to force me to steal over the border in some sort of disguise, where I could safely be caught in ambush. Then they would have pretext enough to bring legal action against me and to prolong the trial to suit their convenience."

"The wretches! The God-forsaken!" broke in the young girl, and clenched her hands.

"So nothing remained but to trust myself to the contrabbandieri in Poretta. Early in the morning, so they tell me, we can reach Pistoja. The duel is arranged for the afternoon, in a garden just outside of the town."

Impetuously she grasped his hand in both of hers. "Do not go down there, Filippo," she said. "They will murder you."

"Of course, that is what they want, child, nothing less. But how do you know it?"

"I know it here and—here!" and with her finger she touched her forehead and her heart.

"You also are a witch, a soothsayer," he continued, laughing. "Yes, I think they do wish to murder me. My adversary is the best shot in Tuscany. They have done me the honor to oppose to me a distinguished foe. Now I, too, will not altogether disgrace myself. Yet who knows how regular the proceedings will be? Who can tell? Or perhaps you have magic enough to prophesy that too? But what good would it do, child? It could not alter facts."

"Now you must drive it out of your mind," he continued after a short silence, "this following the bent of your foolish old love. Perhaps everything has had to turn out so, that I might not leave the world until I had set you free, free from yourself and your unhappy loyalty, poor child. Think, we may have been poorly suited to one another. Your loyalty was given to another Filippo, a young coxcomb with giddy lips, and carefree except for love. What would you have done with a melancholy brooder, a hermit?" During the last half of the sentence he spoke to himself, pacing up and down, but now he went up to her, and as he was about to seize her by the hand he stopped, shocked by the expression of her face. All the gentleness had gone from her manner, all the color from her lips.

"You do not love me!" she said, slowly and dully, as if another spirit were speaking out of her, as if she were listening to her own words in order to learn what was really meant. Then she drew back her hand with a cry, so that the tiny flames in the lamp threatened to go out. And from without the ear was suddenly chilled by an angry whine and howl from the dog.

"You do not love me, no, no!" she cried, as if beside herself. "Can you give yourself over to death rather than into my arms? Can you speak calmly of your death as if it were not mine, too? It were better for me if these eyes were blind rather than see you again, and these ears had become dumb before they were forced to hear the cruel voice by which I live and die. Why did the dog not tear you to pieces before I knew that you had come? Why did your foot not slip on the edge of the precipice? Alas! Alas! Behold my sorrow, O Madonna!"

She flung herself before the picture, lay with her forehead to the ground, her hands spread far from her, and seemed to pray.

Between the murmurs and groans of the unhappy girl the man heard the alarm of the dog, while the moon now gained its full power and illuminated the whole room. And now before he could collect himself or speak a word he felt her arms about his neck again, her mouth on his throat and hot tears falling over his face.

"Do not go to your death, Filippo!" sobbed the poor girl. "If you stay here with me, who will ever find you? Let them talk as they will, the crowd of murderers, the cowardly wretches, more detestable than the wolves of the Apennines! Yes," she said, and looked up at him through her streaming tears, "you will stay. The Madonna has sent you to me—that I might save you. Filippo, I do not know what angry words I spoke, but that they were angry I felt by the icy contraction here at my heart from which the words relieved me. Forgive me for that. It puts me in hell to think that love can be forgotten and loyalty trodden under foot. Let us sit down here and consider the matter. Do you wish a new house? We will build one. A change of company? We will send every one away, even Nina, even the old dog shall go. And if you think then they may betray you—why we will go ourselves, even to-day, now. I know all the paths, and before the sun rises we will be deep among the ravines on our way toward the north, and wandering, wandering to Genoa, to Venice, wherever you will."

"Stop!" said he sternly. "It is enough folly. You can not be my wife, Fenice. Even if they do not kill me to-morrow, it will not be for long, for I know how I am in their toils." Quietly but firmly he released his neck from her arms.

"See! my child," he continued, "things are unhappy enough as they stand, and we ought not to make them worse through want of reason. Perhaps when you hear of my death later, your eyes will be resting on a husband and beautiful children, and you will be thankful the dead man of this night had more wisdom than you, even as in that other night you had more wisdom than he. Let me go to rest now. Go you, too, and take care we do not see each other again in the morning. You have a good reputation, as I learnt from my contrabbandieri on the way here. Should we see each other in the morning, and should you make a scene—you understand, my child? And now, good night, good night, Fenice!" Then once

more he begged her earnestly for her hand. But
she did not give it to him. She looked absolutely
white in the moonlight; her brows and lowered
eyelashes all the darker.

"Have I not sufficiently atoned for having enjoyed seven years ago one long night of too much
happiness? And now he wills that this thou-
sand-times accursed happiness shall make me unhappy again, and this time for the length of an
eternity? No, no, no! I will never let him go!
I would dishonor myself before all men if he
should go away and die."

"Did you not hear," he broke in sharply, "that
it is my will to rest? Why do you talk with such
infatuation, making yourself ill? If you can not
feel that honor must tear me from you, then you
can never be fit for me. I am no doll on your
lap to be fondled and joked with. My paths I
have marked out before me, and they are too
narrow for two. Show me the hide on which I
am to pass the night and then—let us forget each
other!"

"Though you drive me from you with blows, I
will not leave you! If death places himself between us, with these good arms I will save you
from him. In death and life—you are mine,
Filippo!"

"Be still!" he cried aloud. The color rose suddenly to his forehead, as with both arms he pushed
the impetuous figure from him. "Be still! And
now it is over—now and forever. Am I a *thing*

that can be dragged to any one that calls for it—
to any one whose eyes take a fancy to it? You
have been sighing for me for seven years—does
that give you the right to make me untrue to myself in the eighth? If you wished to corrupt me,
your method was badly chosen. Seven years ago
I loved you because you were different from what
you are to-day. If you had flown to my neck
then, and had hoped to win my heart by boldness,
I would have set boldness against boldness, as
I do to-day! Now, all is over between us, and I
know that the pity that moved me before was not
love. For the last time, where is my room?"

Sharply and coldly he said this, and in the silence that followed he felt pain at the tone of his
own voice. Yet he added not a word, wondering
in the stillness that she took it so much more
calmly than he had feared. Far rather would he
now have soothed some stormy outburst of her
sorrow with kinder words. But she went past
him coldly, threw open a heavy wooden door
not far from the hearth, in silence pointed to
the iron bolt, and then returned to the hearth
again.

He entered and bolted the door behind him.
Yet for a moment he stood standing by the door,
to listen to what she might be doing. But there
was not a sound of life in the room and not a stir
could be heard in the whole house save the rest-
lessness of the dog, the pawing of the horses in
their stalls, and the whistling of the wind without

which was fast driving away the last streaks of the mist. The moon in all its glory was now shining in the heavens, and it flooded the room as Filippo drew a great bunch of heather out of a hole in the wall which served as a window. He now plainly saw he was in Fenice's room. There against the wall stood her neat, narrow bed, near it a chest unlocked, a small table, a little wooden bench, the walls hung with pictures of saints and madonnas, a little bowl of holy water under the crucifix by the door.

He now threw himself on the hard bed and felt the storm raging within him. A few minutes, and he raised one foot about to hasten out and tell her that he had hurt her only that he might heal her; then he stamped on the ground, vexed at such effeminate weakness. "It is the one thing that remains," he said to himself, "if crimes and misfortunes are to increase no more. Seven years, poor child!" A heavy comb, decorated with little pieces of metal, lay on a small table; he took it up mechanically in his hand. This brought to mind again the abundance of her hair, the proud neck on which it rested, the noble forehead round which it curled, and the browned cheeks. Then he threw the tempter into the trunk, where he saw the neat dresses, kerchief for the head, and bits of finery of all sorts, folded together carefully and in order. Slowly he let the lid fall again, and then went to the hole in the wall and looked out.

THE YOUNG GIRL OF TREPPI

The room lay in the rear of the house, so that none of the other huts of Treppi obstructed his view over the chasm-cleft highlands. Opposite, stretching behind the ravine, was the naked ridge of rocks, bathed in the moon that must now be standing directly over the house. At one side he saw a few sheds, past which a path ran down into the abyss. A forlorn little pine tree, with bare twigs, was trying to take root among the stones; besides this only heather covered the ground, with here and there some pitiable little bush. "Surely," said he in the stillness, "this is not a place in which to forget what one has loved. I would it were otherwise! Yes, yes, she who has loved me more than finery and flirting and the whispering of coxcombs would be the right wife for me, after all. What eyes would my old Marco make if he saw me suddenly return from my journey with a beautiful wife. Not once would we need to change our abode; and how unhome-like are the innumerable corners of solitude! And it would be good for me, at times—an old grumbler, a laughing child—but folly, folly, Filippo! What would the poor thing do as a widow in Bologna! No, no, none of that! No new sins added to the old mass! I will rise an hour before the others, and steal out and away before a soul in Treppi awakes."

He was about to turn from the window to stretch his form on the bed, worn out from the long ride, when he saw a womanly figure move

out from the shadow of the house into the moonlight. She did not look round, but in his mind there
was no doubt that it was Fenice. With quiet
steps and long, she turned from the house in the
direction of the path that led down into the
ravine. A shudder crept over him, for at the
same moment the suspicion entered his mind that
she intended to harm herself. Without a moment's thought he sprang to the door and tore
violently at the bolt. But the old rusty iron had
imbedded itself so stubbornly in the clamps that
in vain he used every effort. A cold sweat stood
on his brow; he shouted, shook, and pounded
against the door with fists and feet, but could
not force it. At length he gave over and rushed
back to the window hole. The stone was already
yielding to his fury when suddenly he saw again
the figure of the young girl rise on the path and
wind its way toward the hut. She was carrying
something in her hand, which by the uncertain
light he could not make out, only her face he saw
distinctly; it was earnest and thoughtful, but
without passion. Not a look did she cast toward
his window, and again she disappeared into
shadow, while he stood there, breathing heavily
from anxiety and exertion. He heard a distinct
noise, which seemed to come from the direction
of the old dog, but it was neither bark nor whine.
The mystery oppressed him uncomfortably. He
leaned his head far out of the opening, but nothing was he conscious of save the still night in the

mountains. All at once sounded a short, sharp cry, followed by the heartrending moan of the dog, and then long and anxiously he listened; not another sound the whole night long, save once when the door of the neighboring chamber slammed and Fenice's step could be heard on the stone floor. In vain he stood for long at the bolted door, listening, questioning, imploring the girl for one short word. All was quiet next to him. He now threw himself on the bed, as in a fever, and lay there watching and thinking, until at last a few hours before midnight the moon sank and weariness became lord of his thousand fluctuating thoughts. As sleep left him, a twilight surrounded Filippo; yet when his mind was fully awake and he had raised himself in bed, he became aware that it was not like the twilight that comes before sunrise. From one side there stole toward him a feeble ray of sunlight, and he soon noticed that the hole in the wall which he had left open before he went to sleep had now become stuffed with brushwood. He pulled it out and the full morning sun blinded him. In highest wrath at the contrabbandieri, his sleep, and most of all at the young girl to whom he attributed this piece of trickery, he went instantly to the door, whose bolt now easily gave way to a moderate push, and entered the neighboring room.

He met Fenice alone, left sitting at the hearth as if she had been long expecting him. From her face had vanished every trace of yesterday's storm, not one motion of the sorrow, not so much as a line of her violent self-control met his dark eyes.

"You have managed well that I should sleep away the hours," he said sharply.

"Yes," she said, indifferently. "You were tired out. You will arrive in Pistoja early enough, if you do not have to meet the murderers until the afternoon."

"I did not ask you to concern yourself about my weariness. Are you still going to force yourself upon me? It will do you no good, girl. Where are my men?"

"Gone."

"Gone? Do you intend to make a fool of me? Where are they? Silly woman, as if they would go without being paid!" And he strode hastily toward the door, about to go out.

But Fenice remained sitting motionless, and kept speaking in the same even tone: "I have paid them. I told them that you needed sleep and that I would accompany you down there myself; it happens that the supply of wine has given out and I must buy new, an hour this side of Pistoja."

For a moment anger prevented him from speaking. "No!" he broke out at last, "not with you, never with you! Treacherous serpent! It is laughable that you still think to ensnare me in your slippery coils. We are now as completely separated as ever. I despise you that you hold

166

me weak and pitiable enough to be won over by these little artifices. I will not go with you! Let me have one of your servants and then—pay yourself for the price of the contrabbandieri."

He threw a purse to her, and opened the door to search for some one who might conduct him down the mountain. "Put yourself to no trouble," said she, "you will find none of the servants. they are all away in the mountains. And, besides, there is no one in Treppi who could serve you. Poor, feeble, old women, old men and children, they are still in their huts. If you do not believe me—look!

"And apart from all else," she continued, as he stood at the threshold irresolute, in fury and vexation, and turned his back on her. "Why, think you, is the way so impossible and dangerous if I guide you? I had a dream last night by which I see that you are not intended for me. It is true, I shall still always like you a little, and it will give me pleasure still to chat with you for a few hours. Must I, for that reason, be laying snares for you? You are free to go from me wherever you will, to death or to life. Only, I would go along with you a little way. I will swear to you, if that will appease you, that it will be for only a short way—by my life, not so far as Pistoja. Only so far until you have struck the right path. For if you go off on your own account you will soon lose your way, so that you can go neither forward nor back. You ought to know that, indeed, from your former tramps over the mountain."

"Pest!" he murmured, and bit his lip. But he saw that the sun was rising, and after all, perhaps, what serious grounds had he for anxiety? He turned about and looked at her, and believed that he could trust the evidence of the clear-tempered look in her great eyes, that no kind of treachery lurked behind her words. She seemed to him to have become altogether another person since yesterday, and he had to confess that there was a feeling of uneasiness, mingled with his surprise, that yesterday's attack of violent passion had passed over so soon and without leaving a trace. He looked at her a while longer, but she gave cause for no suspicion whatever.

"If you have grown reasonable, then," he said, "let it be so. Come!"

Without any special sign of pleasure, she rose and said: "We must eat first; we will not find anything on the way." She set a plate before him and a jug, and then she herself began to eat, standing by the hearth, but of wine she drank not a drop. He, on the contrary, to make a quick end of the matter, ate a few spoonfuls, gulped down the wine, and lighted his cigar at the coals on the hearth. During all this time not a look had he vouchsafed in her direction, but he saw as he looked at her by chance, for she was standing near him, that there was a bright spot on each of her cheeks and something like triumph in her eyes. She rose impetuously, seized the jug, and at one fling shattered it on the stone floor.

"No one else shall drink out of this," said she, "since your lips have hung upon it."

He started up in surprise; for a moment the suspicion crossed his mind: "Has she given me poison?" But immediately he preferred to believe that it was only the dying flame left of the love-worship she had forsworn, and without further ado he followed her out of the house.

"They have taken the horse on with them to Poretta," she remarked, for by his eyes he seemed to be looking for the animal. "You could not have ridden away, either, without danger. The roads are steeper than yesterday."

She now went on before him, and soon they left behind them the huts that stood out in the sharp sun, lifeless and without the tiniest cloud of smoke issuing from the chimneys.

Now for the first time Filippo noticed the perfect majesty of the wilderness, over which was hanging a clear, transparent sky. Their way, scarcely discernible by the somewhat obscured traces over the hard rocks, lay northward along a wide ridge, and now and then, where the line of the parallel ridge opposite curved downward, a strip of sea gleamed along the horizon on the left. Far and wide was still no vegetation save the dwarfed mountain shrubs and the lichens. But now they left the heights and descended into the ravine which had to be crossed in order to

mount to the opposite ridge. Here they soon
came upon the pines and oaks that sprung up in
the ravine, and heard the rushing of the waters
far below. Fenice was now walking ahead, step-
ping with sure foot over the firmest stones, without looking about or speaking a word. He could
not help but let his eyes hang upon her and admire the supple power of her limbs. Her great
white handkerchief wholly concealed her face
from him, but whenever it became necessary for
them to walk together side by side, he was compelled to look about him and away from her, so
forcibly did the features of the noble scene attract him. Now, in the full sunlight, he noticed
for the first time her peculiar childlike expression,
without being able to say in what it particularly
lay, as if, perhaps, there still remained something
of seven years ago in her face, while everything
else had been developing.

At last he began to speak of herself, and she
gave him frank, reasonable answers. Only that
her voice, which was ordinarily not hard and hollow, as is usually the case with women reared in
the mountains, to-day was monotonous and
sounded most melancholy over things of least
account. These paths over which they were
traveling had of late been very generally fre-
quented by political fugitives, most of whom had,
of course, rested at Treppi on the way. Filippo
inquired of the girl about them and certain others
of his acquaintance whom he described; but few

of them could she call to mind, although she was aware that the smugglers had allowed many a stranger to pass the night at her house. Of one of these she had only too vivid a recollection. At the description of him the blood mounted to her face and she stood still.

"He is a bad one!" she said sullenly. "That night I woke the servants and had him locked out of the house."

During this talk the lawyer did not notice how high the sun was rising and that not a glimpse of the Tuscan plain had yet appeared. He was thinking, too, in a disconnected way, of the approaching end of the day. It was so refreshing to be tramping along this path, overgrown with bushes, fifty feet above the torrent, to feel the fine spray of the waterfall dash up against his face, to see the lizards slipping over the stones, and the graceful butterflies chasing the furtive sunlight, that he was not once conscious of how they were wandering up-stream and not yet turning westward at all. There was a magic in the voice of his guide that made him forget everything that had yesterday, in the company of the smugglers, been so incessantly in his mind. But now, as they ascended out of the ravine, and the boundless, utterly strange mountain wastes, with new heights and cliffs, desolate and parched, lay before them, he awoke all at once from his daydream, stood still and looked into the sky. He now understood clearly that they had been wandering in the opposite direction, and quite two hours farther away from his goal than when they set out.

"Halt!" said Filippo. "I see in time that you have betrayed me after all. Is that the way to Pistoja, you traitress?"

"No," said she, fearlessly, but her eyes fell to the ground.

"Now, then, by all the power of hell, the devil can easily take lessons and learn hypocrisy of you. A curse on my blindness!"

"Man is all-powerful, man is mightier than the devil and the angels, if he loves," she said in a deep, melancholy tone.

"No," he cried, in a flash of sudden fury, "you have not triumphed yet. Do not exult yet, over-confident girl, not yet! What a crazy girl calls love can not break the will of a man. Turn back with me to the place and show me the shortest way—or I will choke you with these hands—you fool, who can not see I must hate you, you who are willing to make me appear before all the world as a good-for-nothing." He stepped up close in front of her, with clenched hands; he completely forgot himself.

"Ah! Do choke me!" She spoke with a loud but trembling voice. "Only do it, Filippo! But when you have done it, you will throw yourself over my body and weep blood from your eyes, that you can not bring me to life again. Your place will be here by me, you will struggle with

the vultures that try to tear my flesh to pieces;
the sun will scorch you by day, the dew of night
will wet you, until you rot away as I do—but to
leave me you are utterly incapable. Do you
think a poor foolish thing that has been brought
up among the mountains will throw away seven
years as easily as she does a day? I know what
those years have cost me, how dear they were, and
that I am paying a good round price when I wish
to buy you with them. Should I let you go to
your death? The idea is one to be laughed at.
Once turn away from me and you will soon be
aware that I am drawing you back to me forever.
For in the wine that you drank to-day there was
mixed a love-charm which no man under the sun
has ever yet withstood."

Royal she looked as she cried out these words,
her arms stretched toward him as if her hand
were holding out a sceptre to one that owed her
allegiance. But he laughed at it and said:
"Your love-charm has rendered you poor service,
for I never hated you more than I do at this
moment. But I am a fool to hate a fool. May
you be cured as well of your love as of your
superstition, when you see me no more. I do
not need your guidance. I see over on yonder
slope a shepherd's hut with the herd about it.
There's a fire gleaming. There they will undoubtedly put me in the right way. Farewell,
poor serpent, farewell!"

. . . .

She answered nothing as he went away, and sat down quietly in the ravine, in the shadow of a rock, in the gloomy green of the fir trees that grew down by the stream, her great eyes lowered to the ground. He had not gone long from her before he found himself without a path, between cliffs and bushes; then, much as he might like to deny it, the words of this strange girl kept exercising on his heart a disturbing influence that turned his thoughts all inward. Meanwhile he kept ever in view the heath-fire in the meadow opposite, working his way through to reach the valley. By the position of the sun he reckoned that it must now be about the tenth hour. But when he had climbed down the mountain steep he found a sunless path beneath, and soon after a narrow bridge that crossed a new mountain stream and led up along the opposite side, and promised to open out into the meadow. He followed this, and at first the path ran steep up, but afterward, by a great circuit, far away to the foot of the mountain. He saw now that this would not bring him straight to his goal; yet over the more direct way hung inaccessible, precipitous crags, and unless he preferred to return, he must trust himself to this path. Now he walked on briskly, at first like one released from the fetters over yonder, and peering out intently every once in a while for the hut that kept continually receding. By and by, as his blood began to pulse more evenly, there came into his mind again all the details of the scene through which he had just passed. The picture of the beautiful girl he now saw before him vividly, and not as before, through the mist of sudden anger. He could not resist a feeling of profound pity. "She is over there now," he said to himself. "The poor, deluded child sits building castles with her magic art. It was for that she left the hut yesterday at night, and by the light of the moon to gather who knows what harmless herbs. I remember; did not even my own brave smugglers, too, point out to me some special white blossoms among the rocks, and say they were powerful in exciting love for love? Innocent flowers, how they have slandered you! And it was for that she shattered the jug, for that the wine tasted so bitter on the tongue. The older innocence grows, the stronger and more worthy of honor it becomes. How like the Cumæan Sibyl she stood before me, so truth-compelling, almost like that Roman as she flung her books into the fire. How beautiful and afflicted your delusions have made you!"

The farther he went, the stronger did he feel the pathetic splendor of her love and the power of her beauty which separation was now beginning to make clear to him.

"I ought not to have made her suffer because she wished in perfect good faith to save me, to set me free from my inevitable duties. I should have taken the hand she offered me and said: 'I love you, Fenice, and if I am still alive, I will

come back to you and take you home.' How
blind I was not to have thought of this way out!
Shame upon the lawyer! I ought to have taken
leave of her with kisses, like a bridegroom, then
she would have had no suspicion that I was deceiving her, instead of which I have insisted with
the stubborn girl and only made matters worse."

Now be became absorbed in the dream of such
a leave-taking and fancied he felt her breath and
the touch of her fresh young lips upon his own.
It was as if he almost heard his name called.
"Fenice!" he cried back passionately, and stood
still with violently beating heart. The stream
rushed beneath him, the branches of the firs hung
motionless, far and wide a shady wilderness.

Her name was again upon his lips, when just
in time the shame of what the world thinks sealed
his mouth—shame and a fear as well. He struck
himself upon the brow. "Am I still so far gone
that I even dream of her while I am awake?" he
cried. "Is she to prove right that no man under
the sun is able to withstand this magic? Then,
indeed, I should be worthy of nothing better than
what she thought to make me, to be called a
Squire of Dames all my life long! No, to hell
with you, beautiful, deceiving she-devil!"

He had regained for the moment his self-control, but now he saw that he had also been led
astray from his path. He could not go back
unless he was willing to run into the arms of danger. So now he concluded to reach again, at any

price, some height from which he could look about him for the lost shepherd's hut. The bank of the stream along which he was walking, rushing far below, was much too steep. So he flung his cloak over his shoulder, chose a secure footing, and at one leap was on the other side of the ravine, whose walls came close together here. In better spirits, he now mounted the opposite slope and soon came out into the broad sunshine. The sun beat on his head cruelly and his tongue was parched with thirst, as with a great effort he worked his way up. Now all at once anxiety came upon him that in spite of all his pains he might never reach the goal. Thicker and thicker the blood mounted to his head; he blamed the devil's wine that he had tossed down in the morning, and again he had to think of the white blossoms they had pointed out to him yesterday on the way. Here they were growing again—his flesh crept. "If it should be true," he thought; "if there are powers that can master our hearts and minds and bend the will of a man to the caprice of a maid—rather let the worst come than this disgrace! Rather death than slavery. But no, no, no, a lie can conquer only him who believes in it. Be a man, Filippo; forward, the height is there before you; only a short time, and this cursed mountain with its ghosts will lie behind you forever!"

And yet he could not cool the fever in his blood. Every stone, every slippery place, every pine-bough hanging heavily before him was a reminder which he had to conquer by force, with an exertion of will out of all proportion. When at last he arrived at the height, holding on by the last bushes and with a swing gained the top, the blood was dripping from his eyes so, and the sudden glare of the sun so dazed him, that he could not look about. Angrily he chafed his forehead, and lifting his hat brushed his hand through the tangled hair. Then again he heard his name called, this time in very truth, and started terrified toward the spot from which they were calling him. And opposite, a few steps from the rock, as he had left her, sat Fenice, looking at him with calm, happy eyes.

"Have you come at last, Filippo!" she said heartily. "I expected you sooner."

"Fantom of Hell!" he cried, beside himself with fear, as all the passion of longing struggled within him, "do you still mock me because I am led astray by pain and the sun is melting everything in my brain? Do you triumph because I am forced to see you once more, in order that I may amuse you once more? If I have found you again, by God Almighty, it is not because I have looked for you, and you shall lose me in spite of it!"

She shook her head, laughing strangely. "It draws you without your knowing it," she said. "You would find me if all the mountains in the world were between us, for in your wine I mixed seven drops of the dog's heart's blood. Poor Fuoco! He loved me and he hated you. So the Filippo that you once were you shall hate as you hated me and shall have no peace again until you love me. Filippo, do you not see now that I have conquered you? Come now, I will show you the way again to Genoa, my beloved, my husband, my hero!"

With that she stood up, and was about to encircle him with her two arms, when suddenly she shrank back from his face. He had become deathly pale, except for the red in the whites of his eyes, his lips moved without giving a sound, his hat had fallen from his head, with his hands he hastily waved off every approach.

"A dog! a dog!" were his first painfully spoken words. "No! no! no! You shall not conquer, demon! Better a dead man than a living dog!" At that rang out a frightful laugh from his lips, and heavily, as if he were struggling by force for every step, his eyes fixed staringly at the girl, he turned, staggering, and fell headlong backward down into the ravine which he had just left.

Before her eyes it was night; with both hands she tore at her heart and sent out a cry that rang through the ravine like the cry of a falcon, as she saw the tall figure disappear over the edge of the precipice. She tottered a few steps, then stood firm and upright, her hands always crushed against her heart. "Madonna!" she cried, without giving a thought to anything. Always looking down ahead of her, impetuously she now approached the ravine and began to climb down the stone wall between the firs. Her lips, breathing heavily, murmured words without meaning; with one hand she gripped fast her heart, with the other she let herself down by the stones and branches. Thus, until she came to the base of the fir trees—there he was lying. He had his eyes closed, his forehead and hair covered with blood, his back leaning against the trunk of a tree. His coat was torn and his right leg, moreover, seemed to be wounded. Whether he lived she could not make out. She took him up in both arms, then she felt that he still moved. His cloak, which he had worn closely about his shoulders, seemed to have broken the force of his fall. "Christ be praised!" she said, breathing once more. It was as if the strength of a giant had come to her, as she climbed up the steep again with the helpless man against her breast. It was long work. Four times she laid him down among the moss and rocks, still the life slept in him. When at last she arrived at the top with her unfortunate burden, her own knees gave way, and she lay for a moment in a faint and in complete unconsciousness. Then she stood up and turned away in the direction in which lay the shepherd's hut. When she had come near enough she set up a shrill call throughout the width of the valley. The echo answered first, then a human voice. She called a second time, and then turned back without waiting for the answer. When she again came to the helpless man, she moaned sorrowfully and dragged him into the shadow of the rock where she had been sitting before and waiting for him. There he found himself when consciousness feebly returned and he first opened his eyes again. He saw two shepherds by him, one an old man, the other a young lad of seventeen years. They were sprinkling water in his face and rubbing his temples. His head was resting softly; he did not know that he was lying in the lap of the young girl.

He seemed altogether to have forgotten her. He heaved a deep sigh that shook him from head to foot, and then closed his eyes again. At last he begged with faltering voice: "One of you good people, will you go down—quickly—to Pistoja. They are waiting for me. May God's mercy reward him who tells the landlord of the Fortuna —how it is with me. I mean—" his voice and consciousness failed again.

"I will go," said the girl. "You two, in the meanwhile, carry the master to Treppi, and lay him on the bed which Nina will show you. She must call the surgeon, the old woman, and have the master healed and bandaged by her. Lift him up, you, Tommaso, by the shoulders; you, Beppo, by the feet. So, lift him! Softly! Softly! But stop—dip this in water and lay it on his brow and wet it again at every spring. Do you understand?"

She tore from her head a great piece of the linen kerchief, soaked it and bound it about the bloody head of Filippo. Then he was lifted up, the men bore him on to Treppi, and the girl, gazing after him with the life entirely gone from her eyes, picked up her skirts quickly and went along the rough path down the mountain.

.   .   .   .

It was about three o'clock in the afternoon when she reached Pistoja. The Fortuna inn lay some hundred feet beyond the city, and at this, the hour of siesta, there was but little sign of life within. In the shadow of the broad overhanging eaves wagons were standing, unhitched, while the drivers were asleep on the cushions; in the great smithy opposite, all work was at rest, and through the thickly dusted trees along the highway not a breeze was stirring. Fenice went over to the spring in front of the house, whose stream, the only busy thing about, was pouring down into the great stone trough, and refreshed her hands and face. Then she drank, slow and deep, to still both thirst and hunger, and went into the tavern.

The landlord lifted himself sleepily from the bench in the wine-room, but lay down again when he saw that it was a girl from Treppi that disturbed his rest.

"What do you want?" he addressed her sharply. "If you want something to eat or some wine, go into the kitchen."

"Are you the landlord?" she asked quietly.

"Who else but me? You know me, I should think—Baldassare Tizzi of the Fortuna. What have you got for me, my pretty daughter?"

"A message from Signor Filippo Mannini, the lawyer."

"Eh, eh, that's it, is it? That's something different, to be sure," and he got up quickly. "Didn't he come himself, child. There are some gentlemen over there waiting for him."

"Then bring me to them."

"Ei ei, the sphinx! Can't a man know what he has to say to the gentlemen?"

"No."

"There, there, very good, child, very good. Every one has his own secret, this pretty stubborn-head as well as the tough skull of old Baldassare. Eh, eh, so he is not coming; that will be very displeasing to the gentlemen; they appear to have important business with him." He became silent and looked at the girl sidewise. But as she gave no sign of taking him into her confidence, but opened the door, he put on his straw hat and went out with her, shaking his head.

A little wine-garden lay at the back of the court through which she passed as the old man continued breaking out into questions and exclamations to which she returned not a word. At the end of the middle arbor-walk lay an unpretentious summer house; the shutters were closed, and on the inside over the glass door hung down a heavy curtain. A few steps from the pavilion, the landlord told Fenice to wait—and he went alone to the door, which opened at his knock. Fenice then saw the curtain thrust aside and a pair of eyes look out at her. Then the old man came back to her and said that the gentlemen would speak with her.

As Fenice entered the pavilion a man who had been sitting at the table with his back to the door rose and shot a quick, piercing glance at her. Two others remained seated on their chairs. On the table she saw flasks of wine and glasses.

"The signor, the lawyer, is not coming, as he promised?" said the men before whom she stood. "Who are you, and what have you brought as evidence of your mission?"

"I am a girl from Treppi, Fenice Cattaneo, sir. Evidence? I have none, other than that I am telling the truth."

"Why does the signor, the lawyer, not come? We thought he was a man of honor."

"He is none the less honorable because he has suffered a violent fall from the cliffs and has been wounded in the head and in the leg, so that he has lost consciousness."

The questioner exchanged glances with the other men, and then continued:

"You tell the truth, to be sure, Fenice Cattaneo, because you know how to lie so badly. If he has lost consciousness, how could he send you here to announce it to us?"

"Speech came back to him for a moment. Then he said that he was expected at the Fortuna; that it should be made known there what had happened to him."

A dry laugh was audible from one of the other men.

"You see," said the speaker, "these gentlemen here put no great faith in your tale. Truly, it is easier to play the poet than the man of honor."

"If you mean, signor, that out of cowardice Signor Filippo does not come, it is an abominable lie, which may Heaven put down to your account," she said firmly, and looked at each of the men in turn.

"You are warm, little one," mocked the man. "Are you, perhaps, the very good friend of the gentleman, the lawyer, heh?"

"No, the Madonna is witness!" said she, in her richest voice. The men whispered together, and she heard one of them say: "The Aerie,[1] too, is in Tuscany. You do not really believe in this trick, do you?" The third interrupted him: "He lies no more in Treppi than—"

"Come and see for yourself," Fenice broke into their whispering. "But you shall not carry weapons, if I am to guide you."

"Little fool," said the first speaker. "Think you that we will risk our lives for such a trim little creature as you are?"

"No, but for him; that I know."

[1] Meaning Treppi among the rock-hills.

"Have you any other special conditions to impose, Fenice Cattaneo?"

"Yes, that a surgeon accompanies us. Is there one among you, Signori?"

She received no answer. Instead of which the three men put their heads together. "As we came by, I saw him by chance in front of his house; it is to be hoped that he has not yet returned to the city," said one of them, and then left the pavilion. He returned after a short time with a fourth, whom the company did not seem to know.

"Will you do us the kindness of going up with us to Treppi?" The spokesman addressed him. "You will be infromed on the way what is the business in hand."

The other bowed silently, and they all left the pavilion. As they passed the kitchen, Fenice provided herself with some bread and took a few bites of it. Then she went on ahead of the company again and struck into the path leading to the mountain. She paid no attention to her companions, who were talking excitedly among themselves, but hurried on as fast as she could, so that they had to call her several times for fear they should lose her from their sight. Then she stopped and waited, and in hopeless brooding gazed out into empty space, her hand pressed close to her heart. So the evening wore on before they arrived at the height.

The village of Treppi looked no livelier than usual. Only the faces of a few children stirred in curiosity at the windows, and a few old women appeared under their doorways as Fenice passed by with her companions. She spoke with no one, but went straight to her home, returning the neighbors' greetings with a curt wave of the hand. Here before the door stood a group of men deep in conversation, servants were busy with packed horses, and contrabbandieri were going to and fro. When they saw the strangers coming, there was a panic among the people. They drew aside and let the company pass. Fenice exchanged a few words with Nina in the great hall and then opened the door of her room. In there, in the dimness, could be seen the wounded man, stretched out on the bed, and kneeling on the ground beside him a very old woman of Treppi.

"How is he getting on, chiaruccia?" (chirurgeon) asked Fenice.

"Not badly, praise the Madonna!" answered the old woman, and with sharp glances inspected the gentlemen who were entering behind the young girl.

Filippo started up from a half sleep and his pale face suddenly glowed: "It is you!" said he.

"Yes, I am bringing the gentlemen with whom you intended to fight, that they may see for themselves that you could not come. There's a surgeon here, also."

The feeble glance of the man lying there stole slowly over the four strange faces. "He is not

among them," he said. "I do not know any of
these gentlemen."

As he spoke, and was about to close his eyes
again, the spokesman stepped out from among
the three and said: "It is enough that we know
you, Signor Filippo Mannini. We have orders
to wait and to arrest you. Letters of yours have
been seized, from which it appears that you have
set foot in Tuscany again not only in order to
settle the duel, but also to establish a certain
society for the purpose of lending aid to your
party at Bologna. You see before you the Commissary of Police and here are my orders."

He drew a paper from his pocket and held it
before Filippo's face. But the latter only stared
at it, as if he understood nothing of the matter,
and fell back again into his sleep-like stupor.

"Examine the wound, Doctor"—the Commissary now turned to the surgeon. "If his condition will allow it at all, we must carry the
gentleman down without delay. I saw some
horses outside there. We can accomplish two
acts of the law at once if we take possession of
them, for they are laden with smuggled goods.
It is a lucky thing one knows what sort of people
visit Treppi when one wants to know it."

As he said this, and the surgeon approached
Filippo, Fenice disappeared from the room. The
old chirurgeon remained quietly sitting and mum-
bling to herself. Voices were heard without and
an unusual disturbance of going to and fro, and

at the hole in the wall faces looked in and quickly disappeared again.

"It is possible," the surgeon now said, "for us to take him down if we bind him tight with a twofold bandage. Frankly, he would recover more rapidly if he were left here in this peaceful spot and in the care of this old witch, whose medicinal herbs put the most learned physician to shame. The fever may endanger his life on the way, and I will in no case take the responsibility, Mr. Commissary."

"Unnecessary, unnecessary," replied the other. "*How* to get rid of him does not enter into the question. So bind your rags about him, as tight as you can, so that none of them may slip, and then forward. We have the moonlight and are taking a young fellow along with us as guide. Meanwhile, go out, Molza, and secure the horses."

The police officer whom the order concerned opened the door of the room quickly and was about to go out when an unexpected sight turned him to stone. The room adjoining was occupied by a crowd of village folk, at whose head stood two contrabbandieri. Fenice was still addressing them as the door opened. Now she stepped to the threshold of the room, and said, with sharp emphasis:

"You will leave this room instantly, gentlemen, and without the wounded man, or you will never see Pistoja again. No blood has ever yet flowed in this house as long as Fenice Cattaneo has been mistress of it, and may the Madonna prevent any such crime for all time to come. Do not try to return, either, with more men. You still bear in mind, perhaps, the spot where one has to climb up, one by one, the rock staircase. A single child can defend this pass, if he rolls down the steep the stones that lie scattered up on top as if sown there. We will place a watch there until this gentleman is in safety. Now, go and boast abroad of your heroism, how you have played a young girl false and wished to murder a wounded man."

The faces of the officers turned paler and paler, and after the last words there followed a pause. Then, as if at a word of command, they all three drew from their pockets the pistols that had up to now been concealed, and deliberately the Commissary said: "We come in the name of the law. If you do not respect it yourself, will you still hinder others from executing it? It may cost six of you your lives if you compel us to procure the law by force."

A murmur passed through the crowd of the others. "Be still, friends," cried the resolute girl. "They dare not do it. They know that every man they shoot will bring a sixfold death upon the murderer. You speak like a fool," she said, turning again to the Commissary. "The fear that sits on your brows speaks, at least, more reasonably. Do as fear advises you. The way is open, gentlemen!"

She stepped back and pointed with her left hand toward the front door of the house. Those in the room whispered a few words together, then with conciliatory bearing they walked through the excited crowd, which with ever-increasing curses made way for them. The surgeon was undecided which he should follow; but at an imperious nod from the young girl, he hastily joined his companions.

This whole scene had been witnessed by the big eyes of the sick man in the chamber, who had half risen. Now the old woman went back to him and smoothed his pillow for him.

"Lie still, my son!" said she, "there is no danger. Sleep, sleep, poor son, the old chiaruccia watches, and that you may be still more secure, that is our Fenice's care, the blessed child! Sleep, sleep!" She crooned him to sleep with monotonous songs, like a child. But he took the name of Fenice with him into his dreams.

. . . .

Filippo was ten days up there in the mountains and in the care of the old woman, slept much by night, and by day, sitting before the door, enjoyed the clear air and the peacefulness of it all. As soon as he was able to write again, he sent a messenger with a letter to Bologna, and the next day received an answer. Whether welcome or unwelcome was not to be read in his pale face. Except to his nurse and the children of Treppi he spoke to no one, and he saw Fenice

daily during the evening, when she was kept busy
about the house. At sunrise she left the house
and remained all day in the mountains. Formerly it had been otherwise, as he gathered from
her chance utterances. But even when she was
at home there was never an opportunity to speak
to her. She went about in general as if perfectly
unconscious of his presence, and appeared to be
ordering her life as formerly, yet her face had
become like stone and her eyes as dead.

When Filippo, one day, enticed by the beautiful weather, had wandered farther than usual
from the house, and with the feeling of new
strength was climbing an easy height, he was
startled as he turned the corner of a rock and
unexpectedly saw Fenice sitting on the moss near
a spring. She had distaff and spindle in her
hands, and during the spinning appeared to be
much absorbed. At Filippo's step she looked up,
but spoke not a word, yet the expression of her
face changed, and she quickly gathered up all
her tools. Then she went away, without heeding
his call, and was soon out of sight.

The morning after this incident, he had just
risen and his first thoughts were again turned to
her, when the door of his room opened and the
young girl calmly appeared before him. She remained standing at the threshold, and signed to
him imperiously with her hand, as he was about
to approach her hastily from the window.

"You are cured once more," she said coldly. "I

have spoken with the old woman. She thinks you have strength to travel again by short day stages and on horseback. You will leave Treppi early in the morning, and never return. This promise I demand of you!"

"I promise it, Fenice, on one condition."

She was silent.

"That you go with me, Fenice!" He spoke with great, uncontrolled emotion.

A dark frown of anger overclouded her brow. But she restrained herself, and said, holding on to the door-knob: "In what way have I deserved to be made sport of? Make the promise without condition. I expect it on your *honor,* Signor!"

"Will you so thrust me aside, after you have instilled your love charm into me to the very core and made me your own forever, Fenice?"

She calmly shook her head. "There is no longer any charm between us," she said in a hollow voice. "You lost blood before the drink worked; the spell is broken. And it is well that it is so, for I have done wrong. Do not let us speak of it any more and only say that you will go. A horse will be ready and a guide for wherever you will."

"If it is no longer magic that binds me to you, there is surely something else, for which you have no remedy. May God be gracious to me—"

"Be still!" she interrupted him, and closed her lips tightly. "I am deaf to such words as you are going to speak. If you think there is something due to me and are trying to pity me—then go and the account is therewith balanced. You shall not think that this poor head of mine can learn nothing. I know now that one can not buy a human being—as little by the pitiable services that go as a matter of course, as by seven years of waiting—which is also a matter of course, before God. You shall not think that you have made me unhappy. You have cured me! Go, and take my thanks with you!"

"Answer me, before God!" he cried, beside himself, and went nearer to her, "have I cured you also of your *love?*"

"No," she said firmly. "What is that to you? That is my affair; you have neither right nor power over it. Go."

With that she stepped back and over the threshold. The next moment he had fallen on the stones at her feet and was clasping her knees.

"If it is true, what you say," he cried in greatest sorrow, "then save me, receive me, take me up to you, or this brain, which only a miracle has kept together, will burst in pieces, along with the heart that you wish to thrust aside. My world is empty, my love the prey of hate, my old and my new home banished me; what have I to live for, if I must also lose you!"

Then he looked up at her and saw the bright tears breaking from her closed eyes. Her face was still motionless; then she took a deep breath, her eyes opened, her lips moved, still without words. At one touch life was again blossoming in her. She bent down over him, her strong arms lifted him up—"You are mine!" she whispered trembling. "So will I be yours."

.   .   .   .

The sun as it rose the next day saw the pair on their way to Genoa where Filippo decided to retire before the plots of his enemies. The tall, pale man rode upon a safe horse, which his wife was leading by the bridle. On both sides extended in the clearness of the autumn the heights and depths of the beautiful Apennines; eagles circled above the ravines, and far away in the distance glistened the sea. And calm and shining like the ocean there the future lay before the wanderers.

THE SIRE DE MALETROIT'S DOOR

BY ROBERT LOUIS STEVENSON

THE SIRE DE MALETROIT'S DOOR

BY ROBERT LOUIS STEVENSON

DENIS DE BEAULIEU was not yet two-and-twenty, but he counted himself a grown man, and a very accomplished cavalier into the bargain. Lads were early formed in that rough, warfaring epoch; and when one has been in a pitched battle and a dozen raids, has killed one's man in an honorable fashion, and knows a thing or two of strategy and mankind, a certain swagger in the gait is surely to be pardoned. He had put up his horse with due care, and supped with due deliberation; and then, in a very agreeable frame of mind, went out to pay a visit in the gray of the evening. It was not a very wise proceeding on the young man's part. He would have done better to remain beside the fire or go decently to bed. For the town was full of the troops of Burgundy and England under a mixed command; and though Denis was there on safe-conduct, his safe-conduct was like to serve him little on a chance encounter.

It was September, 1429; the weather had fallen sharp; a flighty piping wind, laden with showers, beat about the township; and the dead leaves ran riot along the street. Here and there a window was already lighted up; and the noise of men-at-arms making merry over supper within, came forth in fits and was swallowed up and carried away by the wind. The night fell swiftly; the flag of England, fluttering on the spire-top, grew ever fainter and fainter against the flying clouds —a black speck like a swallow in the tumultuous, leaden chaos of the sky. As the night fell the wind rose, and began to hoot under archways and roar amid the tree-tops in the valley below the town.

Denis de Beaulieu walked fast and was soon knocking at his friend's door; but though he promised himself to stay only a little while and make an early return, his welcome was so pleasant, and he found so much to delay him, that it was already long past midnight before he said good-by upon the threshold. The wind had fallen again in the meanwhile; the night was as black as the grave; not a star, nor a glimmer of moonshine, slipped through the canopy of cloud. Denis was ill-acquainted with the intricate lanes of Chateau Landon; even by daylight he had found some trouble in picking his way; and in this absolute darkness he soon lost it altogether. He was certain of one thing only—to keep mounting the hill; for his friend's house lay at the lower end, or tail, of Chateau Landon, while the inn was up at the head, under the great church spire. With this clue to go upon he stumbled and groped forward, now breathing more freely

in open places where there was a good slice of sky
overhead, now feeling along the wall in stifling
closes. It is an eery and mysterious position
to be thus submerged in opaque blackness in an
almost unknown town. The silence is terrifying
in its possibilities. The touch of cold window
bars to the exploring hand startles the man like
the touch of a toad; the inequalities of the pavement shake his heart into his mouth; a piece of
denser darkness threatens an ambuscade or a
chasm in the pathway; and where the air is
brighter, the houses put on strange and bewilder-
ing appearances, as if to lead him farther from his
way. For Denis, who had to regain his inn without attracting notice, there was real danger as
well as mere discomfort in the walk; and he went
warily and boldly at once, and at every corner
paused to make an observation.

He had been for some time threading a lane
so narrow that he could touch a wall with either
hand when it began to open out and go sharply
downward. Plainly this lay no longer in the direction of his inn; but the hope of a little more
light tempted him forward to reconnoiter. The
lane ended in a terrace with a bartizan wall, which
gave an outlook between high houses, as out of
an embrasure, into the valley lying dark and
formless several hundred feet below. Denis
looked down, and could discern a few tree-tops
waving and a single speck of brightness where
the river ran across a weir. The weather was

clearing up, and the sky had lightened, so as to show the outline of the heavier clouds and the dark margin of the hills. By the uncertain glimmer, the house on his left hand should be a place of some pretensions; it was surmounted by several pinnacles and turret-tops; the round stern of a chapel, with a fringe of flying buttresses, projected boldly from the main block; and the door was sheltered under a deep porch carved with figures and overhung by two long gargoyles. The windows of the chapel gleamed through their intricate tracery with a light as of many tapers, and threw out the buttresses and the peaked roof in a more intense blackness against the sky. It was plainly the hotel of some great family of the neighborhood; and as it reminded Denis of a town house of his own at Bourges, he stood for some time gazing up at it and mentally gaging the skill of the architects and the consideration of the two families.

There seemed to be no issue to the terrace but the lane by which he had reached it; he could only retrace his steps, but he gained some notion of his whereabouts, and hoped by this means to hit the main thoroughfare and speedily regain the inn. He was reckoning without that chapter of accidents which was to make this night memorable above all others in his career; for he had not gone back above a hundred yards before he saw a light coming to meet him, and heard loud voices speaking together in the echoing narrows of the lane.

It was a party of men-at-arms going the night
round with torches. Denis assured himself that
they had all been making free with the wine-bowl,
and were in no mood to be particular about safe-
conducts or the niceties of chivalrous war. It was
as like as not that they would kill him like a dog
and leave him where he fell. The situation was
inspiriting but nervous. Their own torches would
conceal him from sight, he reflected; and he
hoped that they would drown the noise of his
footsteps with their own empty voices. If he
were but fleet and silent, he might evade their
notice altogether.

Unfortunately, as he turned to beat a retreat,
his foot rolled upon a pebble; he fell against the
wall with an ejaculation, and his sword rang
loudly on the stones. Two or three voices demanded who went there—some in French, some
in English; but Denis made no reply, and ran the
faster down the lane. Once upon the terrace, he
paused to look back. They still kept calling after
him, and just then began to double the pace in
pursuit, with a considerable clank of armor, and
great tossing of the torchlight to and fro in the
narrow jaws of the passage.

Denis cast a look around and darted into the
porch. There he might escape observation, or—
if that were too much to expect—was in a capital
posture whether for parley or defense. So
thinking, he drew his sword and tried to set his
back against the door. To his surprise, it yielded

behind his weight; and though he turned in a moment, continued to swing back on oiled and noiseless hinges, until it stood wide open on a black interior. When things fall out opportunely for the person concerned, he is not apt to be critical about the how or why, his own immediate personal convenience seeming a sufficient reason for the strangest oddities and revolutions in our sublunary things; and so Denis, without a moment's hesitation, stepped within and partly closed the door behind him to conceal his place of refuge. Nothing was further from his thoughts than to close it altogether; but for some inexplicable reason—perhaps by a spring or a weight—the ponderous mass of oak whipped itself out of his fingers and clanked to, with a formidable rumble and a noise like the falling of an automatic bar.

The round, at that very moment, debouched upon the terrace and proceeded to summon him with shouts and curses. He heard them ferreting in the dark corners; the stock of a lance even rattled along the outer surface of the door behind which he stood; but these gentlemen were in too high a humor to be long delayed, and soon made off down a corkscrew pathway which had escaped Denis's observation, and passed out of sight and hearing along the battlements of the town.

Denis breathed again. He gave them a few minutes' grace for fear of accidents, and then groped about for some means of opening the door and slipping forth again. The inner surface was

quite smooth, not a handle, not a molding, not a
projection of any sort. He got his finger-nails
round the edges and pulled, but the mass was immovable. He shook it, it was as firm as a rock.
Denis de Beaulieu frowned and gave vent to a
little noiseless whistle. What ailed the door? he
wondered. Why was it open? How came it to
shut so easily and so effectually after him? There
was something obscure and underhand about all
this, that was little to the young man's fancy.
It looked like a snare, and yet who could suppose
a snare in such a quiet by-street, and in a house
of so prosperous and even noble an exterior?
And yet—snare or no snare, intentionally or un-
intentionally—here he was, prettily trapped; and
for the life of him he could see no way out of it
again. The darkness began to weigh upon him.
He gave ear; all was silent without, but within
and close by he seemed to catch a faint sighing,
a faint sobbing rustle, a little stealthy creak—
as though many persons were at his side, holding
themselves quite still, and governing even their
respiration with the extreme of slyness. The
idea went to his vitals with a shock, and he faced
about suddenly as if to defend his life. Then,
for the first time, he became aware of a light
about the level of his eyes and at some distance
in the interior of the house—a vertical thread of
light, widening toward the bottom, such as might
escape between two wings of arras over a doorway. To see anything was a relief to Denis; it

was like a piece of solid ground to a man laboring in a morass; his mind seized upon it with avidity; and he stood staring at it and trying to piece together some logical conception of his surroundings. Plainly there was a flight of steps ascending from his own level to that of this illuminated doorway; and indeed he thought he could make out another thread of light, as fine as a needle, and as faint as phosphorescence, which might very well be reflected along the polished wood of a handrail. Since he had begun to suspect that he was not alone, his heart had continued to beat with smothering violence, and an intolerable desire for action of any sort had possessed itself of his spirit. He was in deadly peril, he believed. What could be more natural than to mount the staircase, lift the curtain, and confront his difficulty at once? At least he would be dealing with something tangible; at least he would be no longer in the dark. He stepped slowly forward with outstretched hands, until his foot struck the bottom step; then he rapidly scaled the stairs, stood for a moment to compose his expression, lifted the arras and went in.

He found himself in a large apartment of polished stone. There were three doors; one on each of three sides; all similarly curtained with tapestry. The fourth side was occupied by two large windows and a great stone chimney-piece, carved with the arms of the Malétroits. Denis recognized the bearings, and was gratified to find

himself in such good hands. The room was
strongly illuminated; but it contained little
furniture except a heavy table and a chair or two,
the hearth was innocent of fire, and the pavement
was but sparsely strewn with rushes clearly many
days old.

On a high chair beside the chimney, and directly facing Denis as he entered, sat a little old
gentleman in a fur tippet. He sat with his legs
crossed and his hands folded, and a cup of spiced
wine stood by his elbow on a bracket on the wall.
His countenance had a strongly masculine cast;
not properly human, but such as we see in the
bull, the goat, or the domestic boar; something
equivocal and wheedling, something greedy,
brutal, and dangerous. The upper lip was inordinately full, as though swollen by a blow or a
toothache; and the smile, the peaked eyebrows,
and the small, strong eyes were quaintly and almost comically evil in expression. Beautiful
white hair hung straight all round his head, like a
saint's, and fell in a single curl upon the tippet.
His beard and mustache were the pink of venerable sweetness. Age, probably in consequence
of inordinate precautions, had left no mark upon
his hands; and the Malétroit hand was famous.
It would be difficult to imagine anything at once
so fleshy and so delicate in design; the taper,
sensual fingers, were like those of one of Leo-
nardo's women; the fork of the thumb made a
dimpled protuberance when closed; the nails were

perfectly shaped, and of a dead, surprising whiteness. It rendered his aspect tenfold more redoubtable, that a man with hands like these should keep them devoutly folded like a virgin martyr—that a man with so intent and startling an expression of face should sit patiently on his seat and contemplate people with an unwinking stare, like a god, or a god's statue. His quiescence seemed ironical and treacherous, it fitted so poorly with his looks.

Such was Alain, Sire de Malétroit.

Denis and he looked silently at each other for a second or two.

"Pray step in," said the Sire de Malétroit. "I have been expecting you all the evening."

He had not risen but he accompanied his words with a smile and a slight but courteous inclination of the head. Partly from the smile, partly from the strange musical murmur with which the Sire prefaced his observation, Denis felt a strong shudder of disgust go through his marrow. And what with disgust and honest confusion of mind, he could scarcely get words together in reply.

"I fear," he said, "that this is a double accident. I am not the person you suppose me. It seems you were looking for a visit; but for my part, nothing was further from my thoughts—nothing could be more contrary to my wishes—than this intrusion."

"Well, well," replied the old gentleman indulgently, "here you are, which is the main point. Seat yourself, my friend, and put yourself entirely at your ease. We shall arrange our little affairs presently."

Denis perceived that the matter was still complicated with some misconception, and he hastened to continue his explanations.

"Your door . . ." he began.

"About my door?" asked the other raising his peaked eyebrows. "A little piece of ingenuity." And he shrugged his shoulders. "A hospitable fancy! By your own account, you were not desirous of making my acquaintance. We old people look for such reluctance now and then; when it touches our honor, we cast about until we find some way of overcoming it. You arrive uninvited, but believe me, very welcome."

"You persist in error, sir," said Denis. "There can be no question between you and me. I am a stranger in this countryside. My name is Denis, damoiseau de Beaulieu. If you see me in your house, it is only—"

"My young friend," interrupted the other, "you will permit me to have my own ideas on that subject. They probably differ from yours at the present moment," he added with a leer, "but time will show which of us is in the right."

Denis was convinced he had to do with a lunatic. He seated himself with a shrug, content to wait the upshot; and a pause ensued, during which he thought he could distinguish a hurried gabbling as of prayer from behind the arras immediately opposite him. Sometimes there seemed to be but one person engaged, sometimes two; and the vehemence of the voice, low as it was, seemed to indicate either great haste or an agony of spirit. It occurred to him that this piece of tapestry covered the entrance to the chapel he had noticed from without.

The old gentleman meanwhile surveyed Denis from head to foot with a smile, and from time to time emitted little noises like a bird or a mouse, which seemed to indicate a high degree of satisfaction. This state of matters became rapidly insupportable; and Denis, to put an end to it, remarked politely that the wind had gone down.

The old gentleman fell into a fit of silent laughter, so prolonged and violent that he became quite red in the face. Denis got upon his feet at once, and put on his hat with a flourish.

"Sir," he said, "if you are in your wits, you have affronted me grossly. If you are out of them, I flatter myself I can find better employment for my brains than to talk with lunatics. My conscience is clear; you have made a fool of me from the first moment; you have refused to hear my explanations; and now there is no power under God will make me stay here any longer; and if I can not make my way out in a more decent fashion, I will hack your door in pieces with my sword."

The Sire de Malétroit raised his right hand and

wagged it at Denis with the fore and little fingers extended.

"My dear nephew," he said, "sit down."

"Nephew!" retorted Denis, "you lie in your throat"; and he snapped his fingers in his face.

"Sit down, you rogue!" cried the old gentleman, in a sudden, harsh voice, like the barking of a dog. "Do you fancy," he went on, "that when I had made my little contrivance for the door I had stopped short with that? If you prefer to be bound hand and foot till your bones ache, rise and try to go away. If you choose to remain a free young buck, agreeably conversing with an old gentleman—why, sit where you are in peace, and God be with you."

"Do you mean I am a prisoner?" demanded Denis.

"I state the facts," replied the other. "I would rather leave the conclusion to yourself."

Denis sat down again. Externally he managed to keep pretty calm, but within, he was now boiling with anger, now chilled with apprehension. He no longer felt convinced that he was dealing with a madman. And if the old gentlemen was sane, what, in God's name, had he to look for? What absurd or tragical adventure had befallen him? What countenance was he to assume?

While he was thus unpleasantly reflecting, the arras that overhung the chapel door was raised, and a tall priest in his robes came forth and, giv-

ing a long, keen stare at Denis, said something
in an undertone to Sire de Malétroit.

"She is in a better frame of spirit?" asked the
latter.

"She is more resigned, messire," replied the
priest.

"Now the Lord help her, she is hard to please!"
sneered the old gentleman. "A likely stripling
—not ill-born—and of her own choosing, too?
Why, what more would the jade have?"

"The situation is not usual for a young dam-
sel," said the other, "and somewhat trying to her
blushes."

"She should have thought of that before she
began the dance. It was none of my choosing,
God knows that: but since she is in it, by our
Lady, she shall carry it to the end." And then
addressing Denis, "Monsieur de Beaulieu," he
asked, "may I present you to my niece? She has
been waiting your arrival, I may say, with even
greater impatience than myself."

Denis had resigned himself with a good grace—
all he desired was to know the worst of it as
speedily as possible; so he rose at once, and
bowed in acquiescence. The Sire de Malétroit
followed his example and limped, with the assistance of the chaplain's arm, toward the chapel
door. The priest pulled aside the arras, and all
three entered. The building had considerable
architectural pretensions. A light groining
sprang from six stout columns, and hung down

in two rich pendants from the center of the vault. The place terminated behind the altar in a round end, embossed and honeycombed with a superfluity of ornament in relief, and pierced by many little windows shaped like stars, trefoils, or wheels. These windows were imperfectly glazed, so that the night air circulated freely in the chapel. The tapers, of which there must have been half a hundred burning on the altar, were unmercifully blown about; and the light went through many different phases of brilliancy and semieclipse. On the steps in front of the altar knelt a young girl richly attired as a bride. A chill settled over Denis as he observed her costume; he fought with desperate energy against the conclusion that was being thrust upon his mind; it could not—it should not—be as he feared.

"Blanche," said the Sire, in his most flute-like tones, "I have brought a friend to see you, my little girl; turn round and give him your pretty hand. It is good to be devout; but it is necessary to be polite, my niece."

The girl rose to her feet and turned toward the newcomers. She moved all of a piece; and shame and exhaustion were expressed in every line of her fresh young body; and she held her head down and kept her eyes upon the pavement, as she came slowly forward. In the course of her advance, her eyes fell upon Denis de Beaulieu's feet—feet of which he was justly vain, be it remarked, and wore in the most elegant accouterment even while traveling. She paused—started, as if his yellow boots had conveyed some shocking meaning—and glanced suddenly up into the wearer's countenance. Their eyes met; shame gave place to horror and terror in her looks; the blood left her lips; with a piercing scream she covered her face with her hands and sank upon the chapel floor.

"That is not the man!" she cried. "My uncle, that is not the man!"

The Sire de Malétroit chirped agreeably. "Of course not," he said, "I expected as much. It was so unfortunate you could not remember his name."

"Indeed," she cried, "indeed, I have never seen this person till this moment—I have never so much as set eyes upon him—I never wish to see him again. Sir," she said, turning to Denis, "if you are a gentleman, you will bear me out. Have I ever seen you—have you ever seen me—before this accursed hour?"

"To speak for myself, I have never had that pleasure," answered the young man. "This is the first time, messire, that I have met with your engaging niece."

The old gentleman shrugged his shoulders.

"I am distressed to hear it," he said. "But it is never too late to begin. I had little more acquaintance with my own late lady ere I married her; which proves," he added, with a grimace, "that these impromptu marriages may often produce an excellent understanding in the long run. As the bridegroom is to have a voice in the matter, I will give him two hours to make up for lost time before we proceed with the ceremony." And he turned toward the door, followed by the clergyman.

The girl was on her feet in a moment. "My uncle, you can not be in earnest," she said. "I declare before God I will stab myself rather than be forced on that young man. The heart rises at it; God forbids such marriages; you dishonor your white hair. Oh, my uncle, pity me! There is not a woman in all the world but would prefer death to such a nuptial. Is it possible," she added, faltering—"is it possible that you do not believe me—that you still think this"—and she pointed at Denis with a tremor of anger and contempt—"that you still think *this* to be the man?"

"Frankly," said the old gentleman, pausing on the threshold, "I do. But let me explain to you once for all, Blanche de Malétroit, my way of thinking about this affair. When you took it into your head to dishonor my family and the name that I have borne, in peace and war, for more than three-score years, you forfeited, not only the right to question my designs, but that of looking me in the face. If your father had been alive, he would have spat on you and turned you out of doors. His was the hand of iron. You may bless your God you have only to deal with the hand of velvet, mademoiselle. It was my duty to get you married without delay. Out of pure good-will, I have tried to find your own gallant for you. And I believe I have succeeded. But before God and all the holy angels, Blanche de Malétroit, if I have not, I care not one jack-straw. So let me recommend you to be polite to our young friend: for upon my word, your next groom may be less appetizing."

And with that he went out, with the chaplain at his heels; and the arras fell behind the pair.

The girl turned upon Denis with flashing eyes.

"And what, sir," she demanded, "may be the meaning of all this?"

"God knows," returned Denis, gloomily. "I am a prisoner in this house, which seems full of mad people. More I know not; and nothing do I understand."

"And pray how came you here?" she asked.

He told her as briefly as he could. "For the rest," he added, "perhaps you will follow my example, and tell me the answer to all these riddles, and what, in God's name, is like to be the end of it."

She stood silent for a little, and he could see her lips tremble and her tearless eyes burn with a feverish luster. Then she pressed her forehead in both hands.

"Alas, how my head aches!" she said wearily— "to say nothing of my poor heart! But it is due to you to know my story, unmaidenly as it must

seem. I am called **Blanche de Malétroit**; I have
been without father or mother for—oh! for as
long as I can recollect, and indeed I have been
most unhappy all my life. Three months ago a
young captain began to stand near me every day
in church. I could see that I pleased him; I am
much to blame, but I was so glad that any one
should love me; and when he passed me a letter,
I took it home with me and read it with great
pleasure. Since that time he has written many.
He was so anxious to speak with me, poor fellow!
and kept asking me to leave the door open some
evening that we might have two words upon the
stair. For he knew how much my uncle trusted
me." She gave something like a sob at that, and
it was a moment before she could go on. "My
uncle is a hard man, but he is very shrewd," she
said at last. "He has performed many feats in
war, and was a great person at court, and much
trusted by Queen Isabeau in old days. How he
came to suspect me I can not tell; but it is hard
to keep anything from his knowledge; and this
morning, as we came from mass, he took my
hand into his, forced it open, and read my little
billet, walking by my side all the while. When
he finished, he gave it back to me with great politeness. It contained another request to have
the door left open; and this has been the ruin of
us all. My uncle kept me strictly in my room until
evening, and then ordered me to dress myself as
you see me—a hard mockery for a young girl, do

you not think so? I suppose, when he could not prevail with me to tell him the young captain's name, he must have laid a trap for him: into which, alas! you have fallen in the anger of God. I looked for much confusion; for how could I tell whether he was willing to take me for his wife on these sharp terms? He might have been trifling with me from the first; or I might have made myself too cheap in his eyes. But truly I had not looked for such a shameful punishment as this! I could not think that God would let a girl be so disgraced before a young man. And now I tell you all; and I can scarcely hope that you will not despise me."

Denis made her a respectful inclination.

"Madam," he said, "you have honored me by your confidence. It remains for me to prove that I am not unworthy of the honor. Is Messire de Malétroit at hand?"

"I believe he is writing in the salle without," she answered.

"May I lead you thither, madam?" asked Denis, offering his hand with his most courtly bearing.

She accepted it; and the pair passed out of the chapel, Blanche in a very drooping and shame-faced condition, but Denis strutting and ruffling in the consciousness of a mission, and the boyish certainty of accomplishing it with honor.

The Sire de Malétroit rose to meet them with an ironical obeisance.

"Sir," said Denis, with the grandest possible air," I believe I am to have some say in the matter of this marriage; and let me tell you at once, I will be no party to forcing the inclination of this young lady. Had it been freely offered to me, I should have been proud to accept her hand, for I perceive she is as good as she is beautiful; but as things are, I have now the honor, messire, of refusing."

Blanche looked at him with gratitude in her eyes; but the old gentleman only smiled and smiled, until his smile grew positively sickening to Denis.

"I am afraid," he said, "Monsieur de Beaulieu, that you do not perfectly understand the choice I have offered you. Follow me, I beseech you, to this window." And he led the way to one of the large windows which stood open on the night. "You observe," he went on, "there is an iron ring in the upper masonry, and reeved through that, a very efficacious rope. Now, mark my words: if you should find your disinclination to my niece's person insurmountable, I shall have you hanged out of this window before sunrise. I shall only proceed to such an extremity with the greatest regret, you may believe me. For it is not at all your death that I desire, but my niece's establishment in life. At the same time, it must come to that if you prove obstinate. Your family, Monsieur de Beaulieu, is very well in its way; but if you sprang from Charlemagne, you should

not refuse the hand of a Malétroit with impunity
—not if she had been as common as the Paris road
—not if she were as hideous as the gargoyle over
my door. Neither my niece nor you, nor my own
private feelings, move me at all in this matter.
The honor of my house has been compromised;
I believe you to be the guilty person, at least you
are now in the secret; and you can hardly wonder
if I request you to wipe out the stain. If you
will not, your blood be on your own head! It
will be no great satisfaction to me to have your
interesting relics kicking their heels in the breeze
below my windows, but half a loaf is better than
no bread, and if I can not cure the dishonor, I
shall at least stop the scandal."

There was a pause.

"I believe there are other ways of settling such
imbroglios among gentlemen," said Denis. "You
wear a sword, and I hear you have used it with
distinction."

The Sire de Malétroit made a signal to the
chaplain, who crossed the room with long silent
strides and raised the arras over the third of the
three doors. It was only a moment before he let
it fall again; but Denis had time to see a dusky
passage full of armed men.

"When I was a little younger, I should have
been delighted to honor you, Monsieur de Beaulieu," said Sire Alain; "but I am now too old.
Faithful retainers are the sinews of age, and I
must employ the strength I have. This is one of

the hardest things to swallow as a man grows up
in years; but with a little patience, even this becomes habitual. You and the lady seem to prefer
the salle for what remains of your two hours;
and as I have no desire to cross your preference,
I shall resign it to your use with all the pleasure
in the world. No haste!" he added, holding up
his hand, as he saw a dangerous look come into
Denis de Beaulieu's face. "If your mind revolt
against hanging, it will be time enough two hours
hence to throw yourself out of the window or
upon the pikes of my retainers. Two hours of
life are always two hours. A great many things
may turn up in even as little a while as that.
And, besides, if I understand her appearance, my
niece has something to say to you. You will not
disfigure your last hours by a want of politeness
to a lady?"

Denis looked at Blanche, and she made him an
imploring gesture.

It is likely that the old gentleman was hugely
pleased at this symptom of an understanding;
for he smiled on both, and added sweetly: "If
you will give me your word of honor, Monsieur
de Beaulieu, to await my return at the end of the
two hours before attempting anything desperate,
I shall withdraw my retainers, and let you speak
in greater privacy with mademoiselle."

Denis again glanced at the girl, who seemed
to beseech him to agree.

"I give you my word of honor," he said.

221

Messire de Malétroit bowed, and proceeded to limp about the apartment, clearing his throat the while with that odd musical chirp which had already grown so irritating in the ears of Denis de Beaulieu. He first possessed himself of some papers which lay upon the table; then he went to the mouth of the passage and appeared to give an order to the men behind the arras; and lastly he hobbled out through the door by which Denis had come in, turning upon the threshold to address a last smiling bow to the young couple, and followed by the chaplain with a hand-lamp.

No sooner were they alone than Blanche advanced toward Denis with her hands extended. Her face was flushed and excited, and her eyes shone with tears.

"You shall not die!" she cried, "you shall marry me after all."

"You seem to think, madam," replied Denis, "that I stand much in fear of death."

"Oh, no, no," she said, "I see you are no poltroon. It is for my own sake—I could not bear to have you slain for such a scruple."

"I am afraid," returned Denis, "that you underrate the difficulty, madam. What you may be too generous to refuse, I may be too proud to accept. In a moment of noble feeling toward me, you forget what you perhaps owe to others."

He had the decency to keep his eyes on the

floor as he said this, and after he had finished, so as not to spy upon her confusion. She stood silent for a moment, then walked suddenly away, and falling on her uncle's chair, fairly burst out sobbing. Denis was in the acme of embarrassment. He looked round, as if to seek for inspiration, and seeing a stool, plumped down upon it for something to do. There he sat playing with the guard of his rapier, and wishing himself dead a thousand times over, and buried in the nastiest kitchen-heap in France. His eyes wandered round the apartment, but found nothing to arrest them. There were such wide spaces between the furniture, the light fell so badly and cheerlessly over all, the dark outside air looked in so coldly through the windows, that he thought he had never seen a church so vast, nor a tomb so melancholy. The regular sobs of Blanche de Malétroit measured out the time like the ticking of a clock. He read the device upon the shield over and over again, until his eyes became obscured; he stared into shadowy corners until he imagined they were swarming with horrible animals; and every now and again he awoke with a start, to remember that his last two hours were running, and death was on the march.

Oftener and oftener, as the time went on, did his glance settle on the girl herself. Her face was bowed forward and covered with her hands, and she was shaken at intervals by the convulsive hiccup of grief. Even thus she was not an unpleasant object to dwell upon, so plump and yet so fine, with a warm brown skin, and the most beautiful hair, Denis thought, in the whole world of womankind. Her hands were like her uncle's: but they were more in place at the end of her young arms, and looked infinitely soft and caressing. He remembered how her blue eyes had shone upon him, full of anger, pity, and innocence. And the more he dwelt on her perfections, the uglier death looked, and the more deeply was he smitten with penitence at her continued tears. Now he felt that no man could have the courage to leave a world which contained so beautiful a creature; and now he would have given forty minutes of his last hour to have unsaid his cruel speech.

Suddenly a hoarse and ragged peal of cockcrow rose to their ears from the dark valley below the windows. And this shattering noise in the silence of all around was like a light in a dark place, and shook them both out of their reflections.

"Alas, can I do nothing to help you?" she said, looking up.

"Madame," replied Denis, with a fine irrelevancy, "if I have said anything to wound you, believe me, it was for your own sake and not for mine."

She thanked him with a tearful look.

"I feel your position cruelly," he went on. "The world has been bitter hard on you. Your uncle is a disgrace to mankind. Believe me, madame, there is no young gentleman in all France but would be glad of my opportunity, to die in doing you a momentary service."

"I know already that you can be very brave and generous," she answered. "What I *want* to know is whether I can serve you—now or afterward," she added, with a quaver.

"Most certainly," he answered with a smile. "Let me sit beside you as if I were a friend, instead of a foolish intruder; try to forget how awkwardly we are placed to one another; make my last moments go pleasantly: and you will do me the chief service possible.'

"You are very gallant," she added, with a yet deeper sadness . . . "very gallant . . . and it somehow pains me. But draw nearer, if you please; and if you find anything to say to me, you will at least make certain of a very friendly listener. Ah! Monsieur de Beaulieu," she broke forth—"ah! Monsieur de Beaulieu, how can I look you in the face?" And she fell to weeping again with a renewed effusion.

"Madame," said Denis, taking her hand in both of his, "reflect on the little time I have before me, and the great bitterness into which I am cast by the sight of your distress. Spare me, in my last moments, the spectacle of what I can not cure even with the sacrifice of my life."

"I am very selfish," answered Blanche. "I will be braver, Monsieur de Beaulieu, for your sake. But think if I can do you no kindness in the future—if you have no friends to whom I could carry your adieus. Charge me as heavily as you can; every burden will lighten, by so little, the invaluable gratitude I owe you. Put it in my power to do something more for you than weep."

"My mother is married again, and has a young family to care for. My brother Guichard will inherit my fiefs; and if I am not in error, that will content him amply for my death. Life is a little vapor that passeth away, as we are told by those in holy orders. When a man is in a fair way and sees all life open in front of him, he seems to himself to make a very important figure in the world. His horse whinnies to him; the trumpets blow and the girls look out of the window as he rides into town before his company; he receives many assurances of trust and regard —sometimes by express in a letter—sometimes face to face, with persons of great consequence falling on his neck. It is not wonderful if his head is turned for a time. But once he is dead, were he as brave as Hercules or as wise as Solomon, he is soon forgotten. It is not ten years since my father fell, with many other knights around him, in a very fierce encounter, and I do not think that any one of them, nor so much as the name of the fight, is now remembered. No, no, madame, the nearer you come to it, you see that death is a dark and dusty corner, where a man gets into his tomb and has the door shut after him till the judgment day. I have few friends just now, and once I am dead I shall have none."

"Ah, Monsieur de Beaulieu!" she exclaimed, "you forget Blanche de Malétroit."

You have a sweet nature, madam, and you are pleased to estimate a little service far beyond its worth."

"It is not that," she answered. "You mistake me if you think I am easily touched by my own concerns. I say so, because you are the noblest man I have ever met; because I recognize in you a spirit that would have made even a common person famous in the land."

"And yet here I die in a mousetrap—with no more noise about it than my own squeaking," answered he.

A look of pain crossed her face, and she was silent for a little while. Then a light came into her eyes, and with a smile she spoke again.

"I can not have my champion think meanly of himself. Any one who gives his life for another will be met in Paradise by all the heralds and angels of the Lord God. And you have no such cause to hang your head. For . . . Pray, do you think me beautiful?" she asked, with a deep flush.

"Indeed, madam, I do," he said.

"I am glad of that," she answered heartily.

"Do you think there are many men in France who have been asked in marriage by a beautiful maiden—with her own lips—and who have refused her to her face? I know you men would half despise such a triumph; but believe me, we women know more of what is precious in love. There is nothing that should set a person higher in his own esteem; and we women would prize nothing more dearly."

"You are very good," he said; "but you can not make me forget that I was asked in pity and not for love."

"I am not so sure of that," she replied, holding down her head. "Hear me to an end, Monsieur de Beaulieu. I know how you must despise me; I feel you are right to do so; I am too poor a creature to occupy one thought of your mind, although, alas! you must die for me this morning. But when I asked you to marry me, indeed, and indeed, it was because I respected and admired you, and loved you with my whole soul, from the very moment that you took my part against my uncle. If you had seen yourself, and how noble you looked, you would pity rather than despise me. And now," she went on, hurriedly checking him with her hand, "although I have laid aside all reserve and told you so much, remember that I know your sentiments toward me already. I would not, believe me, being nobly born, weary you with importunities into consent. I too have a pride of my own; and I declare before the holy mother of God, if you should now go back from your word already given, I would no more marry you than I would marry my uncle's groom."

Denis smiled a little bitterly.

"It is a small love," he said, "that shies at a little pride."

She made no answer, although she probably had her own thoughts.

"Come hither to the window," he said with a sigh. "Here is the dawn."

And indeed the dawn was already beginning. The hollow of the sky was full of essential daylight, colorless and clean; and the valley underneath was flooded with a gray reflection. A few thin vapors clung in the coves of the forest or lay along the winding course of the river. The scene disengaged a surprising effect of stillness, which was hardly interrupted when the cocks began once more to crow among the steadings. Perhaps the same fellow who had made so horrid a clangor in the darkness not half an hour before, now sent up the merriest cheer to greet the coming day. A little wind went bustling and eddying among the tree-tops underneath the windows. And still the daylight kept flooding insensibly out of the east, which was soon to grow incandescent and cast up that red-hot cannonball, the rising sun.

Denis looked out over all this with a bit of a

shiver. He had taken her hand, and retained it in his almost unconsciously.

"Has the day begun already?" she said; and then, illogically enough: "the night has been so long! Alas! what shall we say to my uncle when he returns?"

"What you will," said Denis, and he pressed her fingers in his.

She was silent.

"Blanche," he said, with a swift, uncertain, passionate utterance, "you have seen whether I fear death. You must know well enough that I would as gladly leap out of that window into the empty air as to lay a finger on you without your free and full consent. But if you care for me at all do not let me lose my life in a misapprehension; for I love you better than the whole world; and though I will die for you blithely, it would be like all the joys of Paradise to live on and spend my life in your service."

As he stopped speaking, a bell began to ring loudly in the interior of the house; and a clatter of armor in the corridor showed that the retainers were returning to their post, and the two hours were at an end.

"After all that you have heard?" she whispered, leaning toward him with her lips and eyes.

"I have heard nothing," he replied.

"The captain's name was Florimond de Champdivers," she said in his ear.

"I did not hear it," he answered, taking her supple body in his arms, and covered her wet face with kisses.

A melodious chirping was audible behind, followed by a beautiful chuckle, and the voice of Messire de Malétroit wished his new nephew a good morning.

THE THIEF

BY FEODOR MIKAILOVITCH DOSTOIEVSKI

THE THIEF

BY FEODOR MIKAILOVITCH DOSTOIEVSKI

ONE morning, just as I was about to leave for my place of employment, Agrafena (my cook, laundress, and housekeeper all in one person) entered my room, and, to my great astonishment, started a conversation.

She was a quiet, simple-minded woman, who during the whole six years of her stay with me had never spoken more than two or three words daily, and that in reference to my dinner—at least, I had never heard her.

"I have come to you, sir," she suddenly began, "about the renting out of the little spare room."

"What spare room?"

"The one that is near the kitchen, of course; which should it be?"

"Why?"

"Why do people generally take lodgers? Because."

"But who will take it?"

"Who will take it! A lodger, of course! Who should take it?"

"But there is hardly room in there, mother mine, for a bed; it will be too cramped. How can one live in it?"

Translated by Lizzie B. Gorin. Copyright, 1907, by P. F. Collier & Son.

"But why live in it! He only wants a place to sleep in; he will live on the window-seat."

"What window-seat?"

"How is that? What window-seat? As if you did not know! The one in the hall. He will sit on it and sew, or do something else. But maybe he will sit on a chair; he has a chair of his own—and a table also, and everything."

"But who is he?"

"A nice, worldly-wise man. I will cook for him and will charge him only three rubles in silver a month for room and board—"

At last, after long endeavor, I found out that some elderly man had talked Agrafena into taking him into the kitchen as lodger. When Agrafena once got a thing into her head that thing had to be done; otherwise I knew I would have no peace. On those occasions when things did go against her wishes, she immediately fell into a sort of brooding, became exceedingly melancholy, and continued in that state for two or three weeks. During this time the food was invariably spoiled, the linen was missing, the floors unscrubbed; in a word, a lot of unpleasant things happened. I had long ago become aware of the fact that this woman of very few words was incapable of forming a decision, or of coming to any conclusion based on her own thoughts; and yet when it happened that by some means there had formed in her weak brain a sort of idea or wish to undertake a thing, to refuse her permission to carry out this idea or wish meant simply to kill her morally for some time. And so, acting in the sole interest of my peace of mind, I immediately agreed to this new proposition of hers.

"Has he at least the necessary papers, a passport, or anything of the kind?"

"How then? Of course he has. A fine man like him—who has seen the world— He promised to pay three rubles a month."

On the very next day the new lodger appeared in my modest bachelor quarters; but I did not feel annoyed in the least—on the contrary, in a way I was glad of it. I live a very solitary, hermit-like life. I have almost no acquaintance and seldom go out. Having led the existence of a moor-cock for ten years, I was naturally used to solitude. But ten, fifteen years or more of the same seclusion in company with a person like Agrafena, and in the same bachelor dwelling, was indeed a joyless prospect. Therefore, the presence of another quiet, unobtrusive man in the house was, under these circumstances, a real blessing.

Agrafena had spoken the truth: the lodger was a man who had seen much in his life. From his passport it appeared that he was a retired soldier, which I noticed even before I looked at the passport.

As soon as I glanced at him in fact.

Astafi Ivanich, my lodger, belonged to the

better sort of soldiers, another thing I noticed
as soon as I saw him. We liked each other from
the first, and our life flowed on peacefully and
comfortably. The best thing was that Astafi
Ivanich could at times tell a good story, in-
cidents of his own life. In the general tedious-
ness of my humdrum existence, such a narrator
was a veritable treasure. Once he told me a
story which has made a lasting impression upon
me; but first the incident which led to the
story.

Once I happened to be left alone in the house,
Astafi and Agrafena having gone out on business. Suddenly I heard some one enter, and I
felt that it must be a stranger; I went out into
the corridor and found a man of short stature,
and notwithstanding the cold weather, dressed
very thinly and without an overcoat.

"What is it you want?"

"The Government clerk Alexandrov? Does
he live here?"

"There is no one here by that name, little
brother; good day."

"The porter told me he lived here," said the
visitor, cautiously retreating toward the door.

"Go on, go on, little brother; be off!"

Soon after dinner the next day, when Astafi
brought in my coat, which he had repaired for
me, I once more heard a strange step in the corridor. I opened the door.

The visitor of the day before, calmly and be-

fore my very eyes, took my short coat from the
rack, put it under his arm, and ran out.

Agrafena, who had all the time been looking
at him in open-mouthed surprise through the
kitchen door, was seemingly unable to stir from
her place and rescue the coat. But Astafi Ivanich rushed after the rascal, and, out of breath
and panting, returned empty-handed. The man
had vanished as if the earth had swallowed him.

"It is too bad, really, Astafi Ivanich," I said.
"It is well that I have my cloak left. Otherwise
the scoundrel would have put me out of service
altogether."

But Astafi seemed so much affected by what
had happened that as I gazed at him I forgot all
about the theft. He could not regain his composure, and every once in a while threw down the
work which occupied him, and began once more
to recount how it had all happened, where he
had been standing, while only two steps away
my coat had been stolen before his very eyes, and
how he could not even catch the thief. Then
once more he resumed his work, only to throw
it away again, and I saw him go down to the
porter, tell him what had happened, and reproach
him with not taking sufficient care of the house,
that such a theft could be perpetrated in it.
When he returned he began to upbraid Agrafena.
Then he again resumed his work, muttering to
himself for a long time—how this is the way it
all was—how he stood here, and I there, and how

before our very eyes, no farther than two steps away, the coat was taken off its hanger, and so on. In a word, Astafi Ivanich, though he knew how to do certain things, worried a great deal over trifles.

"We have been fooled, Astafi Ivanich," I said to him that evening, handing him a glass of tea, and hoping from sheer ennui to call forth the story of the lost coat again, which by dint of much repetition had begun to sound extremely comical.

"Yes, we were fooled, sir. It angers me very much, though the loss is not mine, and I think there is nothing so despicably low in this world as a thief. They steal what you buy by working in the sweat of your brow— Your time and labor— The loathsome creature! It sickens me to talk of it—pfui! It makes me angry to think of it. How is it, sir, that you do not seem to be at all sorry about it?"

"To be sure, Astafi Ivanich, one would much sooner see his things burn up than see a thief take them. It is exasperating—"

"Yes, it is annoying to have anything stolen from you. But of course there are thieves and thieves—I, for instance, met an honest thief through an accident."

"How is that? An honest thief? How can a thief be honest, Astafi Ivanich?"

"You speak truth, sir. A thief can not be an honest man. There never was such. I only

240

wanted to say that he was an honest man, it seems to me, even though he stole. I was very sorry for him."

"And how did it happen, Astafi Ivanich?"

"It happened just two years ago. I was serving as house steward at the time, and the baron whom I served expected shortly to leave for his estate, so that I knew I would soon be out of a job, and then God only knew how I would be able to get along; and just then it was that I happened to meet in a tavern a poor forlorn creature, Emelian by name. Once upon a time he had served somewhere or other, but had been driven out of service on account of tippling. Such an unworthy creature as he was! He wore whatever came along. At times I even wondered if he wore a shirt under his shabby cloak; everything he could put his hands on was sold for drink. But he was not a rowdy. Oh, no; he was of a sweet, gentle nature, very kind and tender to every one; he never asked for anything, was, if anything, too conscientious— Well, you could see without asking when the poor fellow was dying for a drink, and of course you treated him to one. Well, we became friendly, that is, he attached himself to me like a little dog—you go this way, he follows—and all this after our very first meeting.

"Of course he remained with me that night; his passport was in order and the man seemed all right. On the second night also. On the third he did not leave the house, sitting on the window-seat of the corridor the whole day, and of course he remained over that night too. Well, I thought, just see how he has forced himself upon you. You have to give him to eat and to drink and to shelter him. All a poor man needs is some one to sponge upon him. I soon found out that once before he had attached himself to a man just as he had now attached himself to me; they drank together, but the other one soon died of some deep-seated sorrow. I thought and thought: What shall I do with him? Drive him out—my conscience would not allow it—I felt very sorry for him: he was such a wretched, forlorn creature, terrible! And so dumb he did not ask for anything, only sat quietly and looked you straight in the eyes, just like a faithful little dog. That is how drink can ruin a man. And I thought to myself: Well, suppose I say to him: 'Get out of here, Emelian; you have nothing to do in here, you come to the wrong person; I will soon have nothing to eat myself, so how do you expect me to feed *you?*' And I tried to imagine what he would do after I'd told him all this. And I could see how he would look at me for a long time after he had heard me, without understanding a word; how at last he would understand what I was driving at, and, rising from the window-seat, take his little bundle—I see it before me now—a red-checked little bundle full of holes, in which he kept God knows what, and which he carted along with him wherever he went; how he would brush and fix up his worn cloak a little, so that it would look a bit more decent and not show so much the holes and patches—he was a man of very fine feelings! How he would have opened the door afterward and would have gone forth with tears in his eyes.

"Well, should a man be allowed to perish altogether? I all at once felt heartily sorry for him; but at the same time I thought: And what about me, am I any better off? And I said to myself: Well, Emelian, you will not feast overlong at my expense; soon I shall have to move from here myself, and then you will not find me again. Well, sir, my baron soon left for his estate with all his household, telling me before he went that he was very well satisfied with my services, and would gladly employ me again on his return to the capital. A fine man my baron was, but he died the same year.

"Well, after I had escorted my baron and his family a little way, I took my things and the little money I had saved up, and went to live with an old woman I knew, who rented out a corner of the room she occupied by herself. She used to be a nurse in some well-to-do family, and now, in her old age, they had pensioned her off. Well, I thought to myself, now it is good-by to you, Emelian, dear man, you will not find me now! And what do you think, sir? When I returned in the evening—I had paid a

visit to an acquaintance of mine—whom should
I see but Emelian sitting quietly upon my trunk
with his red-checked bundle by his side. He was
wrapped up in his poor little cloak, and was
awaiting my home-coming. He must have been
quite lonesome, because he had borrowed a
prayer-book of the old woman and held it upside
down. He had found me after all! My hands
fell helplessly at my sides. Well, I thought,
there is nothing to be done, why did I not drive
him away first off? And I only asked him:
'Have you taken your passport along, Emelian?'
Then I sat down, sir, and began to turn the matter over in my mind: Well, could he, a roving
man, be much in my way? And after I had considered it well, I decided that he would not, and
besides, he would be of very little expense to me.
Of course, he would have to be fed, but what
does that amount to? Some bread in the morning and, to make it a little more appetizing, a
little onion or so. For the midday meal again
some bread and onion, and for the evening again
onion and bread, and some kvass, and, if some
cabbage-soup should happen to come our way,
then we could both fill up to the throat. I ate
little, and Emelian, who was a drinking man,
surely ate almost nothing: all he wanted was
vodka. He would be the undoing of me with
his drinking; but at the same time I felt a curious
feeling creep over me. It seemed as if life would
be a burden to me if Emelian went away. And

so I decided then and there to be his father-bene
factor. I would put him on his legs, I thought,
save him from perishing, and gradually wean
him from drink. Just you wait, I thought. Stay
with me, Emelian, but stand pat now. Obey
the word of command!

"Well, I thought to myself, I will begin by
teaching him some work, but not at once; let him
first enjoy himself a bit, and I will in the mean
while look around and discover what he finds
easiest, and would be capable of doing, because
you must know, sir, a man must have a calling
and a capacity for a certain work to be able to do
it properly. And I began stealthily to observe
him. And a hard subject he was, that Emelian!
At first I tried to get at him with a kind word.
Thus and thus I would speak to him: 'Emelian,
you had better take more care of yourself and
try to fix yourself up a little.

" 'Give up drinking. Just look at yourself,
man, you are all ragged, your cloak looks more
like a sieve than anything else. It is not nice.
It is about time for you to come to your senses
and know when you have had enough.'

"He listened to me, my Emelian did, with
lowered head; he had already reached that state,
poor fellow, when the drink affected his tongue
and he could not utter a sensible word. You
talk to him about cucumbers, and he answers
beans. He listened, listened to me for a long
time, and then he would sigh deeply.

" 'What are you sighing for, Emelian?' I ask him.

" 'Oh, it is nothing, Astafi Ivanich, do not worry. Only what I saw to-day, Astafi Ivanich —two women fighting about a basket of huckleberries that one of them had upset by accident.'

" 'Well, what of that?'

" 'And the woman whose berries were scattered snatched a like basket of huckleberries from the other woman's hand, and not only threw them on the ground, but stamped all over them.'

" 'Well, but what of that, Emelian?'

" 'Ech!' I think to myself, 'Emelian! You have lost your poor wits through the cursed drink!'

" 'And again,' Emelian says, 'a baron lost a bill on the Gorokhova Street—or was it on the Sadova? A muzhik saw him drop it, and says, "My luck," but here another one interfered and says, "No, it is my luck! I saw it first. . . ." '

" 'Well, Emelian?'

" 'And the two muzhiks started a fight, Astafi Ivanich, and the upshot was that a policeman came, picked up the money, handed it back to the baron, and threatened to put the muzhiks under lock for raising a disturbance.'

" 'But what of that? What is there wonderful or edifying in that, Emelian?'

" 'Well, nothing, but the people laughed, Astafi Ivanich.'

" 'E-ch, Emelian! What have the people to

do with it?' I said. 'You have sold your immortal soul for a copper. But do you know what I will tell you, Emelian?'

" 'What, Astafi Ivanich?'

" 'You'd better take up some work, really you should. I am telling you for the hundredth time that you should have pity on yourself!'

" 'But what shall I do, Astafi Ivanich? I do not know where to begin and no one would employ me, Astafi Ivanich.'

" 'That is why they drove you out of service, Emelian; it is all on acount of drink!'

" 'And to-day,' said Emelian, 'they called Vlass the barkeeper into the office.'

" 'What did they call him for, Emelian?' I asked.

" 'I don't know why, Astafi Ivanich. I suppose it was needed, so they called him.'

" 'Ech,' I thought to myself, 'no good will come of either of us, Emelian! It is for our sins that God is punishing us!'

"Well, what could a body do with such a man, sir!

"But he was sly, the fellow was, I tell you! He listened to me, listened, and at last it seems it began to tire him, and as quick as he would notice that I was growing angry he would take his cloak and slip out—and that was the last to be seen of him! He would not show up the whole day, and only in the evening would he return, as drunk as a lord. Who treated him to drinks, or where he got the money for it, God only knows; not from me, surely! . . .

" 'Well,' I say to him, 'Emelian, you will have to give up drink, do you hear? you will have to give it up! The next time you return tipsy, you will have to sleep on the stairs. I'll not let you in!'

"After this Emelian kept to the house for two days; on the third he once more sneaked out. I wait and wait for him; he does not come! I must confess that I was kind of frightened; besides, I felt terribly sorry for him. What had I done to the poor devil! I thought. I must have frightened him off. Where could he have gone to now, the wretched creature? Great God, he may perish yet! The night passed and he did not return. In the morning I went out into the hall, and he was lying there with his head on the lower step, almost stiff with cold.

" 'What is the matter with you, Emelian? The Lord save you! Why are you here?'

" 'But you know, Astafi Ivanich,' he replied, 'you were angry with me the other day; I aggravated you, and you promised to make me sleep in the hall, and I—so I—did not dare—to come in—and lay down here.'

" 'It would be better for you, Emelian,' I said, filled with anger and pity, 'to find a better employment than needlessly watching the stairs!'

" 'But what other employment, Astafi Ivanich?'

" 'Well, wretched creature that you are,' here anger had flamed up in me, 'if you would try to learn the tailoring art. Just look at the cloak you are wearing! Not only is it full of holes, but you are sweeping the stairs with it! You should at least take a needle and mend it a little, so it would look more decent. E-ch, a wretched tippler you are, and nothing more!'

"Well, sir! What do you think! He did take the needle—I had told him only for fun, and there he got scared and actually took the needle. He threw off his cloak and began to put the thread through; well, it was easy to see what would come of it; his eyes began to fill and reddened, his hands trembled! He pushed and pushed the thread—could not get it through: he wetted it, rolled it between his fingers, smoothed it out, but it would not—go! He flung it from him and looked at me.

" 'Well, Emelian!' I said, 'you served me right! If people had seen it I would have died with shame! I only told you all this for fun, and because I was angry with you. Never mind sewing; may the Lord keep you from sin! You need not do anything, only keep out of mischief, and do not sleep on the stairs and put me to shame thereby!'

" 'But what shall I do, Astafi Ivanich; I know myself that I am always tipsy and unfit for anything! I only make you, my be—benefactor, angry for nothing.'

"And suddenly his bluish lips began to tremble, and a tear rolled down his unshaven, pale cheek, then another and another one, and he broke into a very flood of tears, my Emelian. Father in Heaven! I felt as if some one had cut me over the heart with a knife.

" 'E-ch you, sensitive man; why, I never thought! And who *could* have thought such a thing! No, I'd better give you up altogether, Emelian; do as you please.'

"Well, sir, what else is there to tell! But the whole thing is so insignificant and unimportant, it is really not worth while wasting words about it; for instance, you, sir, would not give two broken groschen for it; but I, I would give much, if I had much, that this thing had never happened! I owned, sir, a pair of breeches, blue, in checks, a first-class article, the devil take them—a rich landowner who came here on business ordered them from me, but refused afterward to take them, saying that they were too tight, and left them with me.

"Well, I thought, the cloth is of first-rate quality! I can get five rubles for them in the old-clothes market-place, and, if not, I can cut a fine pair of pantaloons out of them for some St. Petersburg gent, and have a piece left over for a vest for myself. Everything counts with a poor man! And Emelian was at that time in sore straits. I saw that he had given up drinking, first one day, then a second, and a third, and looked so downhearted and sad.

"Well, I thought, it is either that the poor fellow lacks the necessary coin or maybe he has entered on the right path, and has at last listened to good sense.

"Well, to make a long story short, an important holiday came just at that time, and I went to vespers. When I came back I saw Emelian sitting on the window-seat as drunk as a lord. Eh! I thought, so that is what you are about! And I go to my trunk to get out something I needed. I look! The breeches are not there. I rummage about in this place and that place: gone! Well, after I had searched all over and saw that they were missing for fair, I felt as if something had gone through me! I went after the old woman—as to Emelian, though there was evidence against him in his being drunk, I somehow never thought of him!

"'No,' says my old woman; 'the good Lord keep you, gentleman, what do I need breeches for? can I wear them? I myself missed a skirt the other day. I know nothing at all about it.'

"'Well,' I asked, 'has any one called here?'

"'No one called,' she said. 'I was in all the time; your friend here went out for a short while and then came back; here he sits! Why don't you ask him?'

"'Did you happen, for some reason or other, Emelian, to take the breeches out of the trunk?

The ones, you remember, which were made for the landowner?'

" 'No,' he says, 'I have not taken them, Astafi Ivanich.'

" 'What *could* have happened to them?' Again I began to search, but nothing came of it! And Emelian sat and swayed to and fro on the window-seat.

"I was on my knees before the open trunk, just in front of him. Suddenly I threw a side-long glance at him. Ech, I thought, and felt very hot round the heart, and my face grew very red. Suddenly my eyes encountered Emelian's.

" 'No,' he says, 'Astafi Ivanich. You perhaps think that I—you know what I mean—but I have not taken them.'

" 'But where have they gone, Emelian?'

" 'No,' he says, 'Astafi Ivanich, I have not seen them at all.'

" 'Well, then, you think they simply went and got lost by themselves, Emelian?'

" 'Maybe they did, Astafi Ivanich.'

"After this I would not waste another word on him. I rose from my knees, locked the trunk, and after I had lighted the lamp I sat down to work. I was remaking a vest for a government clerk, who lived on the floor below. But I was terribly rattled, just the same. It would have been much easier to bear, I thought, if all my wardrobe had burned to ashes. Emelian, it seems, felt that I was deeply angered. It is always so, sir, when a man is guilty; he always feels beforehand when trouble approaches, as a bird feels the coming storm.

" 'And do you know, Astafi Ivanich,' he suddenly began, 'the leach married the coachman's widow to-day.'

"I just looked at him; but, it seems, looked at him so angrily that he understood: I saw him rise from his seat, approach the bed, and begin to rummage in it, continually repeating: 'Where could they have gone, vanished, as if the devil had taken them!'

"I waited to see what was coming; I saw that my Emelian had crawled under the bed. I could contain myself no longer.

" 'Look here,' I said. 'What makes you crawl under the bed?'

" 'I am looking for the breeches, Astafi Ivanich,' said Emelian from under the bed. 'Maybe they got here somehow or other.'

" 'But what makes you, sir (in my anger I addressed him as if he was—somebody), what makes you trouble yourself on account of such a plain man as I am; dirtying your knees for nothing!'

" 'But, Astafi Ivanich— I did not mean anything— I only thought maybe if we look for them here we may find them yet.'

" 'Mm! Just listen to me a moment, Emelian!'

" 'What, Astafi Ivanich?'

" 'Have you not simply stolen them from me
253

like a rascally thief, serving me so for my bread and salt?' I said to him, beside myself with wrath at the sight of him crawling under the bed for something he knew was not there.

" 'No, Astafi Ivanich.' For a long time he remained lying flat under the bed. Suddenly he crawled out and stood before me—I seem to see him even now—as terrible a sight as sin itself.

" 'No,' he says to me in a trembling voice, shivering through all his body and pointing to his breast with his finger, so that all at once I became scared and could not move from my seat on the window. 'I have not taken your breeches, Astafi Ivanich.'

" 'Well,' I answered, 'Emelian, forgive me if in my foolishness I have accused you wrongfully. As to the breeches, let them go hang; we will get along without them. We have our hands, thank God, we will not have to steal, and now, too, we will not have to sponge on another poor man; we will earn our living.'

"Emelian listened to me and remained standing before me for some time, then he sat down and sat motionless the whole evening; when I lay down to sleep he was still sitting in the same place.

"In the morning, when I awoke, I found him sleeping on the bare floor, wrapped up in his cloak; he felt his humiliation so strongly that he had no heart to go and lie down on the bed.

THE THIEF

"Well, sir, from that day on I conceived a terrible dislike for the man; that is, rather, I hated him the first few days, feeling as if, for instance, my own son had robbed me and given me deadly offense. Ech, I thought, Emelian, Emelian! And Emelian, my dear sir, had gone on a two weeks' spree. Drunk to bestiality from morning till night. And during the whole two weeks he had not uttered a word. I suppose he was consumed the whole time by a deep-seated grief, or else he was trying in this way to make an end to himself. At last he gave up drinking. I suppose he had no longer the wherewithal to buy vodka—had drunk up every copeck—and he once more took up his old place on the window-seat. I remember that he sat there for three whole days without a word; suddenly I see him weep; sits there and cries, but what crying! The tears come from his eyes in showers, drip, drip, as if he did not know that he was shedding them. It is very painful, sir, to see a grown man weep, all the more when the man is of advanced years, like Emelian, and cries from grief and a sorrowful heart.

" 'What ails you, Emelian?' I say to him.

"He starts and shivers. This was the first time I had spoken to him since that eventful day.

" 'It is nothing—Astafi Ivanich.'

" 'God keep you, Emelian; never you mind it all. Let bygones be bygones. Don't take it to heart so, man!' I felt very sorry for him.

255

" 'It is only that—that I would like to do something—some kind of work, Astafi Ivanich.'

" 'But what kind of work, Emelian?'

" 'Oh, any kind. Maybe I will go into some kind of service, as before. I have already been at my former employer's asking. It will not do for me, Astafi Ivanich, to use you any longer. I, Astafi Ivanich, will perhaps obtain some employment, and then I will pay you for everything, food and all.'

" 'Don't, Emelian, don't. Well, let us say you committed a sin; well, it is over! The devil take it all! Let us live as before—as if nothing had happened!' "

" 'You, Astafi Ivanich, you are probably hinting about *that*. But I have not taken your breeches.'

" 'Well, just as you please, Emelian!'

" 'No, Astafi Ivanich, evidently I can not live with you longer. You will excuse me, Astafi Ivanich.'

" 'But God be with you, Emelian,' I said to him; 'who is it that is offending you or driving you out of the house? Is it I who am doing it?'

" 'No, but it is unseemly for me to misuse your hospitality any longer, Astafi Ivanich; 'twill be better to go.'

"I saw that he had in truth risen from his place and donned his ragged cloak—he felt offended, the man did, and had gotten it into his head to leave, and—basta.

" 'But where are you going, Emelian? Listen to sense: what are you? Where will you go?'

" 'No, it is best so, Astafi Ivanich, do not try to keep me back,' and he once more broke into tears; 'let me be, Astafi Ivanich, you are no longer what you used to be.'

" 'Why am I not? I am just the same. But you will perish when left alone—like a foolish little child, Emelian.'

" 'No, Astafi Ivanich. Lately, before you leave the house, you have taken to locking your trunk, and I, Astafi Ivanich, see it and weep— No, it is better you should let me go, Astafi Ivanich, and forgive me if I have offended you in any way during the time we have lived together.'

"Well, sir! And so he did go away. I waited a day and thought: Oh, he will be back toward evening. But a day passes, then another, and he does not return. On the third—he does not return. I grew frightened, and a terrible sadness gripped at my heart. I stopped eating and drinking, and lay whole nights without closing my eyes. The man had wholly disarmed me! On the fourth day I went to look for him; I looked in all the taverns and pot-houses in the vicinity, and asked if any one had seen him. No, Emelian had wholly disappeared! Maybe he has done away with his miserable existence, I thought. Maybe, when in his cups, he has perished like a dog, somewhere under a fence. I came home half dead with fatigue and despair, and decided to go out the next day again to look for him, cursing myself bitterly for letting the foolish, helpless man go away from me. But at dawn of the fifth day (it was a holiday) I heard the door creak. And whom should I see but Emelian! But in what a state! His face was bluish and his hair was full of mud, as if he had slept in the street; and he had grown thin, the poor fellow had, as thin as a rail. He took off his poor cloak, sat down on my trunk, and began to look at me. Well, sir, I was overjoyed, but at the same time felt a greater sadness than ever pulling at my heart-strings. This is how it was, sir: I felt that if a thing like that had happened to me, that is—I would sooner have perished like a dog, but would not have returned. And Emelian did. Well, naturally, it is hard to see a man in such a state. I began to coddle and to comfort him in every way.

" 'Well,' I said, 'Emelian, I am very glad you have returned; if you had not come so soon, you would not have found me in, as I intended to go hunting for you. Have you had anything to eat?'

" 'I have eaten, Astafi Ivanich.'

" 'I doubt it. Well, here is some cabbage soup —left over from yesterday; a nice soup with some meat in it—not the meagre kind. And here you have some bread and a little onion. Go ahead and eat; it will do you good.'

"I served it to him; and immediately realized that he must have been starving for the last three days—such an appetite as he showed! So it was hunger that had driven him back to me. Looking at the poor fellow, I was deeply touched, and decided to run into the nearby dram-shop. I will get him some vodka, I thought, to liven him up a bit and make peace with him. It is enough. I have nothing against the poor devil any longer. And so I brought the vodka and said to him: 'Here, Emelian, let us drink to each other's health in honor of the holiday. Come, take a drink. It will do you good.'

"He stretched out his hand, greedily stretched it out, you know, and stopped; then, after a while, he lifted the glass, carried it to his mouth, spilling the liquor on his sleeve; at last he did carry it to his mouth, but immediately put it back on the table.

" 'Well, why don't you drink, Emelian?'

" 'But no, I'll not, Astafi Ivanich.'

" 'You'll not drink it!'

" 'But I, Astafi Ivanich, I think—I'll not drink any more, Astafi Ivanich.'

" 'Is it for good you have decided to give it up, Emelian, or only for to-day?'

"He did not reply, and after a while I saw him lean his head on his hand, and I asked him: 'Are you not feeling well, Emelian?'

" 'Yes, pretty well, Astafi Ivanich.'

"I made him go to bed, and saw that he was truly in a bad way. His head was burning hot and he was shivering with ague. I sat by him the whole day; toward evening he grew worse. I prepared a meal for him of kvass, butter, and some onion, and threw in it a few bits of bread, and said to him: 'Go ahead and take some food; maybe you will feel better!'

"But he only shook his head: 'No, Astafi Ivanich, I shall not have any dinner to-day.'

"I had some tea prepared for him, giving a lot of trouble to the poor old woman from whom I rented a part of the room—but he would not take even a little tea.

"Well, I thought to myself, it is a bad case. On the third morning, I went to see the doctor, an acquaintance of mine, Dr. Kostopravov, who had treated me when I still lived in my last place. The doctor came, examined the poor fellow, and only said: 'There was no need of sending for me, he is already too far gone, but you can give him some powders which I will prescribe.'

"Well, I didn't give him the powders at all, as I understood that the doctor was only doing it for form's sake; and in the mean while came the fifth day.

"He lay dying before me, sir. I sat on the window-seat with some work I had on hand lying on my lap. The old woman was raking the stove. We were all silent, and my heart was breaking over this poor, shiftless creature, as if he were my own son whom I was losing. I knew that Emelian was gazing at me all the time; I noticed for the earliest morning that he longed to tell me something, but seemingly dared not. At last I looked at him, and saw that he did not take his eyes from me, but that whenever his eyes met mine, he immediately lowered his own.

" 'Astafi Ivanich!'

" 'What, Emelian?'

" 'What if my cloak should be carried over to the old clothes market, would they give much for it, Astafi Ivanich?'

" 'Well, I said, 'I do not know for certain, but three rubles they would probably give for it, Emelian.' I said it only to comfort the simple-minded creature; in reality they would have laughed in my face for even thinking to sell such a miserable, ragged thing.

" 'And I thought that they might give a little more, Astafi Ivanich. It is made of cloth, so how is it that they would not wish to pay more than three rubles for it?'

" 'Well, Emelian, if you wish to sell it, then of course you may ask more for it at first.'

"Emelian was silent for a moment, then he once more called to me.

" 'Astafi Ivanich!'

" 'What is it, Emelian?'

" 'You will sell the cloak after I am no more;

no need of burying me in it, I can well get along without it; it is worth something, and may come handy to you.'

"Here I felt such a painful gripping at my heart as I can not even express, sir. I saw that the sadness of approaching death had already come upon the man. Again we were silent for some time. About an hour passed in this way. I looked at him again and saw that he was still gazing at me, and when his eyes met mine he immediately lowered his.

" 'Would you like a drink of cold water?' I asked him.

" 'Give me some, and may God repay you, Astafi Ivanich.'

" 'Would you like anything else, Emelian?'

" 'No, Astafi Ivanich, I do not want anything, but I—'

" 'What?'

" 'You know that—'

" 'What is it you want, Emelian?'

" 'The breeches— You know— It was I who took them—Astafi Ivanich—'

" 'Well,' I said, 'the great God will forgive you, Emelian, poor, unfortunate fellow that you are! Depart in peace.'

"And I had to turn away my head for a moment because grief for the poor devil took my breath away and the tears came in torrents from my eyes.

" 'Astafi Ivanich!—'

THE THIEF

"I looked at him, saw that he wished to tell me something more, tried to raise himself, and was moving his lips— He reddened and looked at me— Suddenly I saw that he began to grow paler and paler; in a moment he fell with his head thrown back, breathed once, and gave his soul into God's keeping."

THOU SHALT NOT KILL

BY LEOPOLD VON SACHER-MASOCH

THOU SHALT NOT KILL

BY LEOPOLD VON SACHER-MASOCH

COUNTESS MARA BAROVIC was the Circe, Omphale, and Semiramis of the mountainous part of Croatia.

Old and young (men, be it understood) were at her feet; and this despite the fact that she was regarded as plain-looking rather than pretty. Her ugliness, however, was the sort that strikes attention, attracts consideration, and excites interest. Moreover, she boasted a "past" that cast a halo about the present.

It was rumored that one of her lovers had "accidentally" shot her husband while out hunting, and that this accident had occurred at a time when the Count had become "embarrassing."

Besides, she was original.

If it be true that woman is a work of art, as a celebrated poet has said, it must be borne in mind that in these days the agreeable and pleasing in art is no longer "the thing." Cruel, unadorned truth is preferred to draped loveliness, in love as well as in art.

The Countess belonged to the type demanded by the modern school. By her two most ardent admirers, Baron Kronenfels and Mr. De Broda,

she was termed respectively the iconoclast and the
naturalist.

She mounted her horse like a hussar, was a
dashing whip, and indulged a passionate fondness
for hunting. One of her favorite pastimes was
roaming field and forest in the picturesque costume of the Croatian peasant; and she could
apply the horsewhip as dexterously and mer-
cilessly to her creditors as to her refractory
horses.

The fair lady was head over ears in debt.
There was nothing she could longer call her own,
not even the furniture in Château Granic, not
even the false braid which adorned her well-
poised little head.

The young aristocrats who danced attendance
upon her ladyship explained the preference displayed by this Croatian Circe for the "wise men
of the East"—as they called Kronenfels and De
Broda—by the brilliant financial position of her
two Jewish admirers.

Of the two, Baron Kronenfels's noble birth
rested upon the more ancient foundation, and for
that reason, perhaps, he enjoyed a certain priority
in the fair lady's preference. De Broda was a
mere sapling in the forest of aristocracy, having
been but recently ennobled. The unfeigned
adoration he displayed for his armorial bearings
made him the butt of endless practical jokes. His
coat-of-arms glittered wherever it could find a
resting-place. It shone upon the collar of his

dog; it was emblazoned on his cigarettes, made especially for him at Laferme's.

Despite certain differences of taste, Kronenfels and De Broda were good friends, good comrades as well, for they were both officers in the Reserve. But how often does friendship stand its ground against the whispers of jealousy, especially when a woman's favor is the prize at stake? The relationship between the two grew strained and unnatural, and they were both secretly conscious that they were walking along a path where the least deviation from the centre would result in a catastrophe.

.   .   .   .   .   .

The long-looked-for altercation took place one evening at the club. Wine had been flowing freely, the betting had been high. Countess Mara was the subject under discussion, and Baron Roukavina was telling an amusing story in that lady's eventful life.

She had not paid her taxes for years, was threatened with an execution, and had been moving heaven and earth to avert the impending disgrace. She had gone to Agram, from there to Buda-Pesth, importuning ministers, seeking favor with deputies, and had actually got so far as to ask an audience of the king. She had received hopeful promises everywhere, but the danger hung heavier over her head with the passing of every hour.

At this particular juncture, Baron Meyerbach

called on her, and offered to settle her troubles. Meyerbach was an intelligent fellow, with a good heart, and a purse with the proverbial open mouth; but Hungarian aristocracy could not receive him within its inner circle for the simple reason that he was a Jew.

"Have you so much influence?" asked the Countess. Her breath was almost taken away by the offer.

"Do not inquire too closely into my *modus operandi,* Countess," said the Baron. "It must be sufficient for you to know that my success is assured."

"And what do you ask in exchange for this service?"

"Simply this: that for the next two weeks you will take a walk with me every day for an hour in Vaitzen Street; that you will skate with me an hour in the park; and that each evening you will give me the privilege of escorting you to a different theatre."

"And is that all?"

"All."

The Countess yielded willingly to the Baron's terms. At the end of the fortnight, she received a receipt in full for the payment of her taxes—thirty-two thousand florins—and Baron Meyerbach found Hungarian aristocracy ready to receive him with open arms even within its most inner of inner circles. The Countess had launched him.

The story closed in a burst of laughter, and the diplomat Meyerbach's health was drunk repeatedly and variously.

Of all the convivial party, De Broda alone was silent. Finally, with Goethe's words in mind, he said in a low voice: "Everybody seeks money, and everybody clings to it."

Kronenfels flung his cards noisily on the table, looked savagely at De Broda, and said, with an ugly frown: "Do you imply by that that such a woman as Countess Mara Barovic would willingly let herself be blinded by money?"

De Broda shrugged his shoulders.

Springing from his seat, the Baron cried out, scornfully: "You are a Jew."

For a moment, participants and listeners seemed paralyzed with astonishment; then De Broda, every nerve tingling with rage, hurled angrily back at his assailant: "You are another!"

A challenge to a duel was the result of the quarrel. Seconds were chosen on the spot, the weapons were to be pistols, and the oak forest near De Granic was to witness the affair early the following morning.

.   .   .   .   .   .

De Broda had gone home. He was arranging his papers in order, when Rabbi Solomon Zuckermandel walked into his sanctum.

"You are going to fight?" were the old man's first words.

"Yes."

"And with a Jew? No, Mr. De Broda; you can not, you dare not shoot a man! You will not do it."

"Pardon me, Rabbi Solomon, but my knowledge is somewhat deeper than yours in affairs of honor."

"Do you think so!" replied the old man, with an indulgent smile. "Ah, well, we shall see. You think we can wash our honor only in blood? My dear Mr. De Broda, spotless honor needs no washing; and if it has a blemish, it can not be effaced even by blood. The Baron called you a Jew. Is that an insult?"

"In the sense he attached to the word, yes."

"Not so. Neither in that sense nor in any other. Does the name of soldier become an insult because soldiers have deserted their flag? The Jews we call to mind when the word 'Jew' is used in reproach are those who have forsaken their standard. They are no longer Jews. Judaism is the fear of the Lord, love of liberty, love of the family and humanity. The honor of the Jew consists not in spilling blood, but in acting uprightly and doing good."

"You are right; but—"

"No, no. No 'buts.' When God in the midst of thunder and lightning gave the Tables of the Law to Moses on Mount Sinai, there were no 'buts'; He said: *'Thou shalt not kill!'* You are a Jew, Mr. De Broda. In other words: Man, thou shalt not kill!"

THOU SHALT NOT KILL

The young fellow turned toward the window. The rabbi should not see his emotion. But the Jewish heart was touched, and the old man who gave no thought to title and coat-of-arms had conquered the aristocrat's pride and prejudice.

．　．　．　．　．　．　．　．

Midnight had struck when Rabbi Solomon reached Kronenfels's quarters. The letter he handed the Baron from his adversary read as follows:

"DEAR SIR—You have insulted me grossly in calling me a Jew in the presence of a number of gentlemen, and have added to the insult, as it were, by making it at a time when Mr. De Treitschke in Berlin has spoken of the Jews as the schlamassl [the plague of the Germans]. You are, however, an only son, the pride of your family, and I should like to avoid our meeting for to-morrow. You have often seen me hit the ace at a good range; and you know as well that I am no phrase-maker. I propose, therefore, that we shall both shoot in the air, and that we shall mutually exchange our word of honor not to speak of this arrangement.

BRODA."

Kronenfels held the letter to the rabbi.

"What is to be done?" he asked, with a smile.

"Mr. De Broda has proved himself a true Jew," responded Zuckermandel, gently. "Do not let him surpass you. Prove to him that you, too, are of a race which, boasting the most ancient civilization, is above all others from the humanitarian standpoint."

Kronenfels wrote some hurried lines which Rabbi Solomon conveyed to Mr. De Broda before daybreak. The Baron's answer was couched in these words:

273

"DEAR SIR—I was about to address you when I received your note.

"I, too, should deeply regret having a mortal encounter with a young man upon whom so many hopes are placed.

"I accept your proposition.

"Moreover, between ourselves be it said, we are Jews—in other words, descendants of ancestors whose house is more ancient than that of the Lichtensteins or Auerspergs, ancestors who have transmitted to us two qualities which Mr. De Treitschke could scarcely possess, being as it were the offshoot of a somewhat recent civilization: and these are, repugnance to shed blood, and the 'rachmonni'[1] of the Jewish heart.

"KRONENFELS."

The duel took place at six o'clock in the morning, the venerable oaks of De Granic forest casting an air of solemnity over the bloodless scene. The adversaries kept their word; the pistols were discharged in the air; and the witnesses declared that honorable satisfaction had been made. As De Broda and Kronenfels were shaking hands with hearty good-will, the brushwood parted, and old Rabbi Solomon slowly approached the young men. Raising his arms in benediction, he said, and the light of happiness beamed from his eyes: "Gentlemen, you are Jews!"

[1] The exact translation of "rachmonni" is "merciful." It is used as a name of God, because the Jew does not pronounce the proper name of God except in his prayers.

THE BEAUTY SPOT

BY ALFRED LOUIS CHARLES DE MUSSET

THE BEAUTY SPOT

BY ALFRED LOUIS CHARLES DE MUSSET

I

IN 1756, when Louis XV, wearied with the
quarrels between the magistrature and the
grand council, about the "two sous tax," [1]
determined upon holding a special *lit de justice,*
the members of Parliament resigned. Sixteen
of these resignations were accepted, and as many
exiles decreed. "But," said Madame de Pompadour to one of the presidents, "could you
calmly stand by and see a handful of men resist
the authority of the King of France? Would
you not have a very bad opinion of such a policy?
Throw off the cloak of petty pretense, M. le
President, and you will see the situation just as I
see it myself."

It was not only the exiles that had to pay the
penalty of their want of compliance, but also
their relatives and friends. The violation of
mail-secrets was one of the King's amusements.
To relieve the monotony of his other pleasures,
it pleased him to hear his favorite read all the
curious things that were to be found in his sub-
jects' private correspondence. Of course, under

[1] Two sous per livre from the tenth of the revenue.

277

the fallacious pretext of doing his own detective work, he reaped a large harvest of enjoyment from the thousand little intrigues which thus passed under his eyes; but whoever was connected, whether closely or in a remote degree, with the leaders of the factions, was almost invariably ruined.

Every one knows that Louis XV, with all his manifold weaknesses, had one, and only one, strong point: he was inexorable.

One evening, as he sat before the fire with his feet on the mantelpiece, melancholy as was his wont, the marquise, looking through a packet of letters, suddenly burst into a laugh and shrugged her shoulders. The King wished to know what was the matter.

"Why, I have found here," answered she, "a letter, without a grain of common sense in it, but a very touching thing for all that—quite pitiable in fact."

"Whose is the signature?" said the King.

"There is none, it is a love-letter."

"And what is the address?"

"That is just the point. It is addressed to Mademoiselle d'Annebault, the niece of my good friend, Madame d'Estrades. Apparently it has been put in among these papers on purpose for me to see."

"And what is there in it?" the King persisted.

"Why, I tell you it is all about love. There is mention also of Vauvert and of Neauflette. Are

278

there any gentlemen in those parts? Does your
Majesty know of any?"

The King always prided himself upon knowing France by heart, that is, the nobility of
France. The etiquette of his court, which he had
studied thoroughly, was not more familiar to him
than the armorial bearings of his realm. Not a
very wide range of learning; still nothing beyond
it did he reckon worthy the study; and it was a
point of vanity with him, the social hierarchy
being, in his eyes, something like the marble
staircase of his palace; he must set foot on it as
sole lord and master. After having pondered a
few moments, he knitted his brow, as though
struck by an unwelcome remembrance; then, with
a sign to the marquise to read, he threw himself
back in his easy chair, saying with a smile:

"Read on—she is a pretty girl."

Madame de Pompadour assumed her sweetest
tone of raillery and began to read a long letter,
which, from beginning to end, was one rhapsody
of love.

"Just see," said the writer, "how the fates
persecute me! At first everything seemed to
work for the fulfilment of my wishes, and you
yourself, my sweet one, had you not given me
reason to hope for happiness? I must, however,
renounce this heavenly dream, and that for no
fault of mine. Is it not an excess of cruelty to
have let me catch a glimpse of paradise, only to
dash me into the abyss? When some unfortunate

wretch is doomed to death, do they take a barbarous pleasure in placing before his eyes all that
would make him love life and regret leaving it?
Such is, however, my fate: I have no other refuge, no other hope, than the tomb, for, in my dire
misfortune, I can no longer dream of winning
your hand. When fate smiled on me, all my
hopes were that you should be mine; to-day, a
poor man, I should abhor myself if I dared
still to think of such blessedness, and, now
that I can no longer make you happy, though
dying of love for you, I forbid you to love me—"

The Marquise smiled at these last words.

"Madame," said the King, "this is an honorable man. But what prevents him from marrying his lady-love?"

"Permit me, sire, to continue."

"—This overwhelming injustice from the best
of kings surprises me. You know that my father
asked for me a commission as cornet or ensign in
the Guards, and that on this appointment depended the happiness of my life, since it would
give me the right to offer myself to you. The
Duc de Biron proposed my name; but the King
rejected me in a manner the memory of which is
very bitter to me. If my father has his own way
of looking at things (admitting that it is a
wrong one) must I suffer for it? My devotion
to the King is as true, as unbounded, as my love
for you. How gladly would I give proof of both
these sentiments, could I but draw the sword!

Assuredly I feel deeply distressed at my request being refused; but that I should be thus disgraced without good reason is a thing opposed to the well-known kindness of his Majesty."

"Aha!" said the King, "I am becoming interested."

"—If you knew how very dull we are! Ah! my friend! This estate of Neauflette, this country-house of Vauvert, these wooded glades!—I wander about them all day long. I have forbidden a rake to be used; the sacrilegious gardener came yesterday with his iron-shod besom. He was about to touch the sand. But the trace of your steps, lighter than the wind, was not effaced. The prints of your little feet and of your red satin heels were still upon the path; they seemed to walk before me, as I followed your beautiful image, and that charming fantom took shape at times as though it were treading in the fugitive prints. It was there, while conversing with you by the flower-beds, that it was granted me to know you, to appreciate you. A brilliant education joined to the spirit of an angel, the dignity of a queen with the grace of a nymph, thoughts worthy of Leibnitz expressed in language so simple, Plato's bee on the lips of Diana, all this enfolded me as in a veil of adoration. And, during those delicious moments, the darling flowers were blooming about us, I inhaled their breath while listening to you, in their perfume your memory lived. They droop their

heads now; they present to me the semblance of
death!"

"This is all Rousseau and water," said the
King. "Why do you read such stuff to me?"

"Because your Majesty commanded me to do
so, for the sake of Mademoiselle d'Annebault's
beautiful eyes."

"It is true, she has beautiful eyes."

"—And when I return from these walks, I
find my father alone, in the great drawing-room,
near the lighted candle, leaning on his elbow,
amid the faded gildings which cover our moldy
wainscot. It is with pain that he sees me enter.
My grief disturbs his. Athénaïs! At the back
of that drawing-room, near the window, is the
harpsichord over which flitted those sweet fingers
that my lips have touched but once—once, while
yours opened softly to harmonies of celestial
music—opened with such dainty art that your
songs were but a smile. How happy are they—
Rameau, Lulli, Duni, and so many more! Yes,
yes, you love them—they are in your memory—
their breath has passed through your lips. I too
seat myself at that harpsichord, I strive to play
one of those airs that you love;—how cold, how
monotonous they seem to me! I leave them and
listen to their dying accents while the echo loses
itself beneath that lugubrious vault. My father
turns to me and sees me distressed—what can he
do? Some boudoir gossip, some report from the
servants' hall has closed upon us the gates that

lead into the world. He sees me young, ardent, full of life, asking only to live in this world, he is my father, and can do nothing for me."

"One would think," said the King, "that this fellow was starting for the hunt, and that his falcon had been killed on his wrist. Against whom is he inveighing, may I ask?"

"—It is quite true," continued the Marquise, reading in a lower tone. "It is quite true that we are near neighbors, and distant relatives, of the Abbé Chauvelin. . . ."

"That is what it is, is it?" said Louis XV, yawning. "Another nephew of the *enquêtes et requêtes*. My Parliament abuses my bounty; it really has too large a family."

"But if it is only a *distant* relative!"

"Enough; all these people are good for nothing. This Abbé Chauvelin is a Jansenist; not a bad sort of fellow, in his way; but he has dared to resign. Please throw the letter into the fire, and let me hear no more about it."

II

If these last words of the King were not exactly a death-warrant, they were something like a refusal of permission to live. What could a young man without fortune do, in 1756, whose King would not hear his name mentioned? He might have looked for a clerkship, or tried to turn philosopher, or poet, perhaps; but without official dedication, the trade was worth nothing.

And besides, such was not, by any means, the vocation of the Chevalier Vauvert, who had written, with tears, the letter which made the King laugh. At this very moment, alone with his father, in the old château of Neauflette, his look was desperate and gloomy, even to frenzy, as he paced to and fro.

"I must go to Versailles," he said.

"And what will you do there?"

"I know not; but what am I doing here?"

"You keep me company. It certainly can not be very amusing for you, and I will not in any way seek to detain you. But do you forget that your mother is dead?"

"No, sir. I promised her to consecrate to you the life that you gave me. I will come back, but I must go. I really can not stay in this place any longer."

"And why, if I may ask?"

"My desperate love is the only reason. I love Mademoiselle d'Annebault madly."

"But you know that it is useless. It is only Molière who contrives successful matches without dowries. Do you forget too the disfavor with which I am regarded?"

"Ah! sir, that disfavor! Might I be allowed, without deviating from the profound respect I owe you, to ask what caused it? We do not belong to the Parliament. We pay the tax; we do not order it. If the Parliament stints the King's purse, it is his affair, not ours. Why should M. l'Abbé Chauvelin drag us into his ruin?"

"Monsieur l'Abbé Chauvelin acts as an honest man. He refuses to approve the 'dixième' tax because he is disgusted at the prodigality of the court. Nothing of this kind would have taken place in the days of Madame de Chateauroux! She was beautiful, at least, that woman, and did not cost us anything, not even what she so generously gave. She was sovereign mistress, and declared that she would be satisfied if the King did not send her to rot in some dungeon when he should be pleased to withdraw his good graces from her. But this Étioles, this le Normand, this insatiable Poisson!"

"What does it matter?"

"What does it matter! say you? More than you think. Do you know that now, at this very time, while the King is plundering us, the fortune of this grisette is incalculable? She began by contriving to get an annuity of a hundred and eighty thousand livres—but that was a mere bagatelle, it counts for nothing now; you can form no idea of the startling sums that the King showers upon her; three months of the year can not pass without her picking up, as though by chance, some five or six hundred thousand livres—yesterday out of the salt-tax, to-day out of the increase in the appropriation for the Royal mews. Although she has her own quarters in the royal residences, she buys La Selle, Cressy, Aulnay, Brimborion, Marigny, Saint-Remy, Bellevue, and a number of other estates—mansions in Paris, in Fontainebleau, Versailles, Compiègne —without counting secret hoards in all the banks of Europe, to be used in case of her own disgrace or a demise of the crown. And who pays for all this, if you please?"

"That I do not know, sir, but, certainly, not I."

"It *is* you, as well as everybody else. It is France, it is the people who toil and moil, who riot in the streets, who insult the statue of Pigalle. But Parliament will endure it no longer, it will have no more new imposts. As long as there was question of defraying the cost of the war, our last crown was ready; we had no thought of bargaining. The victorious King could see clearly that he was beloved by the whole kingdom, still more so when he was at the point of death. Then all dissensions, all faction, all ill-feeling ceased. All France knelt before the sick-bed of the King, and prayed for him. But if we pay, without counting, for his soldiers and his doctors, we will no longer pay for his mistresses; we have other things to do with our money than to support Madame de Pompadour."

"I do not defend her, sir. I could not pretend to say either that she was in the wrong or in the right. I have never seen her."

"Doubtless; and you would not be sorry to see her—is it not so?—in order to have an opinion on the subject? For, at your age, the head judges through the eyes. Try it then, if the fancy takes you. But the satisfaction will be denied you."

"Why, sir?"

"Because such an attempt is pure folly; because this marquise is as invisible in her little boudoir at Brimborion as the Grand Turk in his seraglio; because every door will be shut in your face. What are you going to do? Attempt an impossibility? Court fortune like an adventurer?"

"By no means, but like a lover. I do not intend to supplicate, sir, but to protest against an injustice. I had a well-founded hope, almost a promise, from M. de Biron; I was on the eve of possessing the object of my love, and this love is not unreasonable; you have not disapproved of it. Let me venture, then, to plead my own cause. Whether I shall appeal to the King or to Madame de Pompadour I know not, but I wish to set out."

"You do not know what the court is, and you wish to present yourself there."

"I may perhaps be the more easily received for the very reason that I am unknown there."

"You unknown, Chevalier. What are you thinking about? With such a name as yours! We are gentlemen of an old stock, Monsieur; you could not be unknown."

"Well, then, the King will listen to me."

"He will not even hear you. You see Versailles in your dreams, and you will think your-

self there when your postilion stops his horses at
the city gates. Suppose you get as far as the
antechamber—the gallery, the Oeil de Bœuf;
perhaps there may be nothing between his Majesty and yourself but the thickness of a door;
there will still be an abyss for you to cross. You
will look about you, you will seek expedients,
protection, and you will find nothing. We are
relatives of M. de Chauvelin, and how do you
think the King takes vengeance on such as we?
The rack for Damiens, exile for the Parliament,
but for us a word is enough, or, worse still—silence. Do you know what the silence of the King
is, when, instead of replying to you, he mutely
stares at you, as he passes, and annihilates you?
After the Grève, and the Bastille, this is a degree of torture which, though less cruel in appearance, leaves its mark as plainly as the hand
of the executioner. The condemned man, it is
true, remains free, but he must no longer think of
approaching woman or courtier, drawing-room,
abbey, or barrack. As he moves about every door
closes upon him, every one who is anybody turns
away, and thus he walks this way and that, in an
invisible prison."

"But I will so bestir myself in my prison that I
shall get out of it."

"No more than any one else! The son of M.
de Meynières was no more to blame than you.
Like you, he had received promises, he entertained most legitimate hopes. His father, a de-

voted subject of his Majesty, an upright man if
there is one in the kingdom, repulsed by his sovereign, bowed his gray head before the *grisette,*
not in prayer, but in ardent pleading. Do you
know what she replied? Here are her very words,
which M. de Meynières sends me in a letter:
'The King is the master, he does not deem it
appropriate to signify his displeasure to you per-
sonally; he is content to make you aware of it by
depriving your son of a calling. To punish you
otherwise would be to begin an unpleasantness,
and he wishes for none; we must respect his will.
I pity you, however; I realize your troubles. I
have been a mother; I know what it must cost you
to leave your son without a profession!' This is
how the creature expresses herself; and you wish
to put yourself at her feet!"

"They say they are charming, sir."

"Of course they say so. She is not pretty, and
the King does not love her, as every one knows.
He yields, he bends before this woman. She
must have something else than that wooden head
of hers to maintain her strange power."

"But they say she has so much wit."

"And no heart!—Much to her credit, no
doubt."

"No heart! She who knows so well how to de-
claim the lines of Voltaire, how to sing the music
of Rousseau! She who plays Alzire and Colette!
No heart. Oh, that can not be! I will never believe it."

"Go then and see, since you wish it. I advise, I do not command, but you will only be at the expense of a useless journey.—You love this D'Annebault young lady very much then?"

"More than my life."

"*Alors,* be off!"

III

It has been said that journeys injure love, because they distract the mind; it has also been said that they strengthen love, because they give one time to dream over it. The chevalier was too young to make such nice distinctions. Weary of the carriage, when half-way on his journey, he had taken a saddle-hack and thus arrived toward five o'clock in the evening at the "Sun" Inn—a sign then out of fashion, since it dated back to the time of Louis XIV.

There was, at Versailles, an old priest who had been rector of a church near Neauflette; the chevalier knew him and loved him. This curé, poor and simple himself, had a nephew, who held a benefice, a court abbé, who might therefore be useful. So the chevalier went to this nephew who —man of importance as he was—his chin ensconced in his "rabat," received the newcomer civilly, and condescended to listen to his request.

"Come!" said he, "you arrive at a fortunate moment. This is to be an opera-night at the court, some sort of fête or other. I am not going, because I am sulking so as to get something out

of the marquise; but here I happen to have a note
from the Duc d'Aumont; I asked for it for some
one else, but never mind, you can have it. Go to
the fête; you have not yet been presented, it is
true, but, for this entertainment, that is not necessary. Try to be in the King's way when he goes
into the little *foyer*. One look, and your fortune
is made."

The chevalier thanked the abbé, and, worn out
by a disturbed night and a day on horse-back, he
made his toilet at the inn in that negligent manner which so well becomes a lover. A maid-
servant, whose experience had been decidedly
limited, dressed his wig as best she could, covering his spangled coat with powder. Thus he
turned his steps toward his luck with the hopeful
courage of twenty summers.

The night was falling when he arrived at the
château. He timidly advanced to the gate and
asked his way of a sentry. He was shown the
grand staircase. There he was informed by the
tall Swiss that the opera had just commenced,
and that the King, that is to say, everybody, was
in the hall.[2]

"If Monsieur le Marquis will cross the court,"
added the doorkeeper (he conferred the title of

[2] This does not refer to the present theatre, built by Louis XV,
or rather by Madame de Pompadour, but only completed in 1769
and inaugurated in 1770, for the marriage of the Duc de Berri
(Louis XVI) with Marie Antoinette. The "hall" in question was
a sort of portable theatre, that was moved into this or that gallery or apartment, after the manner in vogue in the days of
Louis XIV.

"Marquis" at a venture), "he will be at the play in an instant. If he prefers to go through the apartments—"

The chevalier was not acquainted with the palace. Curiosity prompted him, at first, to reply that he would cross the apartments; then, as a lackey offered to follow as a guide, an impulse of vanity made him add that he needed no escort. He, therefore, went forward alone, but not without a certain emotion of timidity.

Versailles was resplendent with light. From the ground-floor to the roof there glittered and blazed lustres, chandeliers, gilded furniture, marbles. With the exception of the Queen's apartments, the doors were everywhere thrown open. As the chevalier walked on he was struck with an astonishment and an admiration better imagined than described, for the wonder of the spectacle that offered itself to his gaze was not only the beauty, the sparkle of the display itself, but the absolute solitude which surrounded him in this enchanted wilderness.

To find one's self alone in a vast enclosure, be it temple, cloister, or castle, produces a strange, even a weird feeling. The movement—whatever it be—seems to weigh upon the solitary individual; its walls gaze at him! its echoes are listening to him; the noise of his steps breaks in upon a silence so deep that he is impressed by an involuntary fear and dares not advance without a feeling akin to awe. Such were the chevalier's

first impressions, but curiosity soon got the upper
hand and drew him on. The candelabra of the
Gallery of Mirrors, looking into the polished sur-
faces, saw their flames redoubled in them. Every
one knows what countless thousands of cherubs,
nymphs, and shepherdesses disport themselves on
the panelings, flutter about on the ceilings, and
seem to encircle the entire palace as with an immense garland. Here, vast halls, with canopies
of velvet shot with gold and chairs of state still
impressed with the stiff majesty of the "great
King"; there, creased and disordered ottomans,
chairs in confusion around a card-table; a never-
ending succession of empty salons, where all this
magnificence shone out the more that it seemed
entirely useless. At intervals were half-concealed
doors opening upon corridors that extended as
far as the eye could reach, a thousand staircases,
a thousand passages crossing each other as in a
labyrinth; colonnades, raised platforms built for
giants, boudoirs ensconced in corners like children's hiding-places, an enormous painting of
Vanloo near a mantel of porphyry; a forgotten
patch-box, lying beside a piece of grotesque
Chinese workmanship; here a crushing grandeur,
there an effeminate grace; and everywhere, in the
midst of luxury, of prodigality, and of indolence,
a thousand intoxicating odors, strange and di-
verse, mingle perfumes of flowers and women, an
enervating warmth, the very material and sensible
atmosphere of pleasure itself.

To be in such a place, amid such marvels, at twenty, and to be there alone, is surely quite sufficient cause for temporary intoxication. The chevalier advanced at haphazard, as in a dream.

"A very palace of fairies," he murmured, and, indeed, he seemed to behold, unfolding itself before him, one of those tales in which wandering knights discover enchanted castles. Were they indeed mortal creatures that inhabited this matchless abode? Were they real women who came and sat on these chairs and whose graceful outlines had left on those cushions that slight impress, so suggestive, even yet, of indolence? Who knows but that, behind those thick curtains, at the end of some long dazzling gallery, there may perhaps soon appear a princess asleep for the last hundred years, a fairy in hoops, an Armida in spangles, or some court hamadryad that shall issue forth from this marble column, or burst from out of that gilded panel?

Bewildered, almost overpowered, at the sight of all these novel objects, the young chevalier, in order the better to indulge his reverie, had thrown himself on a sofa, and would doubtless have forgotten himself there for some time had he not remembered that he was in love. What, at this hour, was Mademoiselle d'Annebault, his beloved, doing—left behind in her old château?

"Athénaïs!" he exclaimed suddenly, "why do I thus waste my time here? Is my mind wander-

ing? Great heavens! Where am I? And what
is going on within me?"

He soon rose and continued his travels through
this *terra incognita,* and of course lost his way.
Two or three lackeys, speaking in a low voice,
stood before him at the end of a gallery. He
walked toward them and asked how he should
find his way to the play.

"If M. le Marquis," he was answered (the same
title being still benevolently granted him), "will
give himself the trouble to go down that staircase and follow the gallery on the right, he will
find at the end of it three steps going up; he will
then turn to the left, go through the Diana salon,
that of Apollo, that of the Muses, and that of
Spring; he will go down six steps more, then,
leaving the Guards' Hall on his right and crossing over to the Ministers' staircase, he will not
fail to meet there other ushers who will show him
the way."

"Much obliged," said the chevalier, "with such
excellent instruction, it will certainly be my fault
if I do not find my way."

He set off again boldly, constantly stopping,
however, in spite of himself, to look from side to
side, then once more remembering his love. At
last, at the end of a full quarter of an hour, he
once more found, as he had been told, a group of
lackeys.

"M. le Marquis is mistaken," they informed
him; "it is through the other wing of the château

that he should have gone, but nothing is easier for him than to retrace his steps. M. le Marquis has but to go down this staircase, then he will cross the salon of the Nymphs, that of Summer, that of—"

"I thank you," said the chevalier, proceeding on his way. "How foolish I am," he thought, "to go on asking people in this fashion like a rustic. I am making myself ridiculous to no purpose, and even supposing — though it is not likely — that they are not laughing at me, of what use is their list of names, and the pompous sobriquets of these salons, not one of which I know?"

He made up his mind to go straight before him as far as possible. "For," after all," said he to himself, "this palace is very beautiful and prodigiously vast, but it is not boundless, and, were it three times as large as our rabbit enclosure, I must at last reach the end of it."

But it is not easy in Versailles to walk on for a long time in one direction, and this rustic comparison of the royal dwelling to a rabbit enclosure doubtless displeased the nymphs of the place, for they at once set about leading the poor lover astray more than ever, and, doubtless, to punish him, took pleasure in making him retrace his steps over and over again, constantly bringing him back to the same place, like a countryman lost in a thicket of quickset; thus did they shut him in in this Cretan labyrinth of marble and gold.

THE BEAUTY SPOT

In the "Antiquities of Rome," by Piranesi, there is a series of engravings which the artist calls "his dreams," and which are supposed to reproduce his own visions during a fit of delirious fever. These engravings represent vast Gothic halls; on the flagstones are strewn all sorts of engines and machines, wheels, cables, pulleys, levers, catapults, the expression of enormous power and formidable resistance. Along the walls you perceive a staircase, and upon this staircase, climbing, not without trouble, Piranesi himself. Follow the steps a little higher and they suddenly come to an end before an abyss. Whatever has happened to poor Piranesi, you think that he has, at any rate, reached the end of his labors, for he can not take another step without falling; but lift your eyes and you will see a second staircase rising in the air, and upon these stairs Piranesi again, again on the brink of a precipice.

Look now still higher, and another staircase still rises before you, and again poor Piranesi continuing his ascent, and so on, until the everlasting staircase and the everlasting Piranesi disappear together in the skies; that is to say, in the border of the engraving.

This allegory, offspring of a nightmare, represents with a high degree of accuracy the tedium of useless labor and the species of vertigo which is brought on by impatience. The chevalier, wandering incessantly from salon to salon and from gallery to gallery, was at last seized with a fit of downright exasperation.

"Parbleu," said he, "but this is cruel! After having been so charmed, so enraptured, so enthralled, to find myself alone in this cursed palace." (It was no longer a palace of fairies!) "I shall never be able to get out of it! A plague upon the infatuation which inspired me with the idea of entering this place, like Prince Fortunatus with his boots of solid gold, instead of simply getting the first lackey I came across to take me to the play at once!"

The chevalier experienced this tardy feeling of repentance for his rashness at a moment when, like Piranesi, he was half-way up a staircase, on a landing between three doors. Behind the middle one, he thought he heard a murmur so sweet, so light, so voluptuous, that he could not help listening. At the very instant when he was tremblingly advancing with the indiscreet intention of eavesdropping, this door swung open. A breath of air, balmy with a thousand perfumes, a torrent of light that rendered the very mirrors of the gallery lustreless struck him so suddenly that he perforce stepped back.

"Does Monsieur le Marquis wish to enter?" asked the usher who had opened the door.

"I wish to go to the play," replied the chevalier.

"It is just this moment over."

At the same time, a bevy of beautiful ladies, their complexions delicately tinted with white and carmine, escorted by lords, old and young, who led them, not by the arm, nor by the hand, but by the tips of their fingers, began filing out from the Palace Theatre, taking care to walk side-wise, in order not to disarrange their hoops.

All of these brilliant people spoke in a low voice, with an air half grave, half gay, a mixture of awe and respect.

"What can this be?" said the Chevalier, not guessing that chance had luckily brought him to the little *foyer*.

"The King is about to pass," replied the usher. There is a kind of intrepidity, which hesitates at nothing; it comes but too easily, it is the courage of vulgar people. Our young provincial, although he was reasonably brave, did not pos-sess this faculty. At the mere words, "The King is about to pass," he stood motionless and almost terror-stricken.

King Louis XV, who when out hunting would ride on horseback a dozen leagues with ease, was, in other respects, as is known, royally indolent. He boasted, not without reason, that he was the first gentleman of France, and his mistresses used to tell him, not without truth, that he was the best built and the most handsome. It was something to remember to see him leave his chair, and deign to walk in person. When he crossed the *foyer*, with one arm laid, or rather stretched, on the shoulder of Monsieur d'Argenson, while his red heel glided over the polished floor (he had made his laziness the fashion), all whisperings ceased; the courtiers lowered their heads, not daring to bow outright, and the fine ladies, gently bending their knees within the depths of their immense furbelows, ventured that coquettish good-night which our grandmothers called a courtesy, and which our century has replaced by the brutal English shake of the hand.

But the King paid attention to nothing, and saw only what pleased him. Alfieri, perhaps, was there, and it is he who thus describes, in his memoirs, his presentation at Versailles:

"I well knew that the king never spoke to strangers who were not of striking appearance; all the same I could not brook the impassible and frowning demeanor of Louis XV. He scanned from head to foot the man who was being presented to him, and it looked as if he received no impression by so doing. It seems to me, however, that if one were to say to a giant, 'Here is an ant I present to you,' he would smile on looking at it, or perhaps say, 'Oh! what a little creature.'"

The taciturn monarch thus passed among these flowers of feminine loveliness, and all this court, alone in spite of the crowd. It did not require of the chevalier much reflection to understand that he had nothing to hope from the King, and that the recital of his love would obtain no success in that quarter.

"Unfortunate that I am!" thought he. "My father was but too well informed when he told me that within two steps of the king I should see an abyss between him and me. Were I to venture to ask for an audience, who would be my patron? Who would present me? There he is—the absolute master, who can by a word change my destiny, assure my fortune, fulfil my desires. He is there before me; were I to stretch out my hand I could touch his embroidered coat—and I feel myself farther from him than if I were still buried in the depths of my native province! Oh! If I could only speak to him! Only approach him! Who will come to my help?"

While the chevalier was in this unhappy state of mind he saw entering with an air of the utmost grace and delicacy a young and attractive woman, clad very simply in a white gown, without diamonds or embroideries and with a single rose in her hair. She gave her hand to a lord *tout à l'ambre,* as Voltaire expresses it, and spoke softly to him behind her fan. Now chance willed it that, in chatting, laughing, and gesticulating, this fan should slip from her and fall beneath a chair, immediately in front of the chevalier. He at once hurried to pick it up, and as in doing so he had set one knee on the floor, the young lady appeared to him so charming that he presented her the fan without rising. She stopped, smiled, and passed on, thanking him with a slight movement of the head, but at the look she had given the chevalier he felt his heart beat without knowing why. He was right. This young lady was *la petite d'Etioles,* as the malcontents still called her, while others in speaking of her said "la Marquise" in that reverent tone in which one says "The Queen."

IV

"She will protect me! She will come to my rescue! Ah! how truly the abbé spoke when he said that one look might decide my life. Yes, those eyes, so soft and gentle, that little mouth, both merry and sweet, that little foot almost hidden under the *pompon*— Yes, here is my good fairy!"

Thus thought the chevalier, almost aloud, as he returned to the inn. Whence came this sudden hope? Did his youth alone speak, or had the eyes of the marquise told a tale?

He passed the greater part of the night writing to Mademoiselle d'Annebault such a letter as we heard read by Madame de Pompadour to her lord.

To reproduce this letter would be a vain task. Excepting idiots, lovers alone find no monotony in repeating the same thing over and over again.

At daybreak the chevalier went out and began roaming about, carrying his dreams through the streets. It did not occur to him to have recourse once more to the protecting abbé, and it would not be easy to tell the reason which prevented his doing so. It was like a blending of timidity and audacity, of false shame and romantic honor.

And, indeed, what would the abbé have replied to
him, if he had told his story of the night before?
"You had the unique good fortune to pick up
this fan; did you know how to profit by it? What
did the marquise say to you?"

"Nothing."

"You should have spoken to her."

"I was confused; I had lost my head."

"That was wrong; one must know how to
seize an opportunity; but this can be repaired.
Would you like me to present you to Monsieur
So-and-so, one of my friends; or perhaps to
Madame Such-a-one? That would be still better.
We will try and secure for you access to this
marquise who frightened you so, and then"—and
so forth.

Now the chevalier little relished anything of
this kind. It seemed to him that, in telling his
adventure, he would, so to speak, soil and mar it.
He said to himself that chance had done for him
something unheard of, incredible, and that it
should remain a secret between himself and Fortune. To confide this secret to the first comer
was, to his thinking, to rob it of its value, and to
show himself unworthy of it. "I went alone
yesterday to the castle at Versailles," thought he,
"I can surely go alone to Trianon?" This was,
at the time, the abode of the favorite.

Such a way of thinking might, and even should,
appear extravagant to calculating minds, who
neglect no detail, and leave as little as possible to

chance; but colder mortals, if they were ever young, and not everybody is so, even in youth, have known that strange sentiment, both weak and bold, dangerous and seductive, which drags us to our fate. One feels one's self blind, and wishes to be so; one does not know where one is going and yet walks on. The charm of the thing consists in this recklessness and this very ignorance; it is the pleasure of the artist in his dreams, of the lover spending the night beneath the windows of his mistress; it is instinct of the soldier; it is, above all, that of the gamester.

The chevalier, almost without knowing it, had thus taken his way to Trianon. Without being very *paré,* as they said in those days, he lacked neither elegance nor that indescribable air which forbids a chance lackey, meeting one, from daring to ask where one is going. It was, therefore, not difficult for him, thanks to information he had obtained at the inn, to reach the gate of the château—if one can so call that marble *bonbonnière,* which has seen so many pleasures and pains in bygone days. Unfortunately, the gate was closed, and a stout Swiss wearing a plain coat was walking about, his hands behind his back, in the inner avenue, like a person who is not expecting any one.

"The King is here!" said the chevalier to himself, "or else the marquise is away. Evidently, when the doors are closed, and valets stroll about, the masters are either shut in or gone out."

What was to be done? Full as he had been, a moment earlier, of courage and confidence, he now felt, all at once, confused and disappointed. The mere thought, "The King is here!" alone gave him more alarm than those few words, on the night before: "The King is about to pass!" For then he was but facing the unknown, and now he knew that icy stare, that implacable, impassible majesty.

"Ah! Bon Dieu! What a figure I should cut if I were to be so mad as to try and penetrate this garden, and find myself face to face with this superb monarch, sipping his coffee beside a rivulet."

At once the sinister shadow of the Bastille seemed to fall before the poor lover; instead of the charming image that he had retained of the marquise and her smile, he saw dungeons, cells, black bread, questionable water; he knew the story of Latude, thirty years an inmate of the Bastille. Little by little his hope seemed to be taking to itself wings.

"And yet," he again said to himself, "I am doing no harm, nor the King either. I protest against an injustice; but I never wrote or sang scurrilous songs. I was so well received at Versailles yesterday, and the lackeys were so polite. What am I afraid of? Of committing a blunder? I shall make many more which will repair this one."

He approached the gate and touched it with

his finger. It was not quite closed. He opened it, and resolutely entered.

The gatekeeper turned round with a look of annoyance.

"What are you looking for? Where are you going?"

"I am going to Madame de Pompadour."

"Have you an audience?"

"Yes."

"Where is your letter?"

He was no longer the "marquis" of the night before, and, this time, there was no Duc d'Aumont. The chevalier lowered his eyes sadly, and noticed that his white stockings and Rhinestone buckles were covered with dust. He had made the mistake of coming on foot, in a region where no one walked. The gatekeeper also bent his eyes, and scanned him, not from head to foot, but from foot to head. The dress seemed neat enough, but the hat was rather askew, and the hair lacked powder.

"You have no letter. What do you wish?"

"I wish to speak to Madame de Pompadour."

"Really! And you think this is the way it is done?"

"I know nothing about it. Is the King here?"

"Perhaps. Go about your business and leave me alone."

The chevalier did not wish to lose his temper, but, in spite of himself, this insolence made him turn pale.

"I sometimes have told a lackey to go away,"
he replied, "but a lackey never said so to me."

"Lackey! I a lackey?" exclaimed the enraged
gatekeeper.

"Lackey, doorkeeper, valet, or menial, I care
not, and it matters little."

The gatekeeper made a step toward the chevalier with clenched fists and face aflame. The
chevalier, brought to himself by the appearance of a threat, lifted the handle of his sword
slightly.

"Take care, fellow," said he, "I am a gentleman, and it would cost me but thirty-six livres
to put a boor like you under ground."

"If you are a nobleman, monsieur, I belong to
the King; I am only doing my duty; so do not
think—"

At this moment the flourish of a hunting-horn
sounding from the Bois de Satory was heard
afar, and lost itself in the echo. The chevalier
allowed his sword to drop into its scabbard, no
longer thinking of the interrupted quarrel.

"I declare," said he, "it is the King starting
for the hunt! Why did you not tell me that before?"

"That has nothing to do with me, nor with you
either."

"Listen to me, my good man. The King is
not here; I have no letter, I have no audience.
Here is some money for you; let me in."

He drew from his pocket several pieces of

gold. The gatekeeper scanned him anew with a superb contempt.

"What is that?" said he, disdainfully. "Is it thus you seek to penetrate into a royal dwelling? Instead of making you go out, take care I don't lock you in."

"*You*—you valet!" said the chevalier, getting angry again and once more seizing his sword.

"Yes, I," repeated the big man. But during this conversation, in which the historian regrets to have compromised his hero, thick clouds had darkened the sky; a storm was brewing. A flash of lightning burst forth, followed by a violent peal of thunder, and the rain began to fall heavily. The chevalier, who still held his gold, saw a drop of water on his dusty shoe as large as a crown piece.

"Peste!" said he, "let us find shelter. It would never do to get wet."

He turned nimbly toward the den of Cerberus, or, if you please, the gatekeeper's lodge.

Once in there, he threw himself unceremoniously into the big armchair of the gatekeeper himself.

"Heavens! How you annoy me!" said he, "and how unfortunate I am! You take me for a conspirator, and you do not understand that I have in my pocket a petition for his Majesty! If I am from the country, you are nothing but a dolt."

The gatekeeper, for answer, went to a corner

to fetch his halberd, and remained standing thus with the weapon in his fist.

"When are you going away?" he cried out in a stentorian voice.

The quarrel, in turn forgotten and taken up again, seemed this time to be becoming quite serious, and already the gatekeeper's two big hands trembled strangely on his pike;—what was to happen? I do not know. But, suddenly turning his head—"Ah!" said the chevalier, "who comes here?"

A young page mounted on a splendid horse (not an English one;—at that time thin legs were not the fashion) came up at full speed. The road was soaked with rain; the gate was but half open. There was a pause; the keeper advanced and opened the gate. The page spurred his horse, which had stopped for the space of an instant; it tried to resume its gait, but missed its footing, and, slipping on the damp ground, fell.

It is very awkward, almost dangerous, to raise a fallen horse. A riding-whip is of no use. The kicking of the beast, which is doing its best, is extremely disagreeable, especially when one's own leg is caught under the saddle.

The chevalier, however, came to the rescue without thinking of these inconveniences, and set about it so cleverly that the horse was soon raised and the rider freed. But the latter was covered with mud and could scarcely limp along.

Carried as well as might be to the gatekeeper's

lodge and seated in his turn in the big armchair, "Sir," said he to the chevalier, "you are certainly a nobleman. You have rendered me a great service, but you can render me a still greater one. Here is a message from the King for Madame la Marquise, and this message is very urgent, as you see, since my horse and I, in order to go faster, almost broke our necks. You understand that, wounded as I am, with a lame leg, I could not deliver this paper. I should have, in order to do so, to be carried myself. Will you go there in my stead?"

At the same time he drew from his pocket a large envelope ornamented with gilt arabesques and fastened with the royal seal.

"Very willingly, sir," replied the chevalier, taking the envelope.

And, nimble and light as a feather, he set out at a run and on the tips of his toes.

V

When the chevalier arrived at the château he found another doorkeeper in front of the peristyle:

"By the King's order," said the young man, who this time no longer feared halberds, and, showing his letter, he passed gaily between half a dozen lackeys.

A tall usher, planted in the middle of the vestibule, seeing the order and the royal seal, gravely

inclined himself, like a poplar bent by the wind
—then, smiling, he touched with one of his bony
fingers the corner of a piece of paneling.

A little swinging door, masked by tapestry, at
once opened as if of its own accord. The bony
man made an obsequious sign, the chevalier entered, and the tapestry, which had been drawn
apart, fell softly behind him.

A silent valet introduced him into a drawing-
room, then into a corridor, in which there were
two or three closed doors, then at last into a
second drawing-room, and begged him to wait
a moment.

"Am I here again in the château of Versailles?"
the chevalier asked himself. "Are we going to
begin another game of hide-and-seek?"

Trianon was, at that time, neither what it is
now nor what it had been. It has been said that
Madame de Maintenon had made of Versailles
an oratory, and Madame de Pompadour a boudoir. It has also been said of Trianon that
ce petit château de porcelaine was the boudoir of
Madame de Montespan. Be that as it may, concerning these boudoirs, it appears that Louis XV
put them everywhere. This or that gallery,
which his ancestor walked majestically, was then
divided oddly into an infinity of apartments.
There were some of every color, and the King
went fluttering about in all these gardens of silk
and velvet.

"Do you think my little furnished apartments

are in good taste?" he one day asked the beautiful Comtesse de Sérrant.

"No," said she, "I would have them in blue."

As blue was the King's color, this answer flattered him.

At their next meeting, Madame de Sérrant found the salon upholstered in blue, as she had wished it.

That in which the chevalier now found himself alone was neither blue nor pink, it was all mirrors. We know how much a pretty woman with a lovely figure gains by letting her image repeat itself in a thousand aspects. She bewilders, she envelops, so to speak, him whom she desires to please. To whatever side he turns, he sees her. How can he avoid being charmed? He must either take to flight or own himself conquered.

The chevalier looked at the garden, too. There, behind, the bushes and labyrinths, the statues and the marble vases, that pastoral style which the marquise was about to introduce, and which, later on, Madame Du Barry and Marie Antoinette were to push to such a high degree of perfection, was beginning to show itself. Already there appeared the rural fantasies where the *blasé* conceits were disappearing. Already the puffing tritons, the grave goddesses, and the learned nymphs, the busts with flowing wigs, frozen with horror in their wealth of verdure, beheld an English garden rise from the ground, amid the wondering trees. Little lawns, little streams, little bridges, were soon to dethrone Olympus to replace it by a dairy, strange parody of nature, which the English copy without understanding—very child's play, for the nonce the pastime of an indolent master who tried in vain to escape the ennui of Versailles while remaining at Versailles itself.

But the chevalier was too charmed, too enraptured at finding himself there for a critical thought to present itself to his mind. He was, on the contrary, ready to admire everything, and was indeed admiring, twirling his missive between his fingers as a rustic does his hat, when a pretty waiting-maid opened the door, and said to him softly:

"Come, monsieur."

He had followed her, and after having once more passed through several corridors which were more or less mysterious, she ushered him into a large apartment where the shutters were half-closed. Here she stopped and seemed to listen.

"Still at hide-and-seek!" said the chevalier to himself. However, at the end of a few moments, yet another door opened, and another waiting-maid, who seemed to be even prettier than the first, repeated to him in the same tone the same words:

"Come, monsieur."

If he had been the victim of one kind of emotion at Versailles, he was subject to another, and still deeper feeling now, for he stood on the threshold of the temple in which the divinity dwelt. He advanced with a palpitating heart. A soft light, slightly veiled by thin, gauze curtains, succeeded obscurity; a delicious perfume, almost imperceptible, pervaded the air around him; the waiting-maid timidly drew back the corner of a silk portière, and, at the end of a large chamber furnished with elegant simplicity, he beheld the lady of the fan—the all-powerful marquise.

She was alone, seated before a table, wrapped in a dressing gown, her head resting on her hand, and, seemingly, deeply preoccupied. On seeing the chevalier enter, she rose with a sudden and apparently involuntary movement.

"You come on behalf of the King?"

The chevalier might have answered, but he could think of nothing better than to bow profoundly while presenting to the marquise the letter which he brought her. She took it, or rather seized upon it, with extreme eagerness. Her hands trembled on the envelope as she broke the seal.

This letter, written by the King's hand, was rather long. She devoured it at first, so to speak, with a glance, then she read it greedily, with profound attention, with wrinkled brow and tightened lips. She was not beautiful thus, and no longer resembled the magic apparition of the *petit foyer*. When she reached the end, she seemed to reflect. Little by little her face, which had turned pale, assumed a faint color (at this hour she did not wear rouge), and not only did she regain that graceful air which habitually belonged to her, but a gleam of real beauty illumined her delicate features; one might have taken her cheeks for two rose-leaves. She heaved a sigh, allowed the letter to fall upon the table, and, turning toward the chevalier, said, with the most charming smile:

"I kept you waiting, monsieur, but I was not yet dressed, and, indeed, am hardly so even now. That is why I was forced to get you to come through the private rooms, for I am almost as much besieged here as though I were at home. I would like to answer the King's note. Would it be too much trouble to you to do an errand for me?"

This time he *must* speak; the chevalier had had time to regain a little courage:

"Alas! madame," said he, sadly, "you confer a great favor on me, but, unfortunately, I can not profit by it."

"Why not?"

"I have not the honor to belong to his Majesty."

"How, then, did you come here?"

"By chance; I met on my way a page who had been thrown and who begged me—"

"How 'thrown'?" repeated the marquise, bursting out laughing. She seemed so happy at this moment that gaiety came to her without an effort.

"Yes, madame, he fell from his horse at the gate. I luckily found myself there to help him to rise, and, as his dress was very much disordered, he begged me to take charge of his message."

"And by what chance did you find yourself there?"

"Madame, it was because I had a petition to present to his Majesty."

"His Majesty lives at Versailles."

"Yes, but you live here."

"Oh! So it is you who wished to entrust me with a message."

"Madame, I beg you to believe—"

"Do not trouble yourself, you are not the first. But why do you address yourself to me? I am but a woman—like any other."

As she uttered these words with a somewhat ironical air, the marquise threw a triumphant look upon the letter she had just read.

"Madame," continued the chevalier, "I have always heard that men exercise power, and that women—"

"Guide it, eh? Well, monsieur, there is a queen of France."

"I know it, madame; that is how it happened that I found myself *here* this morning."

The marquise was more than accustomed to such compliments, though they were generally made in a whisper; but, in the present circumstances, this appeared to be quite singularly gratifying to her.

"And on what faith," said she, "on what assurance, did you believe yourself able to penetrate as far as this? For you did not count, I suppose, upon a horse's falling on the way."

"Madame, I believed—I hoped—"

"What did you hope?"

"I hoped that chance—might make—"

"Chance again! Chance is apparently one of your friends; but I warn you that if you have no other, it is a sad recommendation."

Perhaps offended Chance wished to avenge herself for this irreverence, for the chevalier, whom these few questions had more and more troubled, suddenly perceived, on the corner of the table, the identical fan that he had picked up the night before. He took it, and, as on the night before, presented it to the marquise, bending the knee before her.

"Here, madame," he said to her, "is the only friend that could plead for me—"

The marquise seemed at first astonished, and hesitated a moment, looking now at the fan, now at the chevalier.

"Ah! you are right," she said at last, "it is you, monsieur! I recognize you. It is you whom I saw yesterday, after the play, as I went by with M. de Richelieu. I let my fan drop, and you 'found yourself there,' as you were saying."

"Yes, madame."

"And very gallantly, as a true chevalier, you returned it to me. I did not thank you, but I was sure all the same, that he who knows how to pick up a fan with such grace would also know, at the right time, how to pick up the glove. And we are not ill-pleased at that, we women."

"And it is but too true, madame; for, on reaching here just now, I almost had a duel with the gatekeeper."

"Mercy on us!" said the marquise, once more seized with a fit of gaiety. "With the gate-keeper! And what about?"

"He would not let me come in."

"That would have been a pity! But who are you, monsieur? And what is your request?"

"Madame, I am called the Chevalier de Vauvert. M. de Biron had asked in my behalf for a cornetcy in the Guards."

"Oh! I remember now. You come from Neauflette; you are in love with Mademoiselle d'Annebault—"

"Madame, who could have told you?"

"Oh! I warn you that I am much to be feared. When memory fails me, I guess. You are a relative of the Abbé de Chauvelin, and were refused on that account; is not that so? Where is your petition?"

"Here it is, madame; but indeed I can not understand—"

"Why need you understand? Rise and lay

your paper on the table. I am going to answer
the King's letter; you will take him, at the same
time, your request and my letter."

"But, madame, I thought I had mentioned to
you—"

"You will go. You entered here on the business of the King, is not that true? Well, then,
you will enter there in the business of the Marquise de Pompadour, lady of the palace to the
Queen."

The chevalier bowed without a word, seized
with a sort of stupefaction. The world had long
known how much talk, how many ruses and intrigues, the favorite had brought to bear, and
what obstinacy she had shown to obtain this title,
which in reality brought her nothing but a cruel
affront from the Dauphin. She had longed for
it for ten years; she willed it, and she had succeeded. So M. de Vauvert, whom she did not
know, although she knew of his love, pleased her
as a bearer of happy news.

Immovable, standing behind her, the chevalier
watched the marquise as she wrote, first, with all
her heart—with passion—then with reflection,
stopping, passing her hand under her little nose,
delicate as amber. She grew impatient: the presence of a witness disturbed her. At last she
made up her mind and drew her pen through
something; it must be owned that after all it was
but a rough draft.

Opposite the chevalier, on the other side of the

table, there glittered a fine Venetian mirror.
This timid messenger hardly dared raise his eyes.
It would, however, have been difficult not to see
in this mirror, over the head of the marquise, the
anxious and charming face of the new lady of
the palace.

"How pretty she is!" thought he; "it is a pity
that I am in love with somebody else; but
Athénaïs is more beautiful, and moreover it
would be on my part such a horrible disloyalty."

"What are you talking about?" said the marquise. The chevalier, as was his wont, had
thought aloud without knowing it. "What are
you saying?"

"I, madame? I am waiting."

"There; that is done," the marquise went on,
taking another sheet of paper; but at the slight
movement she had made in turning around the
dressing-gown had slipped on her shoulder.

Fashion is a strange thing. Our grandmothers thought nothing of going to court in
immense robes exposing almost the entire bosom,
and it was by no means considered indecent; but
they carefully hid the back of their necks, which
the fine ladies of to-day expose so freely in the
balcony of the opera. This is a newly invented
beauty.

On the frail, white, dainty shoulder of Madame
de Pompadour there was a little black mark that
looked like a fly floating in milk. The chevalier,
serious as a giddy boy who is trying to keep his

countenance, looked at the mark, and the marquise, holding her pen in the air, looked at the chevalier in the mirror.

In that mirror a rapid glance was exchanged, which meant to say on the one side, "You are charming," and on the other, "I am not sorry for it."

However, the marquise readjusted her dressing-gown.

"You are looking at my beauty spot?"

"I am not looking, madame; I see and I admire."

"Here is my letter; take it to the King with your petition."

"But, madame——"

"Well?"

"His Majesty is hunting; I have just heard the horn in the wood of Satory."

"That is true. I did not think of it. Well, tomorrow. The day after; it matters little. No, immediately. Go. You will give that to Lebel. Good-by, monsieur. Try and remember the beauty spot you have just seen; the King alone in the whole kingdom has seen it; and as for your friend, Chance, tell her, I beg of you, to take care and not chatter to herself so loud, as she did just now. Farewell, chevalier."

She touched a little bell, then, lifting a flood of laces upon her sleeve, held out to the young man her bare arm. He once more bent low, and with the tips of his lips scarcely brushed the rosy nails of the marquise. She saw no impoliteness in it—far from it—but, perhaps, a little too much modesty.

At once the little waiting-maids reappeared (the big ones were not yet up), and, standing behind them, like a steeple in the middle of a flock of sheep, the bony man, still smiling, was pointing the way.

VI

Alone, ensconed in an old armchair in the back of his little room at the sign of "the Sun," the chevalier waited the next day, then the next, and no news!

"Singular woman! Gentle and imperious, good and bad, the most frivolous of women, and the most obstinate! She has forgotten me. What misery! She is right;—she is all-powerful, and I am nothing."

He had risen, and was walking about the room.

"Nothing!—no, I am but a poor devil. How truly my father spoke! The marquise was mocking me; that is all; while I was looking at her, it was only the reflection in that mirror, and in my eyes, of her own charms—which are, certainly, incomparable—that made her look so pleased! Yes, her eyes are small, but what grace! And Latour, before Diderot, has taken the dust from a butterfly's wing to paint her portrait. She is not very tall, but her figure is perfectly

322

exquisite. Ah! Mademoiselle d'Annebault! Ah! my beloved friend, is it possible that I, too, should forget?"

Two or three sharp raps at the door awoke him from his grief.

"Who is there?"

The bony man, clad all in black, with a splendid pair of silk stockings, which simulated calves that were lacking, entered, and made a deep bow.

"This evening, Monsieur le Chevalier, there is to be a masked ball at the court, and Madame la Marquise sends me to say that you are invited."

"That is enough, monsieur. Many thanks."

As soon as the bony man had retired, the chevalier ran to the bell; the same maid-servant who, three days before, had done her best to be of service to him, assisted him to put on the same spangled coat, striving to acquit herself even better than before.

And then the young man took his way toward the palace, invited this time, and more quiet outwardly, but more anxious and less bold than when he had made his first steps in that, to him, still unknown world.

VII

Bewildered, almost as much as on the former occasion, by all the splendors of Versailles, which this evening was not empty, the chevalier walked in the great gallery, looking on every

323

side and doing all he could to learn why he was there; but nobody seemed to think of accosting him. At the end of an hour he became wearied and was about to leave, when two masks, exactly alike, seated on a bench, stopped him on his way. One of them took aim at him with her finger as if with a pistol; the other rose and went to him:

"It appears, monsieur," said the mask, carelessly taking his arm, "that you are on very good terms with our marquise."

"I beg your pardon, madame, but of whom are you speaking?"

"You know well enough."

"Not the least in the world."

"Oh! but indeed you do."

"Not at all."

"All the court knows it."

"I do not belong to the court."

"You are playing the child. I tell you it is well known!"

"That may be, madame, but I am ignorant of it."

"You are not ignorant, however, of the fact that the day before yesterday a page fell from his horse at the gate of Trianon. Were you not there by chance?"

"Yes, madame."

"Did you not help him to rise?"

"Yes, madame."

"And did not you enter the château?"

"Certainly."

"And was not a paper given to you?"

"Yes, madame."

"And did you not take it to the King?"

"Assuredly."

"The King was not at Trianon; he was hunting; the marquise was alone—is not that so?"

"Yes, madame."

"She had just risen; she was scarcely clad, excepting, as it is rumored, in a wide dressing-gown."

"People whom one can not prevent from speaking tell all that runs through their heads."

"That is all well enough, but it appears that there passed between your eyes and hers a look which did not offend her."

"What do you mean by that, madame?"

"That you did not displease her."

"I know nothing about that, and I should be distressed that such sweet and rare good-will, which I did not expect, and which touched me to the bottom of my heart, should give occasion to any idle speeches."

"You take fire too quickly, chevalier; one would think that you were challenging the whole court; you would never succeed in killing so many people."

"But, madame, if the page fell, and if I carried his message—allow me to ask why I am interrogated."

The mask pressed his arm and said to him:

"Listen, monsieur."

"As much as you please, madame."

"This is what we are thinking about now: The King no longer loves the marquise, and nobody believes that he ever loved her. She has just committed an imprudence; she has set the whole Parliament against her with her "two sous" tax, and to-day she dares attack a far greater power—the Society of Jesuits. She will fail, but she has weapons, and, before perishing, she will defend herself."

"Well, madame, what can I do?"

"I will tell you. M. de Choiseul has half quarreled with M. de Bernis; neither of them is sure what it is he would like to attempt. Bernis is going away; Choiseul will take his place. A word from you can decide it."

"In what way, madame, pray?"

"By allowing your story of the other day to be told."

"What earthly connection can there be between my visit, the Jesuits, and the Parliament?"

"Write me one word and the marquise is lost. And do not doubt that the warmest interest, the most complete gratitude—"

"I humbly beg your pardon again, madame, but what you are asking of me would be an act of cowardice."

"Is there any honor in politics?"

"I know nothing of all that. Madame de Pompadour let her fan fall before me; I picked it up; I gave it back to her; she thanked me; she permitted me with that peculiar grace of hers to thank her in my turn."

"A truce to ceremonies: time flies; my name is the Countess d'Estrades; you love Mademoiselle d'Annebault, my niece; do not say no, it is useless. You are seeking a cornetcy; you shall have it to-morrow, and if you care for Athénaïs you will soon be my nephew."

"Ah! madame, what excess of goodness!"

"But you must speak."

"No, madame."

"I have been told that you love that little girl."

"As much as it is possible to love; but if ever my love is to declare itself in her presence my honor must also be there."

"You are very obstinate, chevalier! Is that your final reply?"

"It is the last, as it was the first."

"You refuse to enter the Guards? You refuse the hand of my niece?"

"Yes, madame, if that be the price."

Madame d'Estrades cast upon the chevalier a piercing look, full of curiosity; then seeing in his face no sign of hesitation she slowly walked away, losing herself in the crowd.

The chevalier, unable to make anything of this singular adventure, went and sat down in a corner of the gallery.

"What does that woman mean to do?" said he to himself. "She must be a little mad. She wishes to upset the state by means of a silly calumny, and she proposes to me that in order to merit the hand of her niece I should dishonor myself. But Athénaïs would no longer care for me, or, if she lent herself to such an intrigue, I would no longer care for her. What! Strive to harm this good marquise, to defame her, to blacken her character. Never! no, never!"

Always intent upon his own thoughts, the chevalier very probably would have risen and spoken aloud, but just then a small rosy finger touched him on the shoulder.

He raised his eyes and saw before him the pair of masks who had stopped him.

"You do not wish to help us a little then?" said one of the masks, disguising her voice. But although the two costumes were exactly alike, and all seemed calculated to mislead, the chevalier was not deceived. Neither the look nor the tone was the same.

"Will you answer, sir?"

"No, madame."

"Will you write."

"Neither will I write."

"It is true that you are obstinate. Good-night, lieutenant."

"What do you say, madame?"

"There is your commission and your marriage contract." And she threw the fan to him.

It was the one which the chevalier had already twice picked up. The little cupids of Boucher sported on the parchment of the gilded mother-of-pearl masterpiece. There was no longer any doubt; it was the fan of Madame de Pompadour.

"Heavens! Marquise, is it possible?"

"Very possible," said she, raising the little piece of black veil on her chin.

"I know, madame, how to answer—"

"It is not necessary. You are a loyal gentleman, and we shall see each other again, for we are to be in the same house. The King has placed you in the 'cornette blanche.' Remember that for a petitioner there is no greater eloquence than to know how to be silent if need be—"

"And forgive us," added she, laughing as she ran away, "if before bestowing upon you our niece's hand, we thought it expedient to find out your true worth." [3]

[3] Madame d'Estrades not long after was disgraced, together with M. d'Argenson, for having conspired, this time seriously, against Madame de Pompadour.

A NEW-YEAR'S EVE CONFESSION

CONFESSION

BY HERMANN SUDERMANN

A NEW-YEAR'S EVE CONFESSION

BY HERMANN SUDERMANN

THANKS be to God, dear lady, that I may once more sit beside you for a peaceful chat. The holiday tumult is past, and you have a little leisure for me again.

Oh, this Christmas season! I believe that it was invented by some evil demon expressly to annoy us poor bachelors, to show us the more clearly all the desolation of our homeless existence. For others a source of joy, it is for us a torture. Of course, I know, we are not all entirely lonely—for us also the joy of making others happy may blossom, that joy upon which rests the whole secret of the blessed holiday mood. But the pleasure of joining in the happiness of others is tainted for us by a touch of self-irony partly, and also by that bitter longing to which—in contrast to homesickness—I would give the name of "marriage sickness."

Why didn't I come to pour out my heart to you? you ask, you pitying soul, you—you that can give of your sympathy in the same rich measure that others of your sex save for their dainty

Translated by Grace Isabel Colbron.

malices. There's a reason. You remember what Speidel says in his delightful "Lonely Sparrows," which you sent me the day after Christmas, with a true perception of my state of mind? "The bachelor by instinct," he says, "does not desire comfort. Once he is unhappy, he wishes to have the full enjoyment of his unhappiness."

Beside the "lonely sparrow" whom Speidel portrays, there is another sort of bachelor, the so-called "friend of the family." By this I do not mean those professional wreckers of homes, in whose eyes the serpent glitters as they settle down comfortably at the hospitable hearthstone. I mean the good uncle, papa's former school friend, who rocks the baby on his knee while he reads the magazine essays to mama, carefully omitting all the doubtful portions.

I know men who give up their entire lives to the service of some family whose friendship they have won—men who live on without desire by the side of a beautiful woman whom in their hearts they secretly adore.

You doubt me? Oh, it is the words "without desire" that disturb you? You are right, perhaps. In the depth of even the tamest heart some wild desire lies, but—understand me here—it lies bound in chains.

As an instance I would like to tell you about a conversation which took place day before yesterday, on New Year's Eve, between two old, two very old, gentlemen. It is my secret how I came to know of this conversation, and I ask you not to let it go any further. May I begin, then?

Picture to yourself, as a setting for my story, a high-ceilinged room, old-fashioned in furnishings, lighted by a green-shaded, impertinently bright hanging-lamp of the sort our parents had in use before the era of petroleum. The cone of light that goes out from the flame falls upon a round, white-clothed table, upon which stands the various ingredients for a New-Year's punch, while several drops of oil show out broadly in the centre of the table.

My two old gentlemen sat half in the shadow of the green lamp-shade, moldering ruins both, from long-past days, bowed and trembling, gazing before them with the dull glance of the dimming eyes of age. One, the host, is evidently an old officer, as you would recognize at once from his carefully wound cravat, his pointed, sharply-cut mustache, and his martial eyebrows. He sits holding the handle of his roller-chair like a crutch tightly clasped in both hands. He is motionless except for his jaws, which move up and down ceaselessly with the motion of chewing. The other, who sits near him on the sofa, a tall, spare figure, his narrow shoulders crowned by the high-domed head of a thinker, draws occasional thin puffs of smoke from a long pipe which is just about to go out. Among the myriad wrinkles of his smooth-shaven, dried-up face, framed in a wreath of snow-white curls, there lurked a quiet, gentle smile, a smile which the peace of resignation alone can bring to the face of age.

The two were silent. In the perfect stillness of the room the soft bubbling of the burning oil mingled with the soft bubbling of the tobacco juice. Then, from the darkness of the background, the hanging clock began to announce hoarsely the eleventh hour. "This is the hour when she would begin to make the punch," said the man with the domed forehead. His voice was soft, with a slight vibration.

"Yes, this is the time," repeated the other. The sound of his speech was hard, as if the rattle of command still lingered in it.

"I did not think it would be so desolate without her," said the first speaker again.

The host nodded, his jaws moving.

"She made the New Year's punch for us four-and-forty times," continued his friend.

"Yes, it's as long as that since we moved to Berlin, and you became our friend," said the old soldier.

"Last year at this time we were all so jolly together," said the other. "She sat in the armchair there, knitting socks for Paul's eldest. She worked busily, saying she must finish it by twelve o'clock. And she did finish it. Then we drank our punch and spoke quite calmly of death. And two months later they carried her away. As you know, I have written a fat book on the 'Immortality of the Idea.' You never cared much about it—I don't care for it myself now that your wife is dead. The entire Idea of the Universe means nothing to me now."

"Yes, she was a good wife," said the husband of the dead woman; "she cared for me well. When I had to go out for service at five o'clock in the morning, she was always up before me to look after my coffee. Of course she had her faults. When she got into philosophizing with you—h'm."

"You never understood her," murmured the other, the corners of his mouth trembling in controlled resentment. But the glance that rested long on his friend's face was gentle and sad, as if a secret guilt pressed upon his soul.

After a renewed pause, he began:

"Franz, there is something I want to tell you, something that has long troubled me, something that I do not want to carry with me to my grave."

"Well, fire away," said the host, taking up the long pipe that stood beside his chair.

"There was once—something—between your wife and me."

The host let his pipe fall back again, and stared at his friend with wide-opened eyes.

"No jokes please, doctor," he said finally.

"It is bitter earnest, Franz," replied the other. "I have carried it about with me these forty years, but now it is high time to have it out with you."

"Do you mean to say that the dead woman was untrue to me?" cried the husband angrily.

"For shame, Franz," said his friend with a soft, sad smile.

The old soldier murmured something and lit his pipe.

"No, she was as pure as God's angels," continued the other. "It is you and I who are the guilty ones. Listen to me. It is now forty-three years ago; you had just been ordered here as captain to Berlin, and I was teaching at the University. You were a gay bird then, as you know."

"H'm," remarked the host, raising his trembling old hand to his mustache.

"There was a beautiful actress with great black eyes and little white teeth—do you remember?"

"*Do* I? Bianca was her name," answered the other as a faded smile flashed over his weather-beaten, self-indulgent face. "Those little white teeth could bite, I can tell you."

"You deceived your wife, and she suspected it. But she said nothing and suffered in silence. She was the first woman who had come into my life since my mother's death. She came into it like a shining star, and I gazed up to her in adoration as one might adore a star. I found the courage to ask her about her trouble. She smiled and said that she was not feeling quite strong yet—you remember it was shortly after

the birth of your Paul. Then came New-Year's
Eve—forty-three years ago to-night. I came in
at eight o'clock as usual. She sat over her em-
broidery and I read aloud to her while we waited
for you. One hour after another passed and still
you did not come. I saw that she grew more and
more uneasy, and began to tremble. I trembled
with her. I knew where you were, and I feared
you might forget the hour of midnight in the
arms of that woman. She had dropped her work,
I read no longer. A terrible silence weighed
upon us. Then I saw a tear gather under her
eyelid and drop slowly down upon the embroid-
ery in her lap. I sprang up to go out and look
for you. I felt myself capable of tearing you
away from that woman by force. But at the
same moment she sprang up also from her seat—
this very same place where I am sitting now.

"'Where are you going?' she cried, terror in
every feature. 'I am going to fetch Franz,' I
said. And then she screamed aloud: 'For God's
sake, *you* stay with me at least—don't you for-
sake me also.'

"And she hurried to me, laid both hands on
my shoulders and buried her tear-bedewed face
on my breast. I trembled in every fibre, no
woman had ever stood so near me before. But
I controlled myself, and soothed and comforted
her—she was so sadly in need of comfort. You
came in soon after. You did not notice my emotion, your cheeks were burning, your eyes heavy

with the fatigue of love. Since that evening a change had come over me, a change that frightened me. When I had felt her soft arms around my neck, when I had felt the fragrance of her hair, the shining star fell from its heaven, and—a woman stood before me, beautiful, breathing love. I called myself a villain, a betrayer, and to soothe my conscience somewhat I set about separating you from your mistress. Fortunately I had some money at my disposal. She was satisfied with the sum I offered her, and—"

"The devil!" exclaimed the old soldier in surprise; "then you were the cause of that touching farewell letter that Bianca sent me—in which she declared that she must give me up,—although her heart would break?"

"Yes, I was the cause of it," said his friend. "But listen, there is more to tell. I had thought to purchase peace with that money, but the peace did not come. The wild thoughts ran riot all the more madly in my brain. I buried myself in my work—it was just about that time that I was working out the plan of my book on the 'Immortality of the Idea'—but still could not find peace. And thus the year passed and New-Year's Eve came round again. Again we sat together here, she and I. You were at home this time, but you lay sleeping on the sofa in the next room. A merry Casino dinner had tired you. And as I sat beside her, and my eyes rested on her pale face, then memory came over me with irresistible power. Once more I would feel her head on my breast, once more I would kiss her—and then—the end, if need be. Our eyes meet for an instant; I seemed to see a secret understanding, an answer in her glance. I could control myself no longer; I fell at her feet and buried my burning face in her lap.

"I lay there motionless for two seconds perhaps, then I felt her soft hand rest cool upon my head, and her voice, soft and gentle, spoke the words: 'Be brave, dear friend; yes, be brave—do not deceive the man sleeping so trustfully in the next room.' I sprang up and gazed about, bewildered. She took a book from the table and handed it to me. I understood, opened it at random, and began to read aloud. I do not know what it was I read, the letters danced before my eyes. But the storm within my soul began to abate, and when twelve o'clock struck, and you came in sleepily for the New-Year's wishes, it was as if that moment of sin lay far, far behind me, in days that had long passed.

"Since that day I have been calmer. I knew that she did not return my love, and that I had only pity to hope from her. Years passed, your children grew up and married, we three grew old together. You gave up your wild life, forgot the other women, and lived for one alone, as I did. It was not possible that I should ever cease to love her, but my love took on another shape; earthly desires faded, and a bond of the spirit grew up between us. You have often laughed when you heard us philosophizing together. But if you had known how close were our souls at such moments you would have been very jealous. And now she is dead, and before the next New-Year's Eve comes round we two may follow her. It is, therefore, high time that I rid myself of this secret and say to you, 'Franz, I sinned against you once, forgive me.' "

He held out an imploring hand toward his friend; but the other answered, grumbling: "Nonsense. There is nothing to forgive. What you told me there, I knew it long ago. She confessed it herself forty years ago. And now I will tell you why I ran after other women until I was an old man—because she told me then that you were the one and only love of her life."

The friend stared at him without speaking, and the hoarse clock began to strike—midnight.

THE RED ROOM

BY H. G. WELLS

THE RED ROOM

BY H. G. WELLS

"I CAN assure you," said I, "that it will take a very tangible ghost to frighten me." And I stood up before the fire with my glass in my hand.

"It is your own choosing," said the man with the withered arm, and glanced at me askance.

"Eight-and-twenty years," said I, "I have lived, and never a ghost have I seen as yet."

The old woman sat staring hard into the fire, her pale eyes wide open. "Ay," she broke in, "and eight-and-twenty years you have lived, and never seen the likes of this house, I reckon. There's a many things to see, when one's still but eight-and-twenty." She swayed her head from side to side. "A many things to see and sorrow for." I suspected these old people were trying to enhance the spectral terrors of their house by this droning insistence. I put down my empty glass on the table, and, looking about the room, caught a glimpse of myself abbreviated and broadened to an impossible sturdiness, in the queer old mirror beside the china cupboard. "Well," I said, "if I see anything to-night, I shall be so much the wiser. For I come to the business with an open mind."

345

"It's your own choosing," said the man with the withered arm once more.

I heard the faint sound of a stick and a shambling step on the flags in the passage outside. The door creaked on its hinges as a second old man entered, more bent, more wrinkled, more aged even than the first. He supported himself by the help of a crutch, his eyes were covered by a shade, and his lower lip, half averted, hung pale and pink from his decaying yellow teeth. He made straight for an armchair on the opposite side of the table, sat down clumsily, and began to cough. The man with the withered hand gave the newcomer a short glance of positive dislike; the old woman took no notice of his arrival, but remained with her eyes fixed steadily on the fire.

"I said—it's your own choosing," said the man with the withered hand, when the coughing had ceased for a while.

"It's my own choosing," I answered.

The man with the shade became aware of my presence for the first time, and threw his head back for a moment, and sidewise, to see me. I caught a momentary glimpse of his eyes, small and bright and inflamed. Then he began to cough and splutter again.

"Why don't you drink?" said the man with the withered arm, pushing the beer toward him. The man with the shade poured out a glassful with a shaking hand, that splashed half as much again on the deal table. A monstrous shadow of him crouched upon the wall, and mocked his action as he poured and drank. I must confess I had scarcely expected these grotesque custodians. There is, to my mind, something inhuman in senility, something crouching and atavistic; the human qualities seem to drop from old people insensibly day by day. The three of them made me feel uncomfortable with their gaunt silences, their bent carriage, their evident unfriendliness to me and to one another. And that night, perhaps, I was in the mood for uncomfortable impressions. I resolved to get away from their vague foreshadowings of the evil things upstairs.

"If," said I, "you will show me to this haunted room of yours, I will make myself comfortable there."

The old man with the cough jerked his head back so suddenly that it startled me, and shot another glance of his red eyes at me from out of the darkness under the shade, but no one answered me. I waited a minute, glancing from one to the other. The old woman stared like a dead body, glaring into the fire with lack-lustre eyes.

"If," I said, a little louder, "if you will show me to this haunted room of yours, I will relieve you from the task of entertaining me."

"There's a candle on the slab outside the door," said the man with the withered hand, looking at my feet as he addressed me. "But if you go to the Red Room to-night—'

"This night of all nights!" said the old woman, softly.

"—You go alone."

"Very well," I answered, shortly, "and which way do I go?"

"You go along the passage for a bit," said he, nodding his head on his shoulder at the door, "until you come to a spiral staircase; and on the second landing is a door covered with green baize. Go through that, and down the long corridor to the end, and the Red Room is on your left up the steps."

"Have I got that right?" I said, and repeated his directions.

He corrected me in one particular.

"And you are really going?" said the man with the shade, looking at me again for the third time with that queer, unnatural tilting of the face.

"This night of all nights!" whispered the old woman.

"It is what I came for," I said, and moved toward the door. As I did so, the old man with the shade rose and staggered round the table, so as to be closer to the others and to the fire. At the door I turned and looked at them, and saw they were all close together, dark against the firelight, staring at me over their shoulders, with an intent expression on their ancient faces.

"Good-night," I said, setting the door open.

"It's your own choosing," said the man with the withered arm.

THE RED ROOM

I left the door wide open until the candle was well alight, and then I shut them in, and walked down the chilly, echoing passage.

I must confess that the oddness of these three old pensioners in whose charge her ladyship had left the castle, and the deep-toned, old-fashioned furniture of the housekeeper's room, in which they foregathered, had affected me curiously in spite of my effort to keep myself at a matter-of-fact phase. They seemed to belong to another age, an older age, an age when things spiritual were indeed to be feared, when common sense was uncommon, an age when omens and witches were credible, and ghosts beyond denying. Their very existence, thought I, is spectral; the cut of their clothing, fashions born in dead brains; the ornaments and conveniences in the room about them even are ghostly—the thoughts of vanished men, which still haunt rather than participate in the world of to-day. And the passage I was in, long and shadowy, with a film of moisture glistening on the wall, was as gaunt and cold as a thing that is dead and rigid. But with an effort I sent such thoughts to the right-about. The long, drafty subterranean passage was chilly and dusty, and my candle flared and made the shadows cower and quiver. The echoes rang up and down the spiral staircase, and a shadow came sweeping up after me, and another fled before me into the darkness overhead. I came to the wide landing and stopped there for a moment listening to a rustling that I fancied I heard creeping behind me, and then, satisfied of the absolute silence, pushed open the unwilling baize-covered door and stood in the silent corridor.

The effect was scarcely what I expected, for the moonlight, coming in by the great window on the grand staircase, picked out everything in vivid black shadow or reticulated silvery illumination. Everything seemed in its proper position; the house might have been deserted on the yesterday instead of twelve months ago. There were candles in the sockets of the sconces, and whatever dust had gathered on the carpets or upon the polished flooring was distributed so evenly as to be invisible in my candlelight. A waiting stillness was over everything. I was about to advance, and stopped abruptly. A bronze group stood upon the landing hidden from me by a corner of the wall; but its shadow fell with marvelous distinctness upon the white paneling, and gave me the impression of some one crouching to waylay me. The thing jumped upon my attention suddenly. I stood rigid for half a moment, perhaps. Then, with my hand in the pocket that held the revolver, I advanced, only to discover a Ganymede and Eagle, glistening in the moonlight. That incident for a time restored my nerve, and a dim porcelain Chinaman on a buhl table, whose head rocked as I passed, scarcely startled me.

The door of the Red Room and the steps up to it were in a shadowy corner. I moved my candle from side to side in order to see clearly the nature of the recess in which I stood, before opening the door. Here it was, thought I, that my predecessor was found, and the memory of that story gave me a sudden twinge of apprehension. I glanced over my shoulder at the black Ganymede in the moonlight, and opened the door of the Red Room rather hastily, with my face half turned to the pallid silence of the corridor.

I entered, closed the door behind me at once, turned the key I found in the lock within, and stood with the candle held aloft surveying the scene of my vigil, the great Red Room of Lorraine Castle, in which the young Duke had died; or rather in which he had begun his dying, for he had opened the door and fallen headlong down the steps I had just ascended. That had been the end of his vigil, of his gallant attempt to conquer the ghostly tradition of the place, and never, I thought, had apoplexy better served the ends of superstition. There were other and older stories that clung to the room, back to the half-incredible beginning of it all, the tale of a timid wife and the tragic end that came to her husband's jest of frightening her. And looking round that huge shadowy room with its black window bays, its recesses and alcoves, its dusty brown-red hangings and dark gigantic furniture, one could well understand the legends that had sprouted in its black corners, its germinating darknesses. My candle was a little tongue of light in the vastness of the chamber; its rays failed to pierce to the opposite end of the room, and left an ocean of dull red mystery and suggestion, sentinel shadows and watching darknesses beyond its island of light. And the stillness of desolation brooded over it all.

I must confess some impalpable quality of that ancient room disturbed me. I tried to fight the feeling down. I resolved to make a systematic examination of the place, and so, by leaving nothing to the imagination, dispel the fanciful suggestions of the obscurity before they obtained a hold upon me. After satisfying myself of the fastening of the door, I began to walk round the room, peering round each article of furniture, tucking up the valances of the bed and opening its curtains wide. In one place there was a distinct echo to my footsteps, the noises I made seemed so little that they enhanced rather than broke the silence of the place. I pulled up the blinds and examined the fastenings of the several windows. Attracted by the fall of a particle of dust, I leaned forward and looked up the blackness of the wide chimney. Then, trying to preserve my scientific attitude of mind, I walked round and began tapping the oak paneling for any secret opening, but I desisted before reaching the alcove. I saw my face in a mirror— white.

There were two big mirrors in the room, each with a pair of sconces bearing candles, and on the mantelshelf, too, were candles in china candlesticks. All these I lit one after the other. The fire was laid—an unexpected consideration from the old housekeeper—and I lit it, to keep down any disposition to shiver, and when it was burning well I stood round with my back to it and regarded the room again. I had pulled up a chintz-covered armchair and a table to form a kind of barricade before me. On this lay my revolver, ready to hand. My precise examination had done me a little good, but I still found the remoter darkness of the place and its perfect stillness too stimulating for the imagination. The echoing of the stir and crackling of the fire was no sort of comfort to me. The shadow in the alcove at the end of the room began to display that undefinable quality of a presence, that odd suggestion of a lurking living thing that comes so easily in silence and solitude. And to reassure myself, I walked with a candle into it and satisfied myself that there was nothing tangible there. I stood that candle upon the floor of the alcove and left it in that position.

By this time I was in a state of considerable nervous tension, although to my reason there was no adequate cause for my condition. My mind, however, was perfectly clear. I postulated quite unreservedly that nothing supernatural could happen, and to pass the time I began stringing some rhymes together, Ingoldsby fashion, concerning the original legend of the place. A few

I spoke aloud, but the echoes were not pleasant. For the same reason I also abandoned, after a time, a conversation with myself upon the impossibility of ghosts and haunting. My mind reverted to the three old and distorted people downstairs, and I tried to keep it upon that topic.

The sombre reds and grays of the room troubled me; even with its seven candles the place was merely dim. The light in the alcove flaring in a draft, and the fire flickering, kept the shadows and penumbra perpetually shifting and stirring in a noiseless flighty dance. Casting about for a remedy, I recalled the wax candles I had seen in the corridor, and, with a slight effort, carrying a candle and leaving the door open, I walked out into the moonlight, and presently returned with as many as ten. These I put in the various knick-knacks of china with which the room was sparsely adorned, and lit and placed them where the shadows had lain deepest, some on the floor, some in the window recesses, arranging and rearranging them until at last my seventeen candles were so placed that not an inch of the room but had the direct light of at least one of them. It occurred to me that when the ghost came I could warn him not to trip over them. The room was now quite brightly illuminated. There was something very cheering and reassuring in these little silent streaming flames, and to notice their steady diminution of length offered me an occupation and gave me a reassuring sense of the passage of time.

Even with that, however, the brooding expectation of the vigil weighed heavily enough upon me. I stood watching the minute hand of my watch creep towards midnight.

Then something happened in the alcove. I did not see the candle go out, I simply turned and saw that the darkness was there, as one might start ʻand see the unexpected presence of a stranger. The black shadow had sprung back to its place. "By Jove," said I aloud, recovering from my surprise, "that draft's a strong one"; and taking the matchbox from the table, I walked across the room in a leisurely manner to relight the corner again. My first match would not strike, and as I succeeded with the second, something seemed to blink on the wall before me. I turned my head involuntarily and saw that the two candles on the little table by the fireplace were extinguished. I rose at once to my feet.

"Odd," I said. "Did I do that myself in a flash of absent-mindedness?"

I walked back, relit one, and as I did so I saw the candle in the right sconce of one of the mirrors wink and go right out, and almost immediately its companion followed it. The flames vanished as if the wick had been suddenly nipped between a finger and thumb, leaving the wick neither glowing nor smoking, but black. While I stood gaping the candle at the foot of the bed went out, and the shadows seemed to take another step toward me.

"This won't do!" said I, and first one and then another candle on the mantelshelf followed.

"What's up?" I cried, with a queer high note getting into my voice somehow. At that the candle on the corner of the wardrobe went out, and the one I had relit in the alcove followed.

"Steady on!" I said, "those candles are wanted," speaking with a half-hysterical facetiousness, and scratching away at a match the while, "for the mantel candlesticks." My hands trembled so much that twice I missed the rough paper of the matchbox. As the mantel emerged from darkness again, two candles in the remoter end of the room were eclipsed. But with the same match I also relit the larger mirror candles, and those on the floor near the doorway, so that for the moment I seemed to gain on the extinctions. But then in a noiseless volley there vanished four lights at once in different corners of the room, and I struck another match in quivering haste, and stood hesitating whither to take it.

As I stood undecided, an invisible hand seemed to sweep out the two candles on the table. With a cry of terror I dashed at the alcove, then into the corner and then into the window, relighting three as two more vanished by the fireplace, and then, perceiving a better way, I dropped matches on the iron-bound deedbox in the corner, and caught up the bedroom candlestick. With this I avoided the delay of striking matches, but for all that the steady process of extinction went on, and the shadows I feared and fought against returned, and crept in upon me, first a step gained on this side of me, then on that. I was now almost frantic with the horror of the coming darkness, and my self-possession deserted me. I leaped panting from candle to candle in a vain struggle against that remorseless advance.

I bruised myself in the thigh against the table, I sent a chair headlong, I stumbled and fell and whisked the cloth from the table in my fall. My candle rolled away from me and I snatched another as I rose. Abruptly this was blown out as I swung it off the table by the wind of my sudden movement, and immediately the two remaining candles followed. But there was light still in the room, a red light, that streamed across the ceiling and staved off the shadows from me. The fire! Of course I could still thrust my candle between the bars and relight it.

I turned to where the flames were still dancing between the glowing coals and splashing red reflections upon the furniture; made two steps toward the grate, and incontinently the flames dwindled and vanished, the glow vanished, the reflections rushed together and disappeared, and as I thrust the candle between the bars darkness closed upon me like the shutting of an eye, wrapped about me in a stifling embrace, sealed my vision, and crushed the last vestiges of self-possession from my brain. And it was not only palpable darkness, but intolerable terror. The candle fell from my hands. I flung out my arms in a vain effort to thrust that ponderous blackness away from me, and lifting up my voice, screamed with all my might, once, twice, thrice. Then I think I must have staggered to my feet. I know I thought suddenly of the moonlit corridor, and with my head bowed and my arms over my face, made a stumbling run for the door.

But I had forgotten the exact position of the door, and I struck myself heavily against the corner of the bed. I staggered back, turned, and was either struck or struck myself against some other bulky furnishing. I have a vague memory of battering myself thus to and fro in the darkness, of a heavy blow at last upon my forehead, of a horrible sensation of falling that lasted an age, of my last frantic effort to keep my footing, and then I remember no more.

I opened my eyes in daylight. My head was roughly bandaged, and the man with the withered hand was watching my face. I looked about me trying to remember what had happened, and for a space I could not recollect. I rolled my eyes into the corner and saw the old woman, no longer abstracted, no longer terrible, pouring out some drops of medicine from a little blue phial into a glass. "Where am I?" I said. "I seem to remember you, and yet I can not remember who you are."

THE RED ROOM

They told me then, and I heard of the haunted Red Room as one who bears a tale. "We found you at dawn,' said he, "and there was blood on your forehead and lips."

I wondered that I had ever disliked him. The three of them in the daylight seemed commonplace old folk enough. The man with the green shade had his head bent as one who sleeps.

It was very slowly I recovered the memory of my experience. "You believe now," said the old man with the withered hand, "that the room is haunted?" He spoke no longer as one who greets an intruder, but as one who condoles with a friend.

"Yes," said I, "the room is haunted."

"And you have seen it. And we who have been here all our lives have never set eyes upon it. Because we have never dared. Tell us, is it truly the old earl who—"

"No," said I, "it is not."

"I told you so," said the old lady, with the glass in her hand. "It is his poor young countess who was frightened—"

"It is not," I said. 'There is neither ghost of earl nor ghost of countess in that room; there is no ghost there at all, but worse, far worse, something impalpable—"

"Well?" they said.

"The worst of all the things that haunt poor mortal men," said I; "and that is, in all its nakedness—'Fear!' Fear that will not have light nor sound, that will not bear with reason, that deafens and darkens and overwhelms. It followed me through the corridor, it fought against me in the room—"

I stopped abruptly. There was an interval of silence. My hand went up to my bandages. "The candles went out one after another, and I fled—"

Then the man with the shade lifted his face sideways to see me and spoke.

"That is it," said he. "I knew that was it. A Power of Darkness. To put such a curse upon a home! It lurks there always. You can feel it even in the daytime, even of a bright summer's day, in the hangings, in the curtains, keeping behind you however you face about. In the dusk it creeps in the corridor and follows you, so that you dare not turn. It is even as you say. Fear itself is in that room. Black Fear . . . And there it will be . . . so long as this house of sin endures."

THE LONG EXILE

BY COUNT LEO NIKOLAIEVITCH TOLSTOI

THE LONG EXILE

BY COUNT LEO NIKOLAIEVITCH TOLSTOI

"God sees the truth, but bides his time."

ONCE upon a time there lived in the city of Vladímir a young merchant named Aksénof. He had two shops and a house. Aksénof himself had a ruddy complexion and curly hair; he was a very jolly fellow and a good singer. When he was young he used to drink too much, and when he was tipsy he was turbulent; but after his marriage he ceased drinking, and only occasionally had a spree.

One time in summer Aksénof was going to Nízhni[1] to the great Fair. As he was about to bid his family good-by, his wife said to him:

"Iván Dmítrievitch, do not go to-day; I had a dream, and dreamed that some misfortune befell you."

Aksénof laughed at her, and said: "You are always afraid that I shall go on a spree at the Fair."

His wife said: "I myself know not what I am afraid of, but I had such a strange dream: you seemed to be coming home from town, and you

---

[1] Nízhni Nóvgorod: it means Lower New Town.

Translated by Nathan Haskell Dole. Copyright, 1888, by Thomas Y. Crowell & Co.

took off your hat, and I looked, and your head was all gray."

Aksénof laughed. "That means good luck. See, I am going now. I will bring you some rich remembrances."

And he bade his family farewell and set off.

When he had gone half his journey, he fell in with a merchant of his acquaintance, and the two stopped together at the same tavern for the night. They took tea together, and went to sleep in two adjoining rooms.

Aksénof did not care to sleep long; he awoke in the middle of the night, and in order that he might get a good start while it was cool he aroused his driver and bade him harness up, went down into the smoky hut, settled his account with the landlord, and started on his way.

After he had driven forty versts,[2] he again stopped to get something to eat; he rested in the vestibule of the inn, and when it was noon, he went to the doorstep and ordered the samovár[3] got ready; then he took out his guitar and began to play.

Suddenly a troïka[4] with a bell dashed up to the inn, and from the equipage leaped an official with two soldiers; he comes directly up to Aksénof and asks: "Who are you? Where did you come from?"

[2] Nearly twenty-six and a half miles.
[3] Water-boiler for making Russian tea.
[4] A team of three horses harnessed abreast: the outside two gallop; the shaft horse trots.

Aksénof answers without hesitation, and asks him if he would not have a glass of tea with him.

But the official keeps on with his questions: "Where did you spend last night? Were you alone or with a merchant? Have you seen the merchant this morning? Why did you leave so early this morning?"

Aksénof wondered why he was questioned so closely; but he told everything just as it was, and he asks. "Why do you ask me so many questions? I am not a thief or a murderer. I am on my own business; there is nothing to question me about."

Then the official called up the soldiers, and said: "I am the police inspector, and I have made these inquiries of you because the merchant with whom you spent last night has been stabbed. Show me your things, and you men search him."

They went into the tavern, brought in the trunk and bag, and began to open and search them. Suddenly the police inspector pulled out from the bag a knife, and demanded: "Whose knife is this?"

Aksénof looked and saw a knife covered with blood taken from his bag, and he was frightened.

"And whose blood is that on the knife?"

Aksénof tried to answer, but he could not articulate his words:

"I—I—don't—know— I— That knife—it is—not mine—"

Then the police inspector said: "This morning the merchant was found stabbed to death in

his bed. No one except you could have done it.
The tavern was locked on the inside, and there
was no one in the tavern except yourself. And
here is the bloody knife in your bag, and your
guilt is evident in your face. Tell me how you
killed him and how much money you took from
him." Aksénof swore that he had not done it,
that he had not seen the merchant after he had
drunken tea with him, that the only money that he
had with him—eight thousand rubles—was his
own, and that the knife was not his.

But his voice trembled, his face was pale, and
he was all quivering with fright, like a guilty
person.

The police inspector called the soldiers, commanded them to bind Aksénof and take him to
the wagon.

When they took him to the wagon with his
feet tied, Aksénof crossed himself and burst into
tears.

They confiscated Aksénof's possessions and his
money, and took him to the next city and threw
him into prison.

They sent to Vladímir to make inquiries about
Aksénof's character, and all the merchants and
citizens of Vladímir declared that Aksénof, when
he was young, used to drink and was wild, but
that now he was a worthy man. Then he was
brought up for judgment. He was sentenced for
having killed the merchant and for having robbed
him of twenty thousand rubles.

Aksénof's wife was dumfounded by the event, and did not know what to think. Her children were still small, and there was one at the breast. She took them all with her and journeyed to the city where her husband was imprisoned.

At first they would not grant her admittance, but afterward she got permission from the chief, and was taken to her husband.

When she saw him in his prison garb, in chains together with murderers, she fell to the floor, and it was a long time before she recovered from her swoon. Then she placed her children around her, sat down amid them, and began to tell him about their domestic affairs, and to ask him about everything that had happened to him.

He told her the whole story.

She asked: "What is to be the result of it?"

He said: "We must petition the Czar. It is impossible that an innocent man should be condemned."

The wife said that she already had sent a petition to the Czar, but that the petition had not been granted. Aksénof said nothing, but was evidently very much downcast.

Then his wife said: "You see the dream that I had, when I dreamed that you had become gray-headed, meant something, after all. Already your hair has begun to turn gray with trouble. You ought to have stayed at home that time." And she began to tear her hair, and said: "Ványa,[5]

[5] Diminutive of Iván, John.

my dearest husband, tell your wife the truth: Did you commit that crime or not?"

Aksénof said: "So you, too, have no faith in me!" And he wrung his hands and wept.

Then a soldier came and said that it was time for the wife and children to go. And Aksénof for the last time bade farewell to his family.

When his wife was gone, Aksénof began to think over all that they had said. When he remembered that his wife had also distrusted him, and had asked him if he had murdered the merchant, he said to himself: "It is evident that no one but God can know the truth of the matter, and He is the only one to ask for mercy, and He is the only one from whom to expect it."

And from that time Aksénof ceased to send in petitions, ceased to hope, and only prayed to God. Aksénof was sentenced to be knouted, and then to exile with hard labor. And so it was done.

He was flogged with the knout, and then, when the wounds from the knout were healed, he was sent with other exiles to Siberia.

Aksénof lived twenty-six years in the mines. The hair on his head had become white as snow, and his beard had grown long, thin, and gray. All his gaiety had vanished.

He was bent, his gait was slow, he spoke little, he never laughed, and he spent much of his time in prayer.

Aksénof had learned while in prison to make boots, and with the money that he earned he bought the "Book of Martyrs,"[6] and used to read it when it was light enough in prison, and on holidays he would go to the prison church, read the Gospels, and sing in the choir, for his voice was still strong and good.

The authorities liked Aksénof for his submissiveness, and his prison associates repected him and called him "Grandfather" and the "man of God." Whenever they had petitions to be presented, Aksénof was always chosen to carry them to the authorities; and when quarrels arose among the prisoners, they always came to Aksénof as umpire.

Aksénof never received any letters from home, and he knew not whether his wife and children were alive.

One time some new convicts came to the prison. In the evening all the old convicts gathered around the newcomers, and began to ply them with questions as to the cities or villages from which this one or that had come, and what their crimes were.

At this time Aksénof was sitting on his bunk, near the strangers, and, with bowed head, was listening to what was said.

One of the new convicts was a tall, healthy looking old man of sixty years, with a close-cropped gray beard. He was telling why he had been arrested. He said:

"And so, brothers, I was sent here for nothing. I unharnessed a horse from a postboy's sledge,

[6] Chetyá Minyéï.

and they caught me in it, and insisted that I was stealing it. 'But,' says I, 'I only wanted to go a little faster, so I whipped up the horse. And besides, the driver was a friend of mine. It's all right,' says I. 'No,' say they; 'you were stealing it.' But they did not know what and where I had stolen. I have done things which long ago would have sent me here, but I was not found out; and now they have sent me here without any justice in it. But what's the use of grumbling? I have been in Siberia before. They did not keep me here very long though—"

"Where did you come from?" asked one of the convicts.

"Well, we came from the city of Vladímir; we are citizens of that place. My name is Makár, and my father's name was Semyón."

Aksénof raised his head and asked:

"Tell me, Semyónitch,[7] have you ever heard of the Aksénofs, merchants in Vladímir city? Are they alive?"

"Indeed, I heard of them! They are rich merchants, though their father is in Siberia. It seems he was just like any of the rest of us sinners. And now tell me, Grandfather, what you were sent here for?"

Aksénof did not like to speak of his misfortune; he sighed, and said:

"Twenty-six years ago I was condemned to hard labor on account of my sins."

[7] Son of Semyón.

Makár Semyónof said:

"But what was your crime?"

Aksénof replied: "I must, therefore, have deserved this."

But he would not tell or give any further particulars; the other convicts, however, related why Aksénof had been sent to Siberia. They told how on the road some one had killed a merchant, and put the knife into Aksénof's luggage, and how he had been unjustly punished for this.

When Makár heard this, he glanced at Aksénof, clasped his hands round his knees, and said:

"Well, now, that's wonderful! You have been growing old, Grandfather!"

They began to ask him what he thought was wonderful, and where he had seen Aksénof. But Makár did not answer; he only repeated:

"A miracle, boys! how wonderful that we should meet again!"

And when he said these words, it came over Aksénof that perhaps this man might know who it was that had killed the merchant. And he said:

"Did you ever hear of that crime, Semyónitch, or did you ever see me before?"

"Of course I heard of it! The country was full of it. But it happened a long time ago. And I have forgotten what I heard," said Makár.

"Perhaps you heard who killed the merchant?" asked Aksénof.

Makár laughed, and said:

"Why, of course the man who had the knife in his bag killed him. If any one put the knife in your things and was not caught doing it—it would have been impossible. For how could they have put the knife in your bag? Was it not standing close by your head? And you would have heard it, wouldn't you?"

As soon as Aksénof heard these words he felt convinced that this was the very man who had killed the merchant.

He stood up and walked away. All that night he was unable to sleep. Deep melancholy came upon him, and he began to call back the past in his imagination.

He imagined his wife as she had been when for the last time she had come to see him in the prison. She seemed to stand before him exactly as though she were alive, and he saw her face and her eyes, and he seemed to hear her words and her laugh.

Then his imagination brought up his children before him; one a little boy in a little fur coat, and the other on his mother's breast.

And he imagined himself as he was at that time, young and happy. He remembered how he had sat on the steps of the tavern when they arrested him, and how his soul was full of joy as he played on his guitar.

And he remembered the place of execution where they had knouted him, and the knoutsman, and the people standing around, and the chains and the convicts, and all his twenty-six years of prison life, and he remembered his old age. And such melancholy came upon Aksénof that he was tempted to put an end to himself.

"And all on account of this criminal!" said Aksénof to himself.

And then he began to feel such anger against Makár Semyónof that he almost fell upon him, and was crazy with desire to pay off the load of vengeance. He repeated prayers all night, but could not recover his calm. When day came he walked by Makár and did not look at him.

Thus passed two weeks. Aksénof was not able to sleep, and such melancholy had come over him that he did not know what to do.

One time during the night, as he happened to be passing through the prison, he saw that the soil was disturbed under one of the bunks. He stopped to examine it. Suddenly Makár crept from under the bunk and looked at Aksénsof with a startled face.

Aksénof was about to pass on so as not to see him, but Makár seized his arm, and told him how he had been digging a passage under the wall, and how every day he carried the dirt out in his boot-legs and emptied it in the street when they went out to work. He said:

"If you only keep quiet, old man, I will get you out too. But if you tell on me, they will flog me; but afterward I will make it hot for you. I will kill you."

When Aksénof saw his enemy, he trembled all

over with rage, twitched away his arm, and said: "I have no reason to make my escape, and to kill me would do no harm; you killed me long ago. But as to telling on you or not, I shall do as God sees fit to have me."

On the next day, when they took the convicts out to work, the soldiers discovered where Makár had been digging in the ground; they began to make a search, and found the hole. The chief came into the prison and asked every one, "Who was digging that hole?"

All denied it. Those who knew did not name Makár, because they were aware that he would be flogged half to death for such an attempt.

Then the chief came to Aksénof. He knew that Aksénof was a truthful man, and he said: "Old man, you are truthful; tell me before God who did this."

Makár was standing near, in great excitement, and did not dare to look at Aksénof.

Aksénof's hands and lips trembled, and it was some time before he could speak a word. He said to himself: "If I shield him— But why should I forgive him when he has been my ruin? Let him suffer for my sufferings! But shall I tell on him? They will surely flog him? But what difference does it make what I think of him? Will it be any the easier for me?"

Once more the chief demanded:

"Well, old man, tell the truth! Who dug the hole?"

Aksénof glanced at Makár, and then said:

"I can not tell, your Honor. God does not bid me tell. I will not tell. Do with me as you please; I am in your power."

In spite of all the chief's efforts, Aksénof would say nothing more. And so they failed to find out who dug the hole.

On the next night as Aksénof was lying on his bunk, and almost asleep, he heard some one come along and sit down at his feet.

He peered through the darkness and saw that it was Makár.

Aksénof asked:

"What do you wish of me? What are you doing here?"

Makár remained silent. Aksénof arose, and said:

"What do you want? Go away, or else I will call the guard."

Makár went up close to Aksénof and said in a whisper:

"Iván Dmítritch,[8] forgive me!"

Aksénof said: "What have I to forgive you?"

"It was I who killed the merchant and put the knife in your bag. And I was going to kill you too, but there was a noise in the yard; I thrust the knife in your bag, and slipped out of the window."

Aksénof said nothing, and he did not know what to say. Makár got down from the bunk, knelt on the ground, and said:

[8] Son of Dmitry (or Dmítrievitch; see page 363).

"Iván Dmítritch, forgive me, forgive me for Christ's sake. I will confess that I killed the merchant—they will pardon you. You will be able to go home." Aksénof said:

"It is easy for you to say that, but how could I endure it? Where should I go now? My wife is dead! my children have forgotten me. I have nowhere to go."

Makár did not rise; he beat his head on the ground, and said:

"Iván Dmítritch, forgive me! When they flogged me with the knout, it was easier to bear than it is now to look at you. And you had pity on me after all this—you did not tell on me. Forgive me for Christ's sake! Forgive me though I am a cursed villain!"

And the man began to sob.

When Aksénof heard Makár Semyónof sobbing, he himself burst into tears, and said:

"God will forgive you; maybe I am a hundred times worse than you are!"

And suddenly he felt a wonderful peace in his soul. And he ceased to mourn for his home, and had no desire to leave the prison, but only thought of his last hour.

Makár would not listen to Aksénof, and confessed his crime.

When they came to let Aksénof go home, he was dead.

INDEX OF TITLES

INDEX OF TITLES

INDEX OF TITLES

INDEX OF AUTHORS

INDEX OF AUTHORS

INDEX OF AUTHORS